WHAT HAVE WE DONE

ALSO BY ALEX FINLAY

The Night Shift

Every Last Fear

~~WHAT~~ ~~HAVE~~ ~~WE~~ ~~DONE~~

ALEX FINLAY

MINOTAUR
BOOKS
NEW YORK

First published in the United States by St. Martin's Press, an imprint of St. Martin's Publishing Group

WHAT HAVE WE DONE. Copyright © 2023 by Alex Finlay. All rights reserved. Printed in the United States of America. For information, address St. Martin's Publishing Group, 120 Broadway, New York, NY 10271.

www.minotaurbooks.com

Designed by Omar Chapa

Library of Congress Cataloging-in-Publication Data

Names: Finlay, Alex, author.
Title: What have we done / Alex Finlay.
Description: First edition. | New York : Minotaur Books, 2023.
Identifiers: LCCN 2022048503 | ISBN 9781250863720 (hardcover) |
    ISBN 9781250863737 (ebook)
Classification: LCC PS3606.I5528 W53 2023 | DDC 813/.6—dc23
LC record available at https://lccn.loc.gov/2022048503

Our books may be purchased in bulk for promotional, educational, or business use. Please contact your local bookseller or the Macmillan Corporate and Premium Sales Department at 1-800-221-7945, extension 5442, or by email at MacmillanSpecialMarkets@macmillan.com.

First Edition: 2023
10 9 8 7 6 5 4 3 2 1

For Lisa Erbach Vance,
superagent, cherished friend

~~WHAT~~ ~~HAVE~~ ~~WE~~ ~~DONE~~

PROLOGUE

TWENTY-FIVE YEARS AGO

At the top of a knoll through a break in the trees, five teenagers stand at the edge of a shallow grave. A light rain falls, thunder rumbles in the night sky.

One of the boys raises the gun. It was his idea, after all, he should go first. He aims into the hole, but the gun wobbles in the half-light.

"Do it," another boy says.

But the kid with the gun just stands there, arm extended, the rain beading his face, matting his hair.

At last, the only girl in the group reaches for the weapon—the .22 they bought for twenty-two bucks. She swallows, looks at the rest of them. "We agreed," she says. "We all have to." Her eyes return to the pit, and the gun clenched in her hand makes a noise like a firecracker, a faint *pop*.

The girl passes the weapon down the line. And one by one they each take a shot until the gun reaches the last boy. Lightning brightens the sky for a nanosecond. Long enough to see the tears streaming pale vertical lines down his dirty face. He's the only gentle soul at Savior House group home.

He grips the firearm, his breaths ragged, as his best friend looms over him like the protector he is, laces his finger through the trigger guard on top of the gentle boy's, and another *pop* rends the night.

They all then fall to their knees and drive the wet dirt into the void with their bare hands.

In the dark, the gentle boy utters the words none of them will ever forget:

"What have we done?"

PART 1

THE TARGETS

CHAPTER ONE

JENNA

PRESENT DAY

"There's my girl," Simon says in his chipper morning voice. It's one of the things Jenna adores about her husband, his unrelenting cheerfulness.

She's back from running her five miles and feeling every one of her thirty-nine years. She kisses Simon, then sits at the kitchen table across from her stepdaughter Lulu, who's eating pancakes, her shiny Mary Janes swinging under the chair. As usual, their Labrador, Peanut Butter, is at the five-year-old's feet, waiting for falling scraps.

Simon stands at the stovetop pouring batter for more flapjacks, wearing the apron that has I HAVE NO IDEA WHAT I'M DOING inscribed on the front.

"I thought you have an early meeting," Jenna says, noticing that he's still in his pajamas. He wears the button-up style like a character from a 1950s sitcom.

"I have time. I need to make sure my girls get the most important meal of the day." He pushes his glasses up on his nose.

For most women, the nerdy tax lawyer wouldn't elicit the rush of whatever chemical or emotion crowding Jenna's chest. But this boring numbers man, white-bread as they come, fills that part of Jenna that was empty for so long. She knows they're an odd match. She catches the looks, the whispers, that she must be in it for the money, the gossipers not realizing that Simon isn't exactly Bill Gates, even if he resembles him. In fact, Jenna's numbered Swiss account dwarfs their modest savings and Simon's 401(k).

Her older stepdaughter, Willow, bursts into the kitchen, backpack slung over her shoulder. She's wearing her high school uniform and customary scowl. The skirt looks shorter than regulation—Jenna's sure she's had it altered—but she's always walking a tightrope with Willow, so she doesn't say anything.

Pick your battles.

"Good morning," Jenna says with exaggerated cheeriness that would give even Simon a run for his money.

Willow mumbles something, opens the refrigerator, sighs at some unstated grocery-store failure on Jenna's part.

"Pancakes?" Simon asks, earnestly. He's immune to the seventeen-year-old's morning gloom.

"Can't. Ride's here."

Jenna says, "I can get you some fruit or something for the road."

Willow gives her a *you can't be serious* look before she leaves the kitchen with another mumble and the front door slams.

Jenna gets it. Willow lost her mother. Jenna knows what that feels like. Maybe one day they'll be able to talk about it together.

Simon sets a plate in front of Jenna. Smiles. He doesn't ask her

what's on her agenda today. He never does. They met on Match
.com, a year ago—three years after the girls' biological mother
succumbed to cancer. They married six months later to the consternation of Simon's family and friends. *To hell with them all,*
he always says, the rare times he curses. *And Willow will come
around—just give her time.*

Jenna's not so sure about that.

After breakfast, she kisses Simon goodbye, does the dishes,
gathers Lulu's backpack. At the bus stop, the little girl stays on the
sidelines, still too shy to join the other kids huddled on the pic-
turesque block of their affluent village outside Washington, D.C.

Jenna understands. The other moms still haven't taken to
Jenna either. Simon always jokes that they're intimidated by her
looks. She doesn't think it's that, but she'll keep trying. She smiles
at Karen, the perfectly named queen bee of the neighborhood
moms. The gesture goes unrequited.

Jenna joins the other parents waving to the tiny windows on
the yellow school bus, all seeming part saddened, part elated,
at the departure of their children for a few precious hours. As
the bus disappears in a trail of black exhaust, Jenna notices a
woman across the street who seems to be staring at her. She's
not one of the usual bus-stop parents. She has a pretty heart-
shaped face, high cheekbones. Someone new in the neighborhood maybe. Too young to be a mom. An au pair? Jenna raises
her hand to wave, but the woman turns away. *Not even fellow
outcasts want to be friends.* Jenna watches a long moment as the
woman crosses the street to avoid the other parents chatting
on the sidewalk.

Back at the house, Jenna contemplates a shower. But it's Soul-
Cycle day. She's already done her miles, so she could skip it, but

they prepaid a fortune for the classes. Besides, what else does she have to do other than clean the house, which Simon already keeps immaculate? Tax lawyers, she's learned, are people of precision. Still, there's dry cleaning to pick up, a run to Whole Foods for Simon's favorite steaks, Willow's veggie burgers.

After running her errands, she again considers skipping spin class. Then a text arrives:

> See you at SoulCycle!

That's weird. She's not meeting anyone at class. She doesn't really have any friends. The message is from an unfamiliar number. Maybe it's the next wave of advertising technology. They not only read your mind on your social-media feed; now it's your texts. Maybe it's the person she met in class last week who was friendly to her, though Jenna doesn't recall giving the woman her number.

By noon, she's rushing into the lobby of the SoulCycle on Massachusetts Avenue, downtown. Though the studio is only seven miles from Jenna's house, it took forty minutes to get there. D.C. traffic is brutal, but it's still nothing compared to Shanghai or Kabul. There's a SoulCycle in Bethesda, much closer to home, but old habits from her single days are hard to break. And Emma L is her favorite instructor.

She smiles at the receptionist, signs in.

In the changing room, Jenna opens her locker. She's surprised. There's a cell phone inside. It's the cheap burner-phone variety. She examines the locker's door to make sure she's opened the right one, but it's her monthly rental. And the combination on the lock worked.

Dread courses through her.

The phone pings. The text is three words:

> bathroom second stall

She scoops up the phone, shuts the tiny door to the locker, and heads to the restroom. Class is starting, she can hear music and the instructor's distorted voice coming from the studio. The restroom is empty. Lowering her head, she peers under the row of stalls. No feet.

She faces the second stall, opens the door slowly, the pulsing beat of the music still vibrating through the walls.

A jolt rips through her. Inside the stall is a woman. She's sitting on the toilet tank, her feet resting on the seat.

Another lightning bolt to the chest. It's the young woman from the bus stop. The woman steps gracefully onto the floor and shoves a duffel bag into Jenna's hands.

"I said I was done with all this," Jenna tells her. "They said I was free and they wouldn't—"

"That's above my pay grade."

"Please, I can't."

The woman shakes her head. "You'd better. For Simon, Willow, and Tallulah's sake."

The woman steps past her calmly and disappears.

Jenna's heart is banging in her chest, sweat forming on her forehead. She steadies herself, then unzips the duffel. Inside, there's a pair of movie-starlet sunglasses, a wig of flowing black hair, a denim jacket, and a keycard that says, HAMILTON HOTEL. Handwritten on the sleeve, a room number: 1018.

Five minutes later, Jenna slips out of the SoulCycle studio

and struts down the street in her disguise. The Hamilton's only a block away. Her gut is full of butterflies, but her training is coming back to her. Like riding a bike.

She's not this person anymore. She can't, she won't.

But her family.

Inside room 1018, she finds a rifle with a high-end scope on a tripod positioned at the window.

The phone pings again and Jenna reads the instructions.

The bald man at the Capital Grille's outdoor table won't be making it to dessert.

CHAPTER TWO

DONNIE

Donnie wakes to loud thuds on his cabin door. Each pound reverberates through his head like an explosion. He's on the floor of the tiny room in the belly of the cruise ship. Twenty years ago, he and the band would have been in the concierge suites. He pushes himself away from the vomit puddled on the floor. The ocean is choppy today and it's making him feel even worse.

The thumping continues and he manages to climb to his feet. Wearing only tighty-whities, he opens the door, and the light from the hallway sends another bullet through his skull.

"Donnie, what's going on?" Pixie has a concerned look on her face. "Rehearsal started half an hour ago. Tom is *pissed*."

Before he responds, Pixie pushes her small frame inside. She makes a face at the stench, looks around, and before Donnie can conceal the evidence sets her eyes on the empty bottle of Jägermeister. The razor blade and rolled dollar bill on the table.

"Oh, Donnie," she says. She puts her delicate brown hand on his ghost-white bare shoulder.

"I can't do this right now," he says, with more edge than she deserves.

Pixie's new. She joined the band last year—Tracer's Bullet has only two original members from back in the day, including Donnie. But it's enough for the Legends of Rock Cruise. Pixie's the only bandmate Donnie considers a friend. The rest merely tolerate him.

Her downcast expression is the worst. One thousand percent pity. He's been sober for three months, the longest stretch in a decade. But then he got word last night about Ben. The closest thing he had to a brother. Then he ran into that aging groupie—the one with the same bleached hair she probably had when she raised a lighter to their hit power ballad two decades ago.

"Wanna party?" she'd said, smelling of cigarettes and beer. She didn't have to ask him twice. He doesn't remember much else.

"Can you play? Are you okay?" Pixie's questions return him to the present. "Seriously, I'm worried. Tom seems—"

"Of course I can play." He climbs into his shirt and jeans flung on the floor. Grabbing the handle to his guitar case, he charges out of the cabin.

"Hurry," Pixie says, outpacing him. She moves quickly for such a compact woman. "I told them I was going to the bathroom."

Donnie rushes into the ship's performance hall and is greeted by several exasperated expressions, the most prominent from their singer, Tom Kipling.

"Sorry, y'all, I overslept," Donnie says, opening his guitar case and slinging the strap over his shoulder.

"*Pfft.*" Tom grips the microphone, leaning as if he's being held up by the stand. Donnie has a brief image of a younger man in the same pose. Even then, Tom was always bossing everyone around. The only thing that's changed is Tom's hair plugs, those white Chiclet teeth, and the tighter fit of his leather pants.

"Overslept . . . ," Tom says, with an audible sigh. "It's four o'clock."

"What do you want me to do? I said I'm sorry."

Tom starts to speak but stops himself. Donnie notices Tom tap eyes with Animal, their drummer. "Let's just do the sound check," Tom says, sighing again. He points to the set list taped on the stage floor.

Animal clicks his sticks—*a one, a two, a one-two-three-four*—and Donnie strikes the opening chord to a song he's played so many times he can barely stand it. From his Marshall stack comes what sounds like an elephant being slaughtered. His Les Paul is wildly out of tune, thanks to neglect and a popped string.

Tom waves his arms to cut the music. His sagging jowls quiver. But he doesn't yell at Donnie. That's a surprise. Donnie's spent most of his adult life being yelled at by Tom Kipling, so he's used to it. But this is worse. Tom composes himself, then looks over to their manager, Mickey, at stage right. Mickey gives Tom a nod, and Tom addresses the band.

"Tonight, after the show, you all have a choice to make," Tom says. He spins around and fixes his gaze on Donnie. "It's him or me."

And with that—his aging-rock-star flair for the dramatic on full display—Tom stomps offstage.

Donnie looks at his bandmates. When he sees that even Pixie isn't willing to make eye contact, he knows it's over.

Later, after the last encore—they do two every show—Donnie runs offstage drenched in sweat and feeling euphoric. That sensation never goes away. He's performed well; Tom can't deny that. Donnie got his guitar freshly strung and went over the set list beforehand to be ready for tonight's parade of oldies. He even hit all his marks for the ridiculous choreography.

Backstage, amid the high fives and rapture that follows every performance, he thinks things should be fine. Tom will have cooled off. Donnie can explain what happened—that his best friend, Benny, is dead. Not just dead. Murdered. He'll explain that he's committed to his sobriety—to the band—and they'll give him another chance.

After the meet-and-greet—the selfies and poster signing and awkward conversations with drunk people—the VIP room clears out and Tom calls him over.

"You did well tonight," Tom says.

"Thanks, brother. You were great. You sound like you did when we were kids."

Tom gives a fleeting smile with that row of too-white teeth on his too-tan face. He's like an old house with too many layers of paint. He takes a deep breath. "That's just it, man. We're not kids anymore."

"I get it, Tommy. I promise it won't happen again, I just—"

"I've got three ex-wives to support," Tom interrupts. "My daughter's in her second year at Berkeley. I need this job, man."

"Trust me, so do I," Donnie says. He holds back his resentment at Tom's tales of financial woe. Tom took all the songwriting credits—at the time the rest of the band didn't understand that if your name isn't on the song the money stops. It's the reason Tracer's Bullet broke up. Donnie's the only other member who was desperate enough to come back.

"That's what makes this hard, Don."

"Tommy . . ."

Tom offers a sad expression. "It's done, my friend. I wish you nothing but the best."

"You can't do this to me!" Donnie's voice rises.

A couple of roadies look over.

Tom shakes his head.

Donnie's voice breaks now. "You owe me, man."

"I've gotta go." Tom turns. Donnie grabs his arm roughly and Tom twists around, his face dark now. "I suggest you let go of my arm."

Donnie stares at him a long beat. And releases his grip.

Closing in on midnight, on the promenade deck—the most secluded section of the ship after hours—Donnie takes the last swig of the bottle, hating himself for drinking again. Hating himself for not standing up to Tom. Hating himself for what his life has become. He stares out at the ocean. With the moon hidden by clouds, there's nothing but blackness.

He ponders where he can get another bottle. The ship's bars are closed. There's room service, but his account is maxed out.

A woman appears in the weak light. She's in her early twenties, younger than the band's usual fans, but she's wearing a Tracer T-shirt. Probably someone's kid who grew up with their music. That happens sometimes.

Her face brightens when she sees him.

"Oh my god. Are you Donnie Danger?" She looks around as if she wants to confirm what she's seeing, but no one else is on the deck.

"The one and only," Donnie says. His southern drawl gets more pronounced when he's playing rock star, particularly when he's drinking.

"Will you sign an autograph for me?" she asks.

"I'll do anything you want, sweetheart."

She smiles, her teeth glowing in the dim light.

"*Anything?*" she says seductively. She walks over next to him, leans against the protective railing.

"Your wish is my command, darlin'," Donnie says, trying to muster more southern boy charm, but it's half-assed and lazy.

The woman reaches inside her shirt. He thinks she's going to pull it off. Have him sign her breasts. It's been a while since he's done that, but it's part of the job, who's he to complain?

She doesn't remove her top. Doesn't ask him to sign her ample cleavage. Instead, she's reached into her waistband and pulled out a handgun.

"Well, my *wish*"—she says the word with derision—"is that you jump." She motions the gun at the ocean below them, then trains it back on Donnie.

He chuckles, like she's kidding. She's fucking crazy, but he's always been drawn to crazy women. The gun looks real, but surely it's a fake; she's only playing. Offering a rakish smile, he says, "Look, sweetheart, I don't—"

He's cut off with a hard blow to his head with the butt of the gun. Donnie doubles over. After what feels like a long time but might be only a few seconds, he stands, his legs wobbly. He touches his head. There's red on his fingers. His eyes look into hers. She's definitely *not* playing.

"Jump."

She puts the barrel of the gun to his forehead, its muzzle cool on his skin.

"I don't understand." Donnie's heartbeat swirls in his ears now.

"You don't need to understand." She holds up five fingers with the hand not clutching the gun. She begins ticking off her fingers.

"Five . . ."

"All right, hold on, wait. . . ."

"Four . . ."

"Wait, hold up."

"Three . . ."

"Okay!" He raises his hands.

She retracts the barrel and steps back, motions her chin for him to get up on the rail.

A chill races up Donnie's spine. He hops his ass up, feeling the cold metal through his jeans. He's no longer shit-faced drunk, but he's still unsteady from the terror.

The woman gestures with the gun for him to swing his legs around, and he does, fear seizing him as he sits precariously on the ledge, his feet dangling. On this side of the ship there are no decks below. A straight drop into the ocean. His eyes search for life preservers but find none.

"Two," she says.

He twists his head around. She's displaying an awful peace sign with her fingers.

"Please—What's—I don't understand."

Before he pleads more, he hears her say, "One," and feels the shove into the abyss.

CHAPTER THREE

NICO

Nico clasps the flashlight and swings the ray around the coal mine.

He's been the executive producer for the unexpected reality TV hit *The Miners* for a year now, but he still feels claustrophobic in the cavern. The low ceilings, the fog of coal dust, the rats. The coal company closed Mine B in the 1980s, and it's now only used as one of the show's sets. The cast always grumbles about shoots here, complaining that staging scenes in an inoperable mine takes away from the authenticity of the show. Nico listens patiently to their gripes, fights the urge to remind them that they're hardly living an "authentic" coal miner's life. The star of the show, Roger, who's spent the better part of his life working in a godforsaken hole for $47K a year, drives a Bentley for fuck's sake. But for better or for worse, they're Nico's meal ticket.

Like the cast, his income has skyrocketed with the success of the show—the most popular reality series on cable (take that, *Housewives*!). Not to mention that Nico has become something of a sex symbol with his weekly live recap show, *The Black*, which has thrust him into the national conversation. His DMs from women would make even the Tinder crowd blush. It almost makes living in the boonies of West Virginia worth it. Almost makes being at the beck and call of Roger—who texted Nico to meet him at Mine B tonight for some bizarre reason—less annoying. And, best of all, the influx of cash keeps the bookies and loan sharks off Nico's ass, a refreshing change of pace.

Why the hell did Roger want to meet here, anyway? He probably wants to talk about getting more on-camera time. Complain about his co-stars outside their small enclave where gossip and grievances are more abundant than meth . . . which is saying something in this town.

Nico stares at the railroad tracks and the old handcar that looks like something out of an Indiana Jones movie. The cast complains about the handcar too, since it bears no resemblance to the man-trips that real miners use to travel through the tunnels. But it makes for good television. In the cliff-hanger for Season 1, they filmed a scene in which the brakes just so happened to go out. Nico's convinced that Davis, the network asshole who's been trying to muscle in on Nico's job, had someone grease the brakes. The cast had similar suspicions but forgave Davis the moment the scene went viral on social media. Maybe Nico should be more like Davis. Yeah, he should've hidden a camera for this meeting with Roger tonight. A secret meeting that could stir up trouble with the others. Great content for a new episode, but Nico has his limits when it comes to orchestrating drama. It's the only area of his life where he has limits.

He hears the noise of the elevator, the rickety pile of rusted metal. It's nearly ten o'clock, which means Roger—who insists on being called Maverick (coal miners live for their nicknames)—will have several shots of Jim Beam in him.

The doors to the elevator rattle open. Nico hates that contraption. It's going to be the death of someone, he's convinced. Oh, wouldn't Davis love that? The ratings would go through the roof.

The figure moves toward him.

Holding up the flashlight, Nico says, "Geez, Roger, what's with all the cloak-and-dagger? Your text said—"

Nico stops when the figure clicks on the lamp of a miner's helmet. It's a blinding beam, stronger than a typical head lamp.

Nico squints, holds up a hand to shield his eyes. He can make out that the figure is shorter than six-two Roger. His danger antenna starts sending signals, raising the hairs on the back of his neck.

"This is private property," Nico says in a firm tone, trying to keep the tremor out of his voice. "I know the sheriff, so you'd best be on your way before—"

He stops when the figure's lamp turns off, leaving Nico's eyes spotted by the afterglow. He hears gravel crunching, the figure running at him, then hears a strange sound like a hydraulic pump.

Then there's a fire in his shoulder. He's on the ground.

It's only a millisecond before he scrambles to his feet and hauls ass. After years evading the leg breakers when he couldn't keep up with the vig, he knows what's coming.

Nico races down the tunnel and dives onto the handcar. The beam from the miner's helmet is on him again, his own shadow skittering ahead. He turns quickly and sees the figure walking slowly toward him, Jason from the horror movie, carrying something that looks like a baton or cylinder.

What in the holy fuck? The light is getting closer as he settles into the handcar, his shirt damp with blood and sweat. Nico grabs the lever and tugs down with everything he has. His other arm feels like it's been branded by a cowpoke.

The railcar pushes forward. He needs to get the fuck out of there, crank that lever harder.

He ducks low, puts his weight on the lever, the ray from the assailant's helmet bathing him in light. Nico cranks harder, the railcar picking up pace. He uses his good arm and marshals all his strength to pump the crank. The light behind him is getting dimmer as the car bumps along the tracks.

He thinks he hears footfalls behind him, but he keeps cranking, moving faster. They fixed the brakes on this thing at least, but the tracks will end soon. He'll have to turn and fight if the attacker follows. He does not intend to die in this shitty mine, that's for sure.

He cranks and cranks until the light mercifully disappears.

Deep in the tunnel now, darkness envelops him. He yanks out his iPhone. It won't work down here, but there's a flashlight.

No, it will draw the figure to him. He keeps gliding down the tracks, letting the cart slow, knowing there's a dead end. He doesn't want to plow into the bumper.

His heart continues to pound, he's drenched in panic sweat, but the car finally comes to a stop.

It's pitch-black. He listens, fear and blood loss making him tremble.

More silence.

Then, a joyous sound. The rattle of the elevator's motor. The attacker is leaving. *Thank. Fucking. God.*

He feels a wave of relief, but adrenaline still has him wired. He clicks on the phone's flashlight, gasps at his blood-soaked shirt.

All is quiet, the elevator up top now. He needs to get out of there, get to a hospital, but he decides to wait a little longer to give the attacker time to leave the mine site.

Then he hears it.

A deep, loud *boom*.

The railcar shakes and a snapping sound comes from above.

In a split second, he realizes the grim reality. An explosive detonated.

There's a loud rumble, a cloud of black dust fills the tunnel, and everything goes dark.

CHAPTER FOUR

JENNA

Jenna doesn't want to do this. But she has no choice, she knows. She prays the target is a bad guy. She used to tell herself that they were all bad guys. But the truth is, she had no idea. And the harder truth: The longer she was on the job, the more difficult it became to tell the bad guys from the good. Wealth and power can hide monsters in plain sight.

This isn't happening. She was supposed to be out.

But it *is* happening. The woman's voice tackles her thoughts: *You'd better. For Simon, Willow, and Tallulah's sake.*

If she ever meets that woman again, she will kill her.

She separates the hotel room's drapes an inch and looks outside. It's a direct line of sight to the outdoor deck of the Capital Grille.

The deck is empty, which is unusual for the power-lunch hot spot. It's usually packed when Jenna leaves spin class. Perhaps her target reserved the entire seating area.

She looks at the burner phone again.

Cap Grille, outside table, bald man.

Her thoughts drift to her family at breakfast—to her wonderfully normal husband kissing her goodbye, to her wonderfully angsty teen slamming the door, to her wonderfully adorable five-year-old sneaking food to her wonderfully loveable dog. Then Jenna imagines losing them all by the time she returns home if she doesn't do this.

She examines the rifle, checks the scope. The hotel window presents a problem. She usually would have a two-person team, one to shoot out the glass, the other to take out the mark. But she notices that someone has disabled the suicide-deterence mechanism that ordinarily would prevent the window from opening more than a few inches. She pulls the latch and the window opens far enough to avoid obstructing the shot. She looks for something to take a wind reading and sees that a flag planted on the roof of an office building is limp.

She gets in position.

It isn't long before the restaurant's host leads a small cluster of men to an outdoor table. The men are muscular and seem uncomfortable in their business suits. Ex-military. They examine the area, look up and down Massachusetts Avenue. The target is someone important—important enough to have an advance team, anyway. But not so high-value that he's forbidden from eating outside on a beautiful spring day. One of the advance guys says something into his sleeve, then the target appears. Jenna can't see his face, but he's the only bald head. It might as well be painted with a bull's-eye.

Still, it won't be an easy shot. The bald man sits with his back to her. The bodyguards surround the table. She'll need the perfect opening. Jenna hopes he'll need to use the restroom.

She waits. Still as a stone, like she was taught. She once waited thirteen hours, frozen in place. She shudders, remembering the weight in her chest and, worse, peeling off the adult diaper, its smell somehow shocking.

A bottle of something expensive is brought to the table.

She waits.

Sweat slides down her side. Can she still do this? Physically, yes. She's rusty, but it's a skill that never goes away. Emotionally, though . . . can she do it?

Yes, you have to.

At last, the bald man stands. Throws his napkin on the table. The guards change position, ready to escort him to the restroom.

Through the scope, Jenna gets the first look at his face.

And her heart plummets.

She pulls back from the rifle's scope.

The face is familiar, one that's been on the covers of magazines, the nightly news, endless social-media feeds. One that still looks much the same as it did twenty-five years ago in the dining room of their group home.

Something catches her eye. A reflection—a sharp glimmer from the rooftop of the building across from her, just past the restaurant.

Then it hits her: It's the sun glittering off of another scope.

She's not the only hitter. There's a backup team.

This job felt "off" since the start. This is not how The Corporation operates. Jenna's nerves are on fire. She needs to get out of here.

She presses her eye back to the scope.

In one fluid movement, she sets her aim, takes a breath, and pulls the trigger, light as a feather.

CHAPTER FIVE

The recoil slams into her shoulder. Through the sight she sees that the bald man is already surrounded by his human shields, who quickly shuffle him inside the restaurant. No one is hit. Precisely as Jenna intended.

She wipes down the gun, leaves it where she found it. She's been careful not to touch anything else.

Examining herself in the long mirror near the door, she straightens the wig, puts on the sunglasses, tucks the burner phone in her pocket. After one deep breath, she calmly steps out of the room into the hallway.

Lowering her head in case there are cameras, she moves toward the elevator bank. It's quiet. No one has connected the shooting to the hotel. Yet.

She senses another person in the hall and glances up. The woman's back is to her; she's searching her handbag for her room key.

Something is off. Unnatural.

Jenna turns and walks in the other direction. She takes a quick look over her shoulder and sees the guest—the woman from the bus stop and from the SoulCycle bathroom—in a double-handed firing stance. Jenna dodges to the right, hears the cut of wind from the suppressor. She sprints, zagging left and right and left and around the corner.

She spies the door to the emergency stairs and dashes through it, the woman running close behind.

The stairwell spirals down all ten floors. She won't have time to outpace the woman. Jenna climbs over the railing and hangs, her arms outstretched, body a vertical line. Her chest is hammering. She needs to collect herself. *Remember your training.* Hanging there forever, she gets her bearings.

And she releases her grip.

She drops two floors, whiplashing to a stop when she catches the railing.

She hears movement above. The woman's head appears over the ledge for an instant before it pulls back. The shooter tries the move again, from a different position, hoping to avoid a bullet to the forehead. She peers over once more and gets off a shot. But Jenna's already dropping two more floors, where she again catches the railing. This time one hand slips and leaves her hanging tenuously. With every ounce of strength she has, she reaches for the rail with her free hand. But now her other hand's losing its grip.

There's the sound of the suppressor again, a ricochet of metal on metal, as the bullet bounces around the stairwell. Jenna looks up and sees the woman pointing her gun straight at her.

So she releases again.

Jenna misses the railing on the next floor, then the next blurs past, and she's not going to make it.

But her hand slaps the metal on the next rail down and she lets out a primal roar as her body yanks to a stop when she maintains her grip.

She looks up. The woman's head has vanished. She's going to try to beat Jenna to the ground floor.

Jenna pulls herself up and over the railing, bursts through the door—it has the number 3 on it—and into the hallway. There's a luggage cart nearby. A bellhop appears from the room and stacks a large bag on the cart, then disappears back into the room. Jenna walks slowly as a family appears from the room. A father holding a fussy baby and mom trying to wrangle two toddlers. The bellhop loads another bag and, seeing the squirmy kids, tells the parents to go on ahead to check out, he'll meet them in the lobby. The father palms him a few bills and the family shuttles away. The bellhop disappears into the room again. Jenna has only a few minutes before the police—or, worse, the woman and the backup team—sweep every floor. Confirming the thought, she hears sirens outside.

If they've found the connection to the hotel, it may scare off the woman and her team. But Jenna can't be caught here. The bellhop tugs another bag and lugs it onto the cart, not noticing her.

The luggage includes an oversized bag. The kind with a structured interior made for sporting equipment or something large. It will have to do.

Jenna removes the bag from the cart, unzips it. Inside is a folded baby stroller. She pulls it out and races back to the emergency stairwell and tucks it away there. She's perspiring, the wig is lopsided, but somehow it stayed on during her descent. The bellhop is still inside the room, probably doing a final sweep to make sure he's not leaving anything behind. She doesn't have much time. Jenna dashes toward the cart, climbs into the oversized bag, contorts her body, and zips it shut from the inside.

Her mind trips to Savior House. Hiding in the footlocker from the pack of boys at the group home. *Come out come out wherever you are. . . .*

She's a tiny ball, her limbs ache. She's not as agile as she used to be. But the muscle memory is there again. It's hot and she's dripping with sweat. She hears the hotel room door shut, the bellhop curses under his breath, and she thinks she's been caught. But instead, the bag is hoisted upward and dropped onto the luggage cart.

The cart bumps and jostles as it wheels away, then comes to a stop. She hears the ping of the elevator, and the cart starts rolling again. The interior noise soon turns to the sounds of the street. Cars honking, sirens not too far away. She manages to open the bag a trace, the air feeling good on her face, in her lungs. Her view outside is obstructed, so she listens.

The area is being cordoned off, a valet says to someone. There'll be a slight delay. "Welcome to D.C.," he says, with the nonchalance of someone accustomed to terror-threat drills, presidential motorcades, and protest-march street closures.

The cart rolls a few feet, and she peeks out through the opening. She's trying to control her breathing, and she's feeling nauseated, the inside of the bag sweltering. She sees men in hotel uniforms standing at the curb, looking toward the restaurant. Two cabs are parked, their drivers outside the vehicles. A valet is talking to a uniformed cop. Everyone is looking at the Capital Grille.

Except for one woman.

Jenna's heart sinks. The woman wears large sunglasses concealing much of her face, but it's her. She's staring at a cell phone. She walks slowly, oblivious to the chaos around her. Her eyes move from her phone to the street, then to the phone again. As if she's following directions on Google Maps.

Jenna feels a chill course through her. If this job was a setup—and it was—they never planned to let her out of the hotel alive. They'd want the ability to track her, if necessary. And she's still wearing the clothes, the disguise they gave her. And she has their burner phone.

The woman is getting closer now. She looks up and has a curious expression on her face. Then it turns to revelation.

Jenna manages to unzip the bag, shift her body so she rolls off the cart, and untangles her limbs. She takes a gulp of air and gets to her feet.

"*She has a gun!*" Jenna screams, pointing at the woman. "*She has a gun!*"

Jenna doesn't stick around to see what happens. As she sprints away, she hears screams. Before she rounds the corner, she takes a quick look back.

A uniformed police officer is on the ground, writhing in pain.

And the woman is racing after Jenna.

CHAPTER SIX

DONNIE

Donnie gasps, his mouth filling with water. As soon as he gets a gulp of oxygen, he's back under.

Is this how he's going to die? In the dirty, leaf-filled public swimming pool in Chestertown, Pennsylvania? A fitting end to the pile of dog shit that's been his fourteen years of life so far.

Derek grips his hair, forcing Donnie down again. Donnie's panicking, trying to fight, but at 110 pounds he's no match for Derek and his goons.

Derek lets him above water, Donnie sucks in a morsel of precious air, and he's back under. Donnie should've waited for Ben before going in the pool. Derek and his friends leave Donnie alone when Benny's around.

His eyes feel like they're going to shoot out of his head, torpedoes jetting into the blue haze, his lungs burning. But Derek won't release his grip. This isn't the first time Derek has dunked Donnie under—Donnie has even trained for Derek's attacks, practiced holding his breath. On the walk home from school he can hold his breath from the boarded-up house with the mattress in the yard, past the pit bull raging after him along the chain-link fence, to the corner bodega. But today is different. Derek's grip is more forceful, the time Donnie is submerged longer.

Donnie's thoughts are floating, his head light. He should fight. *I can't die here!* He needs to live. To show them all. That he'll be somebody. He'll be onstage in stadiums and on MTV and everyone who ever called him Twig or Cletus or Redneck will beg for backstage tickets. They'll want his autograph. Brag to their friends that they knew him way back when.

Fight, Donnie. But he's too weak. In the blur of legs and bodies in the over-chlorinated pool, the water splashes violently. Someone cannonballing. His chest hurts from holding his breath.

More splashing.

Then, miraculously, Derek releases his hold. Donnie feels two hands under his armpits and he's yanked out of the water.

Next thing he knows, he's on the concrete lip of the pool. Rolled on his side, someone pounding on his back with an open hand. He hears a cough and feels water jettison from his mouth.

He's on his back now, the wind howling, the world spinning. He makes out the figure looking down at him. Benny. Big, tall Benny, standing there with his hands on his hips, a Superman pose. He *is* Superman, Black Superman, as he'd say.

His best friend nods, and Donnie knows he's going to be okay.

But when his vision clears, he's not at the Chestertown public swimming pool. Derek Brood isn't nursing a bloody lip. There's no battered diving board, no rusted fence surrounding the shadeless, overcrowded slab of concrete. And then it hits him all over again, nearly destroys him: *Ben is dead.*

Donnie tries to sit up, but a voice says, "Whoa, hold on there, amigo."

A man with a beard, standing with other men with beards,

looks down at him. The floor sways and there's the smell of fish and salt, the sound of waves and wind. He's on a vessel, a commercial fishing boat, maybe.

The fishermen look like they've seen a ghost—or a miracle.

"You're one lucky son of a bitch, brother," one of them says.

CHAPTER SEVEN

NICO

A sliver of light from his cell phone's flashlight cuts through the black. Nico needs to preserve the battery. There's no service down here, but maybe if they dig down deep enough searching for him they'll get a faint ping. He knows it's unlikely. His shoulder aches, but the bleeding seems to have stopped. He swings the light toward his feet. Four red beady eyes stare back at him. He's never been so happy to see rats. Scurrying, dirty, disgusting varmints that will unquestionably tear his flesh down to the bone if he dies. But for now, they're a welcome sight: They're alive. There's still oxygen. No deadly CO_2 buildup in this cave of gloom. Yet, anyway.

Nico thinks back to his mandatory mine-safety training. He should have paid more attention. There's been a roof collapse. He's not buried alive, so the biggest risk now is running out of air. The explosion has likely sucked away most of the oxygen, but he's in a chamber. He needs to find a SCSR, the self-contained oxygen self-rescuers. They're stored in receptacles along the mine. And he remembers that he needs to keep his movements to a minimum, use as little air as possible. That won't be a problem. He's sore, groggy. One of the rats scurries onto his leg and he kicks it away, sending a searing pain through him.

He wonders if anyone is searching for him or if they even know he's missing. They have to know about the mine collapse. The crew has sensors that detect problems underground. MSHA, WVOMHST, NIOSH, and the other alphabet soup of mine-safety agencies are probably on-site. The showrunner will make sure the cast and crew are accounted for.

The cast.

It was Roger who got Nico into this mess—asking him to meet at Mine B after hours. But it wasn't Roger who attacked him, Nico is sure of that. He never got a clear look, but if Nico has to guess, it was a woman. *Who is she?* And what in the hell was that weapon that pierced into him with such ease?

He clicks off the phone's flashlight. It's frightening in the dark, but the iPhone is already on low-power mode. His mouth is dry and his shoulder is screaming.

He's supposed to bang on the roof bolts; they have equipment to listen for it. He wonders for a moment what the Vegas odds-makers would set his chances of survival.

He shakes his head. Even now, his thoughts return to gambling. He should make a promise—an oath—that if he gets out of this jam he'll never make another bet again. Maybe a 12-step program will stick this time. *What were those twelve steps?* Another instance when he should've paid better attention.

In the disorienting darkness, his mind meanders. He's in a black hole, time relative, impossible to gauge. He resists the urge to check the phone again. With his good arm, he reaches into his front pocket. He feels the ridges of the old silver dollar. Some good-luck charm it turned out to be. He should flip the coin: Heads he'll survive, tails . . . He decides against it.

In the haze, the first of the 12 Steps comes to him: *Admit we are powerless over gambling, that our lives have become unmanageable.*

Nico has never been one to think he's powerless—he can stop gambling whenever he wants. But he's got to admit, things have become unmanageable. He's literally hit rock bottom—hundreds of feet down in a mine, no less. Maybe one of O'Leary's boys came to send a message and set off a charge in the mine.

But that doesn't make any sense. He owes $395,000 plus the vig. He'd been up to a half mil in debt, which O'Leary's people found unacceptable, but he'd scraped together $100K. He had to do something bad to get that down payment, but you do what you gotta do. He's current at the moment, so there's no reason to murder him. He learned this much from his old man, who was one of O'Leary's soldiers back in the day: You don't kill the goose that lays the golden egg. You break its wing, rest the blade of the axe on its neck. Reset the debtor's priorities. You don't blow him up.

His stomach growls. A loud rumble that reminds him of something else that's terrifying. He has no food. No water. His mind jumps to the safety course again. There was a lot of discussion in the class about a group of Chilean miners trapped for months who survived by drinking water from industrial tanks used to wash dirty miners' gloves. Is there a water source down here?

He remembers the funny story about how one of the Chilean miners had both his wife and his mistress show up at the rescue site, a reality show in the making as the world wondered who would win his heart when he emerged. Who did the guy pick? Nico can't remember.

There will be no one outside holding vigil for Nico, he knows that much. Beyond his love of gaming, there are a few constants in the life of Nico Adakai. One: People always think he's an asshole. He's not sure why, he doesn't intend to be one, but there's no denying it. Two: He's a coward, always has been. And three: The people closest to him always leave.

This last thought takes him to another of the 12 Steps: *Make a list of persons we have harmed and become willing to make amends to them all.*

He thinks of his fiancée—correction, *ex*-fiancée—Natalie. She loved him. Really, really loved him. She was willing to work things through, even after discovering the credit cards he'd opened in her name. The thousands in debt he racked up.

"You know, it's not the gambling," she'd said on that last day. "You might be able to overcome that."

"Then what is it?"

"You're incapable of loving anyone."

"That's not true," he said.

"You're always one foot out the door so you can beat the other person at leaving."

Natalie is an elementary school teacher, not a psychologist, but she's watched enough *Dr. Phil* to be on to something. Nico made the mistake of telling Natalie about his mother leaving him behind to escape his abusive father, about his father then disappearing. And he told Natalie about Annie, his first love who vanished without a trace.

In the fog of his thoughts—he must be in shock—his mind frolics to Annie. . . .

Raising her hand in ninth-grade science, one of the only kids listening to the teacher drone on. Sitting on the top of the monkey bars at the seedy park watching the sunset. The way she smelled of bubble gum. Oh, and her laugh. It was high-pitched, cute, and made her seem softer, less damaged by her time in group homes.

The way she'd get exasperated with Nico and the other boys

about their endless "that's what she said" jokes. They were stupid, but "your mama" jokes didn't play well in foster care.

In his mind, he's walking home from school with the others. "How'd you do on the math test?" he asks Annie.

Before she answers, Artemis chimes in. "It wasn't hard at all."

Donnie barks a laugh. "That's what she said."

Nico sleeps.

It's dreamless but restless at the same time.

When he wakes, it takes a moment to remember.

He's in a collapsed mine.

He may never get out.

He hopes they're trying to find him. That, up top, word is out and there's a media circus surrounding the effort to save Nico Adakai. Portable lights, digging equipment, the National Guard, volunteers, network news vans.

He thinks of those Chilean miners again. How long were they trapped? It was sixty-nine days, something he remembers only because of the juvenile fascination with the number sixty-nine.

How'd they escape? There was a drill.

For Nico, they're going to need to work all night, with a big drill, he thinks.

Then he smiles. "That's what she said."

CHAPTER EIGHT

JENNA

Jenna darts around the corner onto K Street, past a coffee shop, and into a CVS. The sound of sirens still floats in the air. She thinks she's lost the woman but can't be sure.

She takes an escalator to the lower level and makes for the back. There's no restroom, but the greeting card aisle is empty. She strips off the jacket and fingers the fabric at the seams, checks the pockets. On the back hem, she finds it. A tiny square the size of an ordinary PC dongle sewn into the denim.

Yanking off the wig, she finds a mirror on a sunglass display stand in the back corner and tries to straighten her hair. It's wet from sweat, disheveled. She finds a bristle brush on a rack and slicks her hair back, runway-model-style. Her cell phone and all her credit cards and money are stowed in the locker at SoulCycle, but she can't go there. She needs to reach Simon. She still has the burner phone. It could also have a tracker—she'll deal with that after. But she needs to warn him.

The burner's screen is blank. She tries to power it on, but nothing happens. It's dead. Or they loaded some self-destruct code on the device. It would be just like Sabine and her Corporation operatives to pull this kind of *Mission Impossible* bullshit.

Back on the main floor, Jenna glances out the window before heading outside. She can't take an Uber without her phone. Maybe she can get a cab. A cabbie won't need money up front and might let her borrow a phone for a quick call. Then she spies a bus pulling to the corner of K and Seventh. She runs over, waits for two elderly women to get on. The driver is already moving before the old ladies have found and swiped their fare cards. Jenna steps past them and the driver says, "You forgot to pay, ma'am."

"Sorry," Jenna says. "I must have left my wallet at my exercise class. I can get off now or at the next stop."

The driver sighs, shakes his head, but plows ahead. Jenna sits on the edge of the seat near the back door. She tucks the jacket with the tracker under the seat, the cell phone and wig stuffed inside. One problem solved. Let that woman follow the bus around for a while.

The bus tugs to a stop, and Jenna jumps out at Ninth and I, near the collection of high-end stores at City Center.

She looks for a cab but doesn't see any, which isn't surprising since Uber and Lyft turned everyone into amateur taxi drivers. She spots a guy in a suit riding one of those motorized scooters that are such a nuisance. He has a hipster beard and is gabbing on his phone, zipping along the sidewalk and around pedestrians too fast.

Jenna decides to do it. As the scooter approaches, she trips forward, knocking into the man. The guy yelps, and they both topple onto the grassy strip separating the sidewalk from the street.

The hipster's eyes are wide as he looks at Jenna, who has jumped to her feet and is brushing herself off. "Oh my gosh, are you okay?" she asks.

A few people walking by watch, then continue on once they see that no one's hurt.

He looks up at her, slightly dazed. His suit pants have a hole in the knee, but he's all right. His head snaps back and forth as if he's making sure no one caught the scene on their phone—the ever-present risk of going viral for one of life's embarrassing moments.

The guy says, "You need to watch where you're—" He stops, apparently computing what's happening as Jenna scoops up his phone and holds it up to his face, unlocking the device.

"What are you—"

Jenna doesn't answer as she darts to the scooter, pulls it from the pavement, and rides away.

He yells after her, but his voice grows distant as she races along Ninth and cuts a sharp right on Mount Vernon Place and past the historic Carnegie Library building that's tragically been converted into an Apple store.

She manages to dial Simon's number as she steers the scooter. It goes to voicemail. Of course . . . a call from an unfamiliar line. When she's a safe distance away, she skids to a stop and furiously thumbs a text.

It says only two words, but Simon will understand:

Alas Babylon.

CHAPTER NINE

DONNIE

Donnie adjusts the angle of the hospital bed upward, laces his hands behind his head with his elbows sticking out. He got lucky: The fishermen were 1990s boys and fans of Tracer's Bullet. They gave him some whiskey and a blanket to get his body temperature up, bandaged the gash on his head, and brought him ashore.

Now he has a half circle of fans around his bed at the University of Miami Hospital. TMZ got wind that Donnie Danger survived a fall from a cruise ship and it didn't take long before his room was filled with flowers and women with big hair. Tracer's Bullet had been one of the only hair bands to emerge—and thrive—during the grunge era, a novelty act that scratched the itch of early Gen Xers not swept away by Kurt Cobain, Pearl Jam, STP, and the rest.

"Could you sign my CD?" a lady asks. She's in her forties with an orange hue to her skin and prominent lines around the eyes from too many years in the sun. With her, a girl in her teens whose eyes are glued to a phone.

"Sure, sweetheart," he says, taking the Sharpie someone gave him. He's in the gown, his skinny white legs tucked under the sheets. "What's your name?"

"Crystal," she says. Like always, he writes: "To beautiful Crystal, stay close to Danger. DD."

She examines the CD cover and cups it to her chest like a treasure.

"And who's this?" He looks at the girl.

"My niece." The girl barely looks up from her phone. "She was at my house when I heard. I'm so glad you're okay."

"You and me both, darlin'."

"How did it happen? I mean, your fall . . ." She says it uncomfortably like she shouldn't ask.

"That is the million-dollar question," Donnie says as he signs a poster for a man with sleeved tattoos. And it is. The last thing he remembers is Tom firing him. And Donnie retrieving his emergency bottle of Jack from his cabin.

The nurse arrives, a look of distaste on her face. "Mr. Danger, you have a visitor."

"The more the merrier," Donnie tells her. He's in full rock-star persona, the only time he feels comfortable in his own skin. The only way to mask the anxiety baked into his bones.

The nurse says, "I'm afraid we need to ask everyone to step out."

"*Boo*," one of his fans says playfully, and the small crowd shuttles out.

A man in a dark suit enters. "Mr., ah, Danger," he says, like it pains him. But it's actually Donnie's last name; he changed it legally after their first album went platinum and he had money burning a hole in his pocket. His real name is Donnie Johnson, but Tom told him, *Don Johnson? You've gotta change that. This isn't Miami Vice.*

"That's me," Donnie says.

The man is tall, olive skinned, his part defined, his posture arrow straight. A lawyer, possibly. Maybe the cruise-ship company thinks Donnie's gonna sue. They've already sent over a giant bouquet of flowers and a perky woman called and told him they'd set him up in a suite at the Fontainebleau hotel so he can recover in style.

He should fall out of a boat more often.

"I'm Special Agent Rodriguez with the Federal Bureau of Investigation."

"The FBI?" Donnie says. "No shit."

The man nods. Doesn't elaborate. "I have a few questions, if you're up for it."

"Sure, boss," Donnie says, his accent thick and folksy when he's Rock Star Donnie.

"What happened?" the agent asks, an open-ended question if there ever was one.

"Afraid I can't tell you much. I hit my nugget on the way down, it seems." He knocks lightly on the side of his head. "Last thing I remember is the show. We killed it." He remembers a little more but doesn't want to get into Tom firing him. His solo pity party afterward with the bottle of Jack. But what came after remains a complete blank.

"You don't remember how you went over?"

Donnie shakes his head. "The doc says it may come back to me, but right now, nothin'."

The FBI agent doesn't seem surprised. He's probably already spoken with the doctor, a pretty Black lady immune to Donnie's charm.

Donnie adds, "There's cameras all over the boat, I imagine the cruise line can—"

"We have the footage," the agent cuts him off. "Mr. Danger . . ." He pauses, cracks his neck. "Is there anyone you can think of who'd want to hurt you?"

Donnie guffaws at that. "Maybe one of my ex-girlfriends." He smiles. "Oh, you're serious. No, I can't think of anyone who'd want to hurt me. I mean, why would they?"

The agent doesn't respond. He pulls out his phone, displays a grainy video. It shows Donnie, his gait unsteady, a bottle clenched in his left hand as he pulls along the stair railing up to the promenade deck with his right.

The agent says, "This is the last footage of you they could find. We think you went over on deck four."

Donnie nods. He has absolutely no recollection of it. "They got cameras there, don't they?"

The agent nods. "The two were disabled, vandalized."

He studies Donnie, like he's looking for a reaction. Maybe they think Donnie disabled the cameras himself. If they've talked to the band, they'd know he was fired. Maybe the FBI thinks he was trying to kill himself. But the agent doesn't ask.

"You were friends with Benjamin Wood?"

This takes him aback. Why would this agent be asking about Benny? Donnie supposes the Feds would be on the case—the murder of a federal judge must be something the FBI covers. But what in the hell does it have to do with Donnie falling off a boat?

"Yeah. We were tight since we were kids. I'm the godfather to his daughter." This reminds him, he needs to call and check in. He called Benny's wife, Mia, several times from the ship's satellite phone, but they all went to voicemail.

"When was the last time you saw him before he was killed?"

"About a month ago. I've been on the road. . . . I visit him in Philly whenever I'm back east."

The agent nods.

"Hey, you mind me asking what this has to do with my, ah, accident?" Donnie asks.

"I don't mind you asking," the agent says. But he doesn't answer the question. Instead, he asks, "Any idea why Judge Wood would have been in Chestertown?" The newspapers said Benny was last seen leaving work, but his body was found in a Dumpster in an industrial area of the dreary Pennsylvania town where they'd been in foster care together. The reports speculated that he'd been the victim of a carjacking.

Donnie shakes his head. He and Benny vowed to never go back to that wretched town.

The agent displays the screen of his phone again. It's a photo of a woman. Grainy footage from a low-end surveillance camera. She's standing outside a marble building.

"You recognize this woman?"

Donnie shakes his head.

Rodriguez says, "Footage shows her outside the Eastern District of Pennsylvania courthouse building on multiple occasions, including three days ago, the last time anyone saw Judge Wood."

"I thought you caught the guy who did it? One of the criminals Benny put away."

The agent sighs. "An arrest has been made. But the investigation is ongoing. The woman is a person of interest, someone we want to speak to. She wasn't originally a high priority, but . . ."

"But what?" Donnie grabs the word, since there's obviously a reason the guy is asking about her.

"We got a facial-recognition hit." The agent swipes his phone again. He pulls up a photo of a white woman. It could be the same woman from outside the courthouse, but it's hard to say. She's young, pronounced cheekbones, cat eyes, sultry.

"Who is she?"

"We're not sure. We got a hit and tracked it to a passport data-base."

Donnie doesn't understand.

"It's a fake passport, but we think it's the same woman."

When it's clear Donnie still isn't getting it, the agent says, "She was a passenger on your cruise."

CHAPTER TEN

JENNA

Jenna ditched the scooter and is fast-walking down Tenth Street when the phone rings. It comes up as only a number, no name. It's not in the scooter guy's contacts. She answers.

"It's me," Simon says. "You're sure?" He's using a burner phone like they discussed when they made this contingency plan.

Their marriage is nothing like the cliché in the movies where the spouse is blindsided by their loved one's secret history. Before Jenna agreed to marry him, she told Simon everything. Well, nearly everything. Enough for him to be clear-eyed and understand the risks of living the rest of his life with her. Actually, there was some cliché to it—he proposed on the promenade outside the Eiffel Tower. She said, *Yes, but* . . .

Using his overly analytical mind, Simon had weighed the costs and benefits. Probably made a spreadsheet of pros and cons.

"Like the movie *Nikita*?" he asked. "You were taken as a kid and trained to . . ."

"Not as glamorous, but yes."

After digesting it all, Simon figured she was safe, that her former employer, a government contractor with no name that its employees called The Corporation, had no reason to come after her. But just in case, they developed an emergency plan.

Simon is an inveterate planner, an occupational hazard. They agreed on a code, something only they would know. Simon chose "Alas Babylon," which is weird, but he said it was from a book he'd read when he was a kid. If either of them ever used the code, they would hightail it out to the Allegheny Mountains of Virginia. A cabin in Bath County that Simon purchased through a web of shell companies. A trail only a tax lawyer could untangle.

"Yes, I'm so sorry."

There's a leaden silence. He's processing.

Jenna says, "You get Lulu. I'm on my way to get Willow. We need to be fast."

Simon is still quiet. He's breathing heavily into the phone. Jenna hears the tapping of computer keys. He's at his desktop.

"Lulu's at school, I can see her on the webcam," he says. Lulu's kindergarten teacher has a live webcam parents can log on to. The high school teachers aren't so generous, but to Willow's consternation, she accepted their locator on her cell phone. "And Willow's pinging at the school."

"Good. Don't bring your phone, it can be tracked. Use the burner. I'm sorry, I—"

"I knew what I was getting into," he cuts her off. "We'll meet you at the—"

"Don't say it." This time she interrupts, not wanting him to reveal where they're headed. It's unnecessary. Both phones are untraceable to them. But there are laser microphones that can pick up conversations four hundred meters away. And she's learned over the years that survival favors the cautious. "I love you," she says, and hangs up, not wanting to hear the pain and fear—and possibly regret at ever meeting her—in his voice.

She needs to get to Willow's school. The scooter hipster's phone will probably work for another fifteen minutes before he gets hold of his carrier and it's disabled. She thumbs the Uber app, orders the car. She's got no money, no credit cards, and soon she'll have no phone. But she and Willow are going to make it to the cabin.

As she waits for the ride, Jenna surveys the area. Tenth Street is like much of downtown D.C.: glass office buildings filled with lawyers and lobbyists amid a smattering of redbrick old row houses converted into coffee shops alongside small roadside parks with benches occupied by the growing homeless population. No one is paying her any mind. Just another Washingtonian staring at her phone, waiting for an Uber or Lyft.

She tries to control her breathing, harness the fear and adrenaline ripping through her. Some of her colleagues at The Corporation loved feeling like this: the high from the chase, the epinephrine from the mission. That's how they got you: The Corporation taught you to crave that feeling; it meant that you were alive, that you had a purpose in this world. But for Jenna, it's always a Proustian moment, something that evokes a buried sensation—the deep sense of dread—rooted in the first time she ever ran for her life. What her stepdaughter Willow might call a trigger.

Her first night at Savior House.

At fifteen, Jenna's heard of scary Chestertown—which is about three burgs over from her modest home in Linwood, Pennsylvania—somewhere her parents and the other grown-ups refer to only in whispers, a place you wouldn't want your car to break down at night.

The social worker pulls to the curb. The group home looks like it was once a grand mansion from another era but now resembles a run-down haunted house from a black-and-white movie or Scooby-Doo cartoon. The social worker introduces her to the man who runs the place—Mr. Brood—a hulking figure who wears a cardigan that gives him the appearance of Mr. Rogers on steroids. It's dinnertime, kids are shuffling to the dining room, but Mr. Brood says she can be excused from dinner, *this one time*. He's stern but isn't mean. More matter-of-fact. He and the social worker talk briefly before the woman shows Jenna to her room. Three beds are in a line, each with a large trunk at the foot. Jenna doesn't say anything, just curls up on the mattress, buries her head in the pillow, which is lumpy and yellowed and has no pillowcase.

She barely had a chance to say goodbye to her parents. Mom and Dad always went bowling on Tuesdays. Jenna should've said, *I love you*, or hugged them. But she'd been talking on the phone with Gigi, stretching the kitchen phone cord so it reached the stairs where she could whisper and giggle and conspire with her friend without her parents eavesdropping. Everything changed in a split second when the police came to the door. No more Friday nights at Blockbuster searching for movies with her dad. No more road trips for Jenna's gymnastics competitions with her mom. No more board games on rainy weekends. No more making dinners together or dumb jokes or the endless mundane things she took for granted and would give anything to get back. She squeezes her eyes tight and cries herself to sleep.

She awakens with a fright—someone touching her arm. Her heart's banging and she can't see who it is at first and is disoriented. Then the crushing reality hits her again. This isn't a nightmare. She's at the group home. Her parents killed in a car accident. She has no one.

There's a girl crouched at her bedside. In a whisper, she says, "We need to hide."

Hide? Jenna doesn't understand. But then from outside the room, there's the sound of male voices. Laughing, heavy footsteps.

"Come out come out wherever you are."

The tone isn't playful like in hide-and-seek. It's creepy. She thinks he's imitating a line from a movie.

Jenna jolts up. She looks around, but there's nowhere to go. The girl's already gone. Jenna jumps to her feet, opens the chest at the foot of the bed. It's small, but she's limber. She balls herself up, closes the lid on top of her, the inside hot from her breath, loud from the banging of her heart.

But the lid juts open. The girl is back, shaking her head, silently telling Jenna that they'll find her there.

The girl takes Jenna's hand, then guides her out of the bedroom. In the upstairs hallway, Jenna hears more noise from downstairs. She's not sure what time it is, but it's dark and the place is otherwise still.

The girl—she has dark black hair and brown skin—puts a finger to her lips. Jenna is terrified now. What is happening? Why is this girl so afraid of them? Where is Mr. Brood?

They step gingerly down the hallway, fear seizing Jenna with every creak of the floorboards.

"Come out come out wherever you are."

The voice floats up the stairs.

The girl stealthily moves into the other bedroom, Jenna following close behind. The room has three more beds in a line.

Three trunks in front of them. The girl goes to a closet at the far end.

The voices grow louder.

The girl opens the closet door. It's empty save for a few clothes hanging on a mismatch of hangers. The girl sweeps aside the clothes and reaches inside. Jenna notices a small gap in the drywall about four feet long. The girl puts her small fingers inside the crevasse and pulls.

A slice of drywall, a makeshift hidden door, comes off and Jenna is startled by two round eyes looking back at them. The girl who led her there says, "Shit."

The girl in the hidden section of the closet says, "You can fit, Marta. Both of you." She pushes herself back, as if willing herself to be smaller.

But Marta clearly knows better.

Marta wedges the section of drywall back to its place and fans the clothes in front of it.

She's starting to panic, Jenna can see. The voices are getting closer.

Jenna needs to take control. Take action. Her gymnastics coach always says, *If you want to be a leader, lead.* She runs to the window and looks outside. There's a small slice of roof covering the porch. But the drop is far.

Jenna pries open the window. Marta is watching her. The voices grow louder. Like a pack of wolves going room to room, looking for food.

Jenna gestures for Marta to come to the open window. But the girl's frozen. Jenna quietly races over, takes Marta's arm, and steers her to the opening. Marta ducks through the window and stands on the small section of roof looking terrified.

"Come out come out . . ."

Jenna darts over to the bed, yanks a thin blanket from it, and climbs out the window, shutting it right as the bedroom light is slapped on.

They move away from the light to the edge. Marta is visibly trembling now.

Jenna hands her an end to the blanket. Gestures for her to grip it tightly. "I'll lower you down," she whispers.

Marta shakes her head violently.

But Jenna gives her a look that says, *It will be okay.*

Voices are coming through the walls. Jenna peers over the ledge. The front lawn isn't overgrown, but it isn't well cared for either. Like someone whips through every few weeks with a mower without regard to what they're plowing over. She confirms it's too far down to jump.

Still holding the blanket, the girl lowers herself so she's sitting on the ledge. She twists her body around so she's facing the house, balancing on her forearms as she grips the blanket.

Jenna plants her feet and begins lowering Marta, the girl gripping the blanket for dear life. Jenna's foot slips, and she worries they'll both go down, but she regains her footing as Marta inches closer to the ground. The blanket is long enough that with outstretched arms Marta will be able to drop without breaking a limb.

Jenna feels a rush of panic as the window makes a loud noise as someone jams it open. The weight on the blanket releases. Jenna makes sure Marta is safely on the ground and then tosses the blanket over the ledge.

A voice booms. "She's outside."

Jenna doesn't look back at the window but instead runs across the roof and leaps to grab the gutter's downspout above, which is old and rusted. She prays it will hold.

There's more voices, but they trail off. They're running downstairs. Trying to catch the girls in the yard. Jenna shimmies down, sliding too fast, the aluminum burning her hands.

Marta has waited for her. The two lace hands and run into the night.

"Are you Clark Stansbury?" The voice jars Jenna back to the present. The driver of a car with an Uber sticker on the side window is looking at her. She remembers she's using the scooter guy's phone, nods, and hurries into the vehicle.

While they drive to Willow's school, Jenna finds herself returning to that first night at the group home, to the dark-haired girl thanking her for getting them out of the house.

"Those boys," she tells Marta. "We need to tell Mr. Brood."

Marta's response takes the wind out of her: "It's not the boys we need to be afraid of."

CHAPTER ELEVEN

DONNIE

"Donnie, how's it hangin'?"

It's Mickey, the manager of Tracer's Bullet. Donnie has the cord to the hospital room's phone pulled tight. He needs to get a new cell phone. His is at the bottom of the Atlantic Ocean. He favors the old flip phones, which are harder to find these days. He has considered getting a smartphone, but he doesn't use social media, doesn't watch television, doesn't surf the interwebs, and doesn't want to start. He's seen too many people addicted to their phones when there are so many better things to be addicted to.

After some small talk, halfhearted concern, Mickey says, "Look, I've got some good news."

"Yeah?"

"Have you talked to Tom?"

"Not since he kicked me out of *my* band," Donnie says. "I've had a buncha fans here, even the frickin' FBI, but nothing from Tom or any of them." Donnie thinks about the FBI agent, the curious image of the woman lingering outside the federal building where Benny worked. He's starting to think she looks familiar, but that's probably the power of suggestion. Still, something has him baffled: If she was on the cruise ship, how would she be outside Benny's office three days ago? They were at sea when Benny died. The agent asked him a lot of questions about whether anyone arrived via helicopter and when they went to port. But there's no way the same woman could be in Pennsylvania when Benny was murdered and on the cruise ship at the same time. Donnie asked the agent about that, but Rodriguez was tight-lipped.

Mickey hesitates. "Tom's probably having a hard time getting hold of you. I got bounced around till they connected me to your room and—"

"What's the good news, Mickey? You said there's good news."

"Look, Tom feels terrible about what happened. He wants to talk. I'm sure he'll reach out today."

Yeah, now that Donnie's getting all this media attention. The nurse told Donnie that he's been all over the TV, and that the morning shows called the hospital asking to interview him. That there are news vans and lots of fans camped outside the hospital. Donnie hasn't turned on the old set mounted to the ceiling, but based on all the visitors, he believes her.

"I'll let Tom talk to you about the band," Mickey says. "I'm calling about something else."

That's interesting. Mickey doesn't usually talk to Donnie at all. He's on Team Tom. The team that let Donnie and the other original members of Tracer's Bullet get screwed out of what was theirs.

"What is it?"

"A book agent reached out to me. Some big publishers are interested in your story, Don."

"My story?"

"Yeah, you know, like an autobiography. They've been selling well. Nikki Sixx has one. Dave Grohl. People eat this shit up now."

But it's not like Donnie was in Mötley Crüe or Nirvana or the Foo Fighters. "All 'cause I fell out of a boat?"

Mickey chuckles. "Who knows? But the advance is six figures."

Donnie thinks about this. His life story. Not an uplifting tale. But six figures, even low six figures, would help with the bills. Put something away for his goddaughter.

"What do I know about writing a book? I write songs, not books."

"That's the beauty of this thing, Don. You don't have to. They got this hotshot writer. All you gotta do is meet with the guy—tell him about your life, feed him some war stories from back in the day—he'll get it all down, lickety-split."

"I don't know, I—"

"Offers like this don't come along every day. You gotta strike while the iron's hot."

Before his plunge off the *Royal Voyager* rotates out of the news cycle.

Donnie is quiet. He thinks about his mom, the group home, terrain he doesn't want to revisit.

"You there?" Mickey says. There's noise in the background, someone saying "check" into a PA system.

Mickey's at rehearsal. Tom's probably there right now. So much for him not having the hospital room's phone number.

"I need to think about it."

Now Mickey is quiet. He clearly thinks it's a no-brainer. "How about this: Meet with the writer, see what you think? The agent already flew him down to Miami from New York."

"I'm checking out of the hospital today, so I won't be—"

"Where you staying? He can be at your hotel by dinnertime."

Donnie realizes that the wheels on this are already in motion.

"Nothing to lose, Don. They'll buy you an expensive meal. No commitment. Just talk to the guy."

"All right. But make it clear I'm not sure about this. I'm staying at the Fontainebleau."

"*Nice.* I love the Fontainebleau," Mickey says. "Sinatra and the Rat Pack used to hang there. I'll tell him to meet you in the Hakkasan Bar in the hotel at seven."

CHAPTER TWELVE

NICO

Nico is burning up. He's in that space between consciousness and dream. Sweat rolls from his brow, his pits feel like a swamp. The wound on his shoulder may be infected. He's at the beach, the magical day with his mom when he was eleven—the blissful ignorance of not knowing that this was her goodbye.

She'd given him a necklace with a pendant. "It's a Saint Christopher, like mine."

"What's a Saint Christopher?"

"He keeps you safe on your journeys."

Nico still wears the necklace, though he's since learned that Saint Christopher, the patron saint of travelers, was demoted by the church for some reason. They probably assumed the guy was an asshole. Nico knows the feeling.

His mind flutters about, a dragonfly hovering over himself. Another bead of sweat travels from his forehead, down his cheek, over his chin. It feels like condensation from a cold beer on a hot summer day.

Summer.

* * *

Then he's back in Chestertown, Pennsylvania, in July.

"It's hot as shit out here," he says. He passes the liter bottle of Mountain Dew to Annie. They sit on top of the octagon-shaped monkey bars in the dilapidated park. The bars are rusted and there's no shade and he hopes he's not sweating too much.

Annie says, "Um, can I ask: Where are your shoes?" She eyes his dirty feet and he's embarrassed, but only a little. "You didn't lose them playing cards with those older kids, did you?"

Nico feigns insult. "No, Donnie's trying out for the talent show tonight," he says. "They keep making fun of him, calling him hill-billy, and he wasn't going to go because of the holes in his shoes. So I . . ." Nico wiggles his toes. If there's one thing Nico hates, it's a bully.

Annie doesn't say anything, but she reaches for his hand, which sends electricity slicing through him.

Nico tries to play it cool, hopes his palm isn't sweaty. His eyes move to the new girl who's on the swing. She's swaying slowly, a distant expression on her face.

"What's up with her?" Nico asks.

Annie shrugs. "I heard her parents died in a car crash."

Nico doesn't say anything. They all have sad stories; all differ-ent, yet all the same.

Annie says, "They gave her the welcome treatment last night. She and Marta slept at the tree house."

Nico releases a sigh. "I heard them fucking around, but I didn't know they were messing with any of you. Where was Mr. Brood?"

"Men's Club." On Wednesday evenings, the businessmen of Chestertown get together to pretend they're big shots.

They'll stay at the park until dark. It's better than the house, which is crowded and where Mr. Brood will put them to work cleaning the bathrooms or doing other made-up chores. But once the sky dusks, it's not safe here.

Annie takes a drink of pop and tosses him the candy. They pooled their money—the four dollars they got from the recycling center. She points across the park. "There's Arty."

Artemis Templeton, another one of the Savior House kids, pulls an old wagon, the wheel wobbling along the broken sidewalk on the perimeter of the park. Inside the wagon is a computer monitor and a tangle of cables and cords. Dumpster diving at the RadioShack again. He says he's going to build the next Microsoft, but bigger. Arty's a strange dude. Probably will be a gazillionaire someday, but strange. The kids call him The Robot because of his monotone inflection.

Annie glances around. She sighs.

There're no kids. No responsible adult would bring their children here to play on the blacktop strewn with broken bottles, used condoms, and even a needle or two. The seesaw is a broken plank.

"You think we'll ever get out of here?" she asks.

"I'd bet on it," Nico tells her.

"You'll bet on anything," she says, smiling. A smile that lights up even this grim place.

She's right, but gambling pays off sometimes. It was a gamble, after all, that Annie would like him. Nico isn't a visionary like Arty. Isn't strong and smart like Ben. Isn't good at guitar like Donnie. Isn't good at anything really, except maybe being a smartass. Maybe that's why his mom didn't come back.

He looks around to make sure nobody's watching. "I, um, got you something." He hands her the small box. She opens it and removes the necklace that has letters spelling out her name: *Annie.*

"That's so sweet. You didn't need to . . ."

"I wanted to."

They sit quietly as the sun goes down.

As they're about to head to the house, Annie says, "The lady's back." She's staring at the verge of the park.

Arty must've seen the woman and gone the long way because he's on the other side now. Mr. Brood is standing with the mysterious woman in the fancy clothes who shows up now and then in her fancy car. She's too stylish to be from the department of children's services. In Nico's three years at Savior House, social workers appear only when they're dropping off a kid.

Nico looks at them. *Who is this lady?*

"Maybe she's Derek's mom," Annie says as Derek Brood walks up to the lady and his father.

"No way this lady gave birth to that pile of ugly."

"We should go," Annie says, eyeing Derek, who's walking in their direction.

"He won't do anything with that lady watching," Nico says.

Annie narrows her eyes, like she knows better.

Nico's pulse quickens as Derek walks purposefully toward the monkey bars. *Be brave. For once in your life, be brave.*

Derek glowers at them. "I heard faggots hung out at this park, but I didn't know sluts did too."

Nico swallows. *Be brave.* He feels for his silver dollar in his pocket. He pulls it out, eyes it in his palm. Tails. He should retreat. No, not in front of Annie.

Quietly, in a barely discernable tone, Nico says, "Douchebags say 'what?'"

Derek scowls. "What?"

This elicits a laugh from Annie.

"What you say, motherfucker?" Derek says.

Nico looks out at the lady and Mr. Brood. Derek won't do anything with them watching. There's always later tonight—*Come out come out wherever you are*—but not now. And Ben and Donnie and Arty will be home later and there's safety in numbers.

"You got something to say, come down here and say it." Derek's angry they're laughing at him.

Nico drains the Mountain Dew bottle. "Why don't you come up here instead?"

Annie laughs again. She stops when Derek runs over, jumps up, and wraps his arms around Nico's legs. He tugs Nico off the cage of metal, and Nico hits the ground hard, knocking the wind out of him.

"*Stop!*" Annie shouts as Derek kicks Nico in the stomach.

Nico feels like he's suffocating as he flops around on the ground. He looks out at Mr. Brood and the woman, expecting them to run over to break it up. But they just watch.

Derek kicks him again. Nico balls up, caging his head with his hands. After years in group homes, he knows you should always protect your head. As he gasps for air, his eyes snag on the woman. She's shaking her head but doing nothing. Annie is screaming, but Derek isn't stopping. He reaches down, grabs Nico's hair, lifting his head so they're looking at each other. His eyes are dark and cold. Nico fears he'll slam his head into the blacktop.

But then Derek goes flying. His feet actually leave the asphalt. Nico turns to see what happened.

It's the new girl.

Derek rises from the blacktop, rage shadowing his features.

But the new girl has already scurried up the play structure. He's chasing her, but she crawls like a spider, moves like a gymnast. As he nears her, she swings around, her feet connecting squarely with Derek's face.

Mr. Brood and the woman finally come over. Nico swears the woman has a faint smile on her face. She points to the new girl.

"You, what's your name?"

The woman has an accent, Nico isn't sure from where. French, maybe.

"Jenna."

The woman nods to Mr. Brood, turns, and disappears.

Nico comes to, still in the mine. His body is radiating heat, he's disoriented. He manages to turn on his cell phone, click on the flashlight. That's when he sees them.

Two dead rats.

CHAPTER THIRTEEN

JENNA

The Uber drops Jenna on Wisconsin, a block from Sidwell Friends School, to avoid the scooter guy tracing her to Willow. She makes it to the front of the building. Two girls wearing the school's uniform bound out the doors. They're smiling and nearly vibrating with teen energy.

Jenna studies the area. She sees nothing suspicious. But this makes her more anxious: the Corporation always makes sure nothing looks suspicious. Jenna escaped. The Corporation doesn't screw up like this.

She straightens herself as she awaits the iris scanner to unlock the school's front doors. Sidwell Friends is an obnoxiously expensive private school, one filled with the spawn of Washington's elite. The parents are generally put together—they have nannies and personal assistants and housekeepers for the hard stuff in life—and the moms are usually dressed to the nines. And they certainly don't show up looking sweaty and disheveled.

Jenna agreed to send Willow to Sidwell for the simple reason that the president's daughter and the children of no fewer than five cabinet officials are students here. It ensures that the school is under heavy Secret Service protection. And her former employer would know that. A stranger caught casing the school would be shoved into a government van before they knew what hit them. But Jenna isn't a stranger. She's a parent. So, disheveled or not, a second scanner, this one for the main office, buzzes her in.

The woman working the front desk says, "Can I help you?" She peers over her glasses pinched on her nose. No smile. Between the overbearing parents and entitled teenagers, Jenna suspects the woman's customer-is-always-right instincts were extinguished long ago.

"Hi. I'm Willow Raines's mom." If Willow had been present, she would've quickly corrected her by saying "*step*mom." But no need to complicate things now. "I totally spaced out that she has a dentist appointment this afternoon, and I need to check her out."

Without saying a word, the receptionist pecks on her computer, probably pulling up Willow's schedule. The woman picks up the phone.

Jenna smiles, tries to look nonchalant. Her daughter is safe at the school. She wonders if Willow would be safer staying put. Maybe, but only briefly. She can't stay here forever. And right now Jenna has the advantage of time.

The receptionist's brow furrows. She murmurs something into the line. Then hangs up.

"Willow has AP Lit sixth period. But her teacher says she didn't come to class. She also missed fourth and fifth periods."

Jenna's heart races. She needs to remain calm. "Oh," she manages. "Maybe she remembered and took an Uber to the doctor."

"You mean *dentist*," the receptionist says, eyeing her now.

"Yes, dental surgeon," Jenna says, recovering from the slip. "I'll track her down," she says absently as she taps on the scooter guy's phone and strides out of the office.

Jenna's thoughts are racing. *Do they have her? If not, where the hell is she?* The receptionist said she missed the two periods before lunch, before Jenna botched the job. And Simon said her phone is pinging at the school.

The bell rings and the hall fills with students. Jenna remembers from parents' night that Willow's locker is near the auditorium. She maneuvers through the kids and finds it. She doesn't see Willow, but she spots a familiar face: Willow's best friend, Lily.

Lily Hurtado usually exudes enthusiasm, but when she notices Jenna her expression turns from curiosity to concern.

Jenna rushes up to her.

"Hi, Ms. Raines," she says sheepishly.

"Hi, Lily. Do you know where Willow is? There's been an emergency and the office says she's missed her last few classes."

Lily looks at her shoes. Worn sneakers with hearts drawn on them with an ink pen.

"She's not in trouble, but if you know where she is, you need to tell me. She's not answering my texts."

"She, um, told me that she and, um, Billy were like gonna skip with some kids."

Billy? Who's Billy? It doesn't matter right now.

"Where, Lily? It's important."

"I don't know."

"Has she done this before?"

Lily looks at her shoes again.

"Where does she usually go?" Jenna's voice must sound angry because the girl is tearing up.

"Last time it was the 7-Eleven on Wisconsin."

Jenna doesn't understand.

Lily shrugs, embarrassed. "Kids hang out in the back."

CHAPTER FOURTEEN

A few blocks from one of the most exclusive private high schools in the country stands a 7-Eleven, which is next to a Popeyes chicken and across the street from a liquor store. Such is the unpredictable landscape of even the affluent sections of Washington, D.C. Jenna paces quickly past a homeless man sitting on the sidewalk eating fried chicken out of a cardboard container and heads down the alley toward the back of the strip of businesses.

There, on a cinder-block wall near a large blue Dumpster, sits a group of kids. One of the teenagers, a boy with floppy hair and the necktie from his school uniform loosened, takes a drink from a brown paper bag and passes it to—you guessed it—Jenna's step-daughter.

Jenna charges over and faces the group.

Willow pauses, makes an exaggerated expression, mouth in a round O, as if unable to believe what she's seeing.

"We need to go," is all Jenna says. The lecture can come later.

"Jenna? Oh. My. God. This isn't happening."

The other kids dart looks at one another, not sure how to proceed.

"Let's go," Jenna says.

But Willow doesn't move. Instead, she sets her jaw. After a brief stare-down with Jenna, she says, "I'm not going anywhere."

The other kids look uncomfortable now. A boy, the one who handed her the brown paper bag, says something to Willow that Jenna can't make out.

"Screw that," Willow says to him. "She's not my mom."

"We don't have time for this," Jenna says. "There's an emergency. You need to come with me."

The other kids have already jumped down from the wall. They gesture for Willow to join them, but she's not budging. She's humiliated, and Jenna gets it, but it's not the time to prove a point. She makes a *get lost* gesture with a flick of her wrist and the other kids scramble away.

"I can't believe you," Willow says. "That was fucking humiliating. You're, like, following me, now?" Her eyes are welling up.

Jenna walks over and looks up at Willow. "Come down. It's not what you think. I can explain. But we need to go *now*. It's not safe."

"What the hell are you talking about?"

They're interrupted when a man appears in the alley. It takes Jenna a moment, but when she sees the ripped knee on his suit pants she realizes it's the guy from the scooter. With him is another hipster who takes a hit on a vape pen, trying to look tough. They must have used the Find My Phone app.

"Lady, I don't know what the hell is going on, but just give me my phone back and I won't call the police. It's got work stuff on it, and I could get in trouble if I have to report it missing."

Willow has hopped down from the wall. She looks to Jenna, then the man, then to Jenna again, a flummoxed expression on her face.

Jenna throws the guy the iPhone. "I'm sorry. It was an emergency," she says.

The hipster catches the device and examines it.

"What is going *on* with you?" Willow is shaking her head. "I'm calling Dad." She reaches in her pocket, then seems to remember she's left the phone at school to avoid the very scenario she's in now—her parents tracking her movements.

Willow says, "How did you know where I—" She stops suddenly, releases a bloodcurdling scream.

Jenna turns and the hipster is on the ground, blood oozing from his head. A woman, the one from SoulCycle and Hamilton Hotel, holds a cylindrical pipe that looks like a large flashlight or toy lightsaber. The woman turns to the hipster's friend, who appears frozen with fear. She puts the end of the tube to his knee and there's a *whoosh* sound and he screams in pain, collapsing. Then she twists the canister, ignoring the cacophony of screams, and puts something inside.

Jenna grabs Willow's arm. Her stepdaughter's face is twisted in confusion and shock. Jenna pulls her to the wall, tells her they need to run. Willow's survival instincts kick in as she grasps the ledge and pulls herself up. Jenna pushes Willow's bottom up and Jenna vaults over the wall after her. On the other side, Jenna hears a plea.

"No, please, no . . . "

There's another *whoosh* sound, then silence.

They run. Up Wisconsin, full speed, past Z-Burger, a Mattress Warehouse, a Chinese food restaurant, and not stopping until Jenna spots a safe place: a bank. The woman with the weird weapon won't risk the armed guards and security cameras. In the lobby of the Chase Bank, Willow's face is depleted of all color; she's shaking, her breaths coming out in rasps.

"Deep breaths," Jenna says, demonstrating in-through-the-nose-out-through-the-mouth several times.

The guard is eyeing them. He comes over.

"Is everything okay, ma'am?"

"Yes. My daughter suffers from panic attacks. She's okay, we just need a moment. Any chance you could get her some water?"

The guard nods and quickly ambles off to get the water.

"Don't leave me," Willow blurts, grasping Jenna's forearm.

"I won't," Jenna says. "Everything's going to be okay. Here's what we're going to do: We're going to calm down. It's a busy street, and the Metro is only a block away. We're going to walk there, together. I'll be right by your side. Can you do that?"

Willow's eyes are large, but she nods.

The guard's back with a Styrofoam cup. Willow takes it, downs the water, her hand shaking so much it nearly spills.

Jenna continues with the nose-mouth breathing, and Willow follows suit.

"I think she's okay," Jenna says to the guard.

He looks at Willow, who nods.

"Thank you so much," Jenna says.

The man returns to his station. Jenna looks out the glass door. She sees a crowd of what look like college students—American University is nearby—strolling past the bank.

She takes Willow by the hand, and they join the group on the sidewalk. The woman doesn't seem to be following. But she could be anywhere.

They make it to the entrance to the Tenleytown subway station and take the stairs adjacent to the escalator.

Still no sign of the woman.

As they reach the platform, Willow makes an unusual sound, a muffled shriek, and Jenna sees the woman making her way through the crowd. Wind pushes through the tunnel, the circular lights lining the track flashing on and off, as the train pulls into the station.

Jenna and Willow try to disappear into the crowd.

The train's doors open and passengers push out, then the masses move forward to board.

Willow starts to get on, but Jenna holds her back.

Along the platform, several train cars down, she and the woman make eye contact. The automated voice from inside the train is warning that the doors are closing. Jenna pulls Willow inside and watches as the woman does the same. Right before the doors close, Jenna pushes Willow through the opening, sliding out after her as the doors shut.

As the train lurches forward, Jenna sees the woman inside. She looks more amused than angry and gives a sarcastic wave as she blurs by.

CHAPTER FIFTEEN

Jenna and Willow walk quickly to the parking garage of a Whole Foods that's near the Metro station. From the second floor, Jenna can see down Wisconsin. District squad cars have clustered in the 7-Eleven's small front lot. Someone found the hipsters. Jenna feels a pang of guilt. If it weren't for her . . . But she needs to push that down, to focus, to think.

Jenna starts trying door handles on parked cars, seeing if any are unlocked.

Willow still looks like she's in shock, punch-drunk. "What are you doing?" she whispers.

"We need a car." It's been years since she's hot-wired a car, and she's worried she's forgotten how. Worse, they'll have to pick something older, unreliable, since newer cars are virtually hot-wire-proof.

"Who *are* you?" Willow says, walking away from Jenna, palms facing out, distancing herself.

Jenna frowns, then realizes that this is *a lot*. "We need a car, we need to get to your dad and Lulu."

Willow replies, "I'm applying to college and I'm *not* going to get caught in a stolen car."

Jenna is almost amused. Tracked by a woman with some type of death-tube weapon, her stepmother's gone crazy, and Willow's mind is on her college applications.

Willow says, "I can ask Billy for his car."

It's not a bad idea. It won't be completely untraceable, but it's unlikely anyone would be tracking the boy's vehicle. Hell, even Jenna didn't know about this boy.

They head back to the school. Out front, Willow says, "Wait here."

Before Jenna can protest, Willow strolls inside. A few excruciating minutes later, she reappears. She leads Jenna to the garage, which is underground. It's filled with luxury sedans, but Willow stops in front of a Jeep Wrangler.

"He'll be here in a minute."

"How'd you—"

"I got my phone from my locker and texted him."

"But—"

"Don't worry. I put it in airplane mode and left it there."

Jenna feels weirdly proud for a moment.

A few minutes later, the boy with floppy hair—the same kid from the 7-Eleven—appears. He looks nervous when he sees Jenna but is soon distracted by Willow. She races over, throws her arms around him. Willow says something Jenna can't hear. The boy—his name is Billy, Jenna reminds herself—hands over his keys. Just. Like. That. With no questions. They must be close.

That's confirmed when Willow gives him a kiss—and it's a *kiss*, not a friendly peck. After, the boy makes eye contact with Jenna, blushes, then offers a small wave and heads back to class.

Willow comes over, swinging the keys on a lanyard. She looks like she's going to say she's driving but thinks better of it.

They climb inside. Jenna lets out a breath, collecting herself.

It's going to be three hours to the cabin. She needs to get there—get Willow to her father and Lulu where it is safe—then figure out what the hell is going on.

Who is the woman with the death tube? And why is she after Jenna?

And why now?

CHAPTER SIXTEEN

DONNIE

Donnie eyes the food tray on the hospital room table. The spinach and sweet potato curry looks like someone sneezed on a pile of mushed carrots. He needs to get the hell out of this place.

He takes a pee, then examines himself in the mirror. He looks like a sight with his bandaged forehead and the hospital scrubs they said he could borrow since he'd arrived from the fishing vessel shirtless and they'd had to cut off his jeans. The cruise ship has docked and Mickey says they're delivering his luggage to the hotel, so that's good. He's not so sure about meeting with this writer, but it's a free meal—and drinks—and he's ready as hell to be out of this place. And who doesn't love Miami Beach? Palm trees, beautiful girls, perfect weather.

The doctor comes by again, ignores his charm offensive, and advises him to stay in the hospital one more night. When he declines, she shakes her head but says someone will come by with the waivers and forms to sign.

As he sits on the bed, his eyes go to the food tray again. He stares at it a long time, trying not to think of Benny, but the memories are everywhere.

They're in line at the school cafeteria as the lunch lady plops a scoop of mush on Donnie's tray.

"No one's seen Marta since yesterday," Donnie says. "She wasn't in homeroom this morning."

Benny listens as they shuffle down the line. He plucks a bruised apple from the pile, the only fruit option to go with today's mystery meat, and takes a bite.

"Maybe she finally ran off," Benny says, with a mouthful. "She's been talking about it."

Donnie makes a face. "Without saying goodbye, man? *No. . . .*"

They make their way into the lunchroom. It's loud as always, the sound of barely supervised teens. There's only one attendant, a lady so old that she probably worked here when the area was a thriving factory town, and she's no match for the heathens of Chestertown High.

They weave through the tables. Benny stops, looks to the far corner. "I'm not in the damn mood for this today."

Donnie follows his line of sight. At the table in the back for the outcasts, Derek Brood and two of his friends are looming over Artemis. Derek is moving in slow jerking movements, imitating a robot. When Artemis doesn't seem to respond, Derek puts a finger on Arty's tray and digs up some mashed potatoes and flicks it, a glob of white sticking to Arty's face. Arty completely ignores him and looks ahead, continues eating. Annie appears to be telling Derek off when one of Derek's friends makes a V with his fingers, puts it to his lips, and waggles his tongue through the gap.

Benny walks over at a quick pace. When he reaches the table, he stumbles like he's tripped over his own feet, and his food tray lands flat on Derek's chest.

Derek jumps back, his shirt covered in slop and spilled milk. "What the fuck?"

"Sorry," Benny says, looking down at Derek. "I tripped."

Benny sits at the table next to Artemis, his back to Derek, not a worry in the world.

Donnie grips his tray, ready to swing it at Derek and his friends if they go after Benny, but instead they leave in a hurry. Donnie smiles at that, puffs out his chest, then sits on the other side of the table next to Annie, across from Artemis and Benny.

Arty sits calmly, the dollop of mashed potatoes still stuck to his cheek. He doesn't react to things like other people.

Donnie slides his tray to the center of the table, signaling to Benny that they can share Donnie's lunch, since Derek's now wearing Benny's.

They sit in silence for a while. Like they're all wondering when life will take a turn for them. When they won't be the outcasts, when they won't have to face the indignities of the lunchroom, when they won't have to go to bed worried about closing their eyes, when they'll have families again.

Nico shows up at the table, no lunch tray in hand. "I went to the office. They said Marta was called in sick."

"Sick? She wasn't in her room this morning," Annie says. "Who would call . . ." She lets the question die.

Nico says, "How many is that now, Arty?"

"What do you mean?" Arty says.

"How many girls gone since we've been at the house?"

Nico and Artemis are the longest tenants at Savior House, and Arty's the obvious mathematician of the pair.

Arty thinks about this. "Six."

"Six damn runaways in three years?" Donnie asks.

Annie says, "How do we know they're runaways?"

"It's the most logical answer," Arty says. "I talked to Mr. Jones and he called the foster care office and was told they looked into everything."

Mr. Jones is a retired computer company executive who's helping Arty with his coding projects, probably the only nice grown-up in any of their lives. Not that they repay him for the kindness: The kids all call him Ned Flanders because of his resemblance to the character on *The Simpsons*.

"Nobody ever talked to me," Ben says. "What kind of investigation is it if no one ever asked us any questions?"

While Arty may be a genius, the next Thomas Edison or something, Benny's the truly smart one. Book *and* street smart, like that O.J. lawyer he admires, or the bald lawyer on *The Practice*.

"You sure we can trust Flanders?" Benny asks. "He and Mr. Brood are friends."

Artemis says, "They're not friends. Mr. Jones says that the state should shut down Savior House, that Mr. Brood only has the job because of his family."

Everyone knows that the Broods are what passes for a political dynasty in corrupt, small-town Chestertown. Mr. Brood's father was its longtime mayor, a position now held by Brood's brother.

Arty continues, "Mr. Jones is in Men's Club with the Broods, but he's not friends with Mr. Brood."

"What about that French lady?" Annie says. "Arty, you said one of the others disappeared after the lady met with Mr. Brood. She was here the other day. We saw her." Annie looks at Nico, who nods.

Arty finally wipes away the mashed potatoes with a paper napkin. "It's unusual," he concedes.

"It's all B.S., is what it is," the voice says. It's the new girl,

Jenna. She's at the far end of the table. Donnie didn't even see her there. She has a way of blending in that's strange.

Ben sits up straight, tightens his jaw. "We gotta figure this shit out."

"Ya think?" Nico says, in that way of his.

Donnie is about to ask, *How?* What could they possibly do? They're just kids.

Arty says, "I'll ask Mr. Jones to call the foster care people again."

"We need to do it soon," Jenna says. "Before another one of us disappears."

By late afternoon, Donnie checks in to his room at the Fontaine-bleau, pleased to find his luggage already in the suite. He riffles through his suitcase for something to wear. He's meeting with a writer, not something he does every day. He considers wearing his one shirt with a collar but opts instead for a concert tee, denim jacket, and ripped jeans. The guy might as well know what he's getting into. He needs to shake off thinking about Savior House, about Benny, about all of it.

At a stand-up table at the Hakkasan Bar & Lounge, looking out of place amid the tanned beautiful people of Miami Beach, is a pasty guy in a button-up shirt. Maybe Donnie should've worn the collar. The man looks timidly at Donnie and raises a hand. Stands.

On closer inspection, he looks less like a writer than a figure skater or ballroom dancer. He has a thin frame, hair that touches his shoulders, and a handsome, angular face.

"Mr. Danger," he says, sticking out his hand. First the FBI, now this guy. Donnie hasn't been called mister this much in years, or ever.

"Mr. Danger's my dad," Donnie says, instinctively carting out the rock-star persona. "Not that I ever met that son of a bitch." He barks a laugh. "Call me Donnie."

"Hi, Donnie, I'm Reeves Rothschild."

"Reeves Rothschild," Donnie repeats, amused. "Sounds like royalty. I feel like I should bow or something."

"A handshake works," Reeves says.

They shake and sit. A waitress with a tight blouse and piercings crawling up her ear asks if they want anything to drink. Donnie thinks on it—maybe just one; it's been a helluva week, after all.

"I'll have a Car Bomb."

The waitress looks confused, then realizes it must be a drink. She nods, looks to Reeves. He hesitates. "I'll have the same."

This makes Donnie smile.

"Thanks for meeting with me," Reeves says. "It's amazing you're already out of the hospital. Are you feeling better?"

"I've got a nasty bump on the head, but otherwise, good as new." There's an awkward silence. Donnie finally says, "So they say you wanna write my story."

"I do." The kid says it like he almost means it.

"Now why in the hell would you wanna do that?" Donnie asks with a crooked smile.

Reeves gives his own sideways grin, acknowledging that maybe this isn't the Great American Novel he's always envisioned.

The waitress arrives with two tall glasses of Guinness, and two shots of Jameson mixed with Baileys Irish Cream.

Reeves has a bemused expression.

"Tell me about yourself," Donnie says, making a show of holding up the shot glass and dropping the liquor into the glass of stout. He quickly chugs the beer before the cream curdles. "Where're you from, Reeves?"

"Westport, Connecticut."

That fits.

Reeves mimics Donnie's move and downs the drink. "I live in New York now," he says, wiping foam from his mouth.

"How long you been a writer?"

Reeves smiles. "My first novel was published five years ago. I was actually in law school—both parents and my two siblings are all lawyers—but I dropped out."

That's one point for the kid. He's passionate, breaking away from what was expected of him. It still doesn't explain why he'd agree to write a book about some washed-up rocker, but still.

Picking up on Donnie's thought, Reeves says, "Look, I know I'm not an obvious choice."

"What, were your parents big fans or somethin'?" Donnie asks.

This amuses Reeves for some reason. "I wouldn't say that."

"Then what?"

"I had this dream, you know? Everyone thought I was crazy dropping out of law school. My father's still furious. And while my first novel received starred reviews and literary awards, it sold fewer than five thousand copies. My publisher dropped me. I'm the joke of my family."

"And you need the money?"

Reeves smiles. "Well, there's that."

"Now that's somethin' I can relate to," Donnie says. He downs the remnants of the drink, raises a hand to catch the waitress's attention.

"But it's more than that," Reeves says. "When my agent called, I thought she was kidding. But then I did some research . . . on you." The writer makes eye contact with Donnie now. "And I think I can do your story justice. I think I understand. . . ."

What it's like to be a joke, Reeves mercifully doesn't say. Donnie examines the kid. Against his better judgment, he asks, "How would this work?"

"However you want. I suggest we get to know one another and perhaps you can tell me about your life. I can identify the parts that I think would make for a good story and write an outline. We can discuss the outline, and then I'll write a first draft and get your feedback."

"That's it?" Donnie asks.

"That's it, though we'll need to spend at least a week together."

Donnie thinks about this. Mickey consulted with one of his contacts in the publishing world, and the terms for the deal are a bit unusual, he said, but so is falling off a cruise ship into the Atlantic, and the money is right.

"Seven days in my life." Donnie laughs, motions to the next round of drinks the waitress sets on the table. "Think you can handle that, Reeves?"

"It'll be like Hemingway in Paris."

Donnie has no idea what that means, but he likes this kid.

They drink more Car Bombs. Talk some more. That leads to dinner, sixteen-ounce dry-aged bone-in rib eye at one of the hotel's fancy restaurants called StripSteak. A woman approaches their table and asks Donnie for a selfie. He hasn't gotten so much attention outside the cruise ship or second-rate venues in years. He offers a crocodile smile for the photo and she scuttles off.

By midnight, Donnie is feeling sloppy, but he's made a decision and he thinks he'll be okay with it when he sobers up. He and Reeves stumble into the hotel lobby. Donnie looks at the writer. "Hemingway, my boy, let's do it."

Reeves's eyes are bloodshot. With slurred speech, he says, "You're sure? We can talk tomorrow if you need to think about—"

"I don't need to think. But I got two conditions."

Reeves waits.

"One, you make me sound smarter than I am."

Reeves hesitates. "I want to tell your real story, not some—"

"I'm just fuckin with you." Donnie cackles. "Even a smart guy like you can only do so much. . . ." Donnie holds up two fingers. Looking at them, he has a strange sensation of panic, but he shakes it off. "Two, though, and I'm not kiddin' on this."

Reeves nods for him to continue.

"We start the story when I'm fifteen, after I was on my own and joined the band. I don't want to get into stuff before then."

Reeves ponders this. "I think we can make that work."

"Good." The last thing Donnie needs is for anyone to start digging into what happened at Savior House.

CHAPTER SEVENTEEN

JENNA

Jenna and Willow drive for a long while in silence. Unsatisfied with Jenna's vague answers to her barrage of questions, Willow has resorted to an old standby: the silent treatment. Willow stares out the window as Jenna races through the questions playing in her mind on a loop: *Why would someone want to kill Artemis Templeton? He's famous, one of those tech billionaires people love to hate. But is that it? Why was I assigned for the hit? Is it because Arty and I were both wards of Savior House twenty-five years ago? Was it The Corporation? If not, how did they know I had been part of the organization? How did they know about my new life, my family?*

Her head is spinning. She needs to get it together. Get Willow safe and then focus on the who, the why.

"Billy seems nice," Jenna says, if only to distract herself, break the quiet. She's not so sure he is nice. Rendezvous at the back of 7-Elevens might speak to the contrary. But he gave Willow his Jeep without question. And the way he looked at her in dopey awe.

Willow ignores her.

Jenna stares at red taillights and heavy traffic on I-81. Once they reach 42 South, it will open up.

"Look, I know this is a lot. . . ."

Willow glances at her with heavy lids, telling her off in a way that only a teenager can. She reaches for the radio, turns it up. She's usually glued to her phone, so this is the best she can do to avoid communicating with Jenna.

Jenna decides to keep trying. She lowers the volume, says, "I know it was scary, what happened. Once I get you safe to your dad, we can all talk about it."

The radio's volume goes up again, and Jenna decides to let it go for now.

Forty minutes later, she merges onto the Woodrow Wilson Parkway. At last, she sees it, mile marker 21, and she pulls to the shoulder. Willow's head leans against the passenger window, her eyes closed.

Jenna checks the mirrors. Only a few stray cars, plenty of distance between the headlights. She searches the glove box, then the center console, but doesn't find what she needs. She gets out and opens the Jeep's back. There's an ice scraper stored there from the winter. It will have to do.

She walks down a small ravine filled with weeds that borders the asphalt shoulder. On the other side of a steel highway guardrail is a handmade cross that has a teddy bear and streamers from balloons that have long since deflated. One of those grim markers. A spot where wayward teens probably were driving too fast and lost control. Or where a drunk driver plowed into unsuspecting motorists. Like Jenna's parents.

Jenna looks around and waits for a car to pass.

Then she falls to her knees and starts digging with the ice scraper.

It takes a minute or two before Willow notices. She comes out of the Jeep, standing a few feet away.

"What the hell are you doing?" Willow swivels her head back and forth as if she's looking for someone to tell her this is all an awful joke. That she's on one of those hidden-camera shows.

She watches as Jenna tugs out a lockbox from the hole, which she carries back to the vehicle like a giant lunch box.

Willow's mouth is agape.

Jenna looks at her stepdaughter, exhales. "You're just going to have to trust me."

Fifteen minutes later, they sit in the Jeep at a Sunoco gas station. It's dark now, and Willow has the lockbox on her lap. Dirt still cakes the box and it's all over Willow's legs and part of her skirt, but she doesn't seem to notice. Willow keeps flipping through the items that came from a document pouch stored in the box. The two passports, one blue, one maroon, both with Jenna's photo on them, both with different names. Then similar counterfeits for Simon, Lulu, and Willow herself. Jenna managed to slip the small handgun out of the box without Willow seeing.

Willow doesn't touch the bundles of cash or the small stack of credit cards secured with a rubber band. She recoils, her hands jerking away as if touching a hot stove, when Jenna reaches over and slides a few twenties from one of the stacks.

Jenna looks around the lot. There's a lone worker in the gas station's convenience store, a pickup truck filling up in the other lane. Jenna opens the Jeep's door but before climbing out says, "You want a water or something?"

Willow shakes her head.

Jenna heads inside, pays for the gas. After, she fills the tank, eyeing Willow in the front seat. Willow has stopped gaping into the lockbox and is staring out the windshield at nothing. *What is going through her teenage mind?*

Back inside the Jeep, Willow finally speaks: "What are you, like in witness protection or something?"

Not a bad guess. She's a more sophisticated teen than Jenna ever was. The kids now have information on virtually any topic a few thumb clicks away. Television and movies have educated them on modern law enforcement. She wishes it were as simple as being in WITSEC.

"I promise, your dad and I will sit down and tell you—"

"That's not fucking good enough, okay!" Willow says. "That lady, she—" Willow's voice quavers. "If I'm in danger, I deserve to know."

Jenna doesn't respond. Her eyes are fixed on the 1980s-era Chevy Camaro with tinted windows. Did she see that car earlier behind them on Route 42?

She pulls out of the station and sees the Camaro, which had stopped for gas, pull behind the Jeep without filling up.

She looks at Willow. "Yes."

"Yes what?"

"Yes, you're in danger," Jenna says, and slams the gas pedal to the floor.

CHAPTER EIGHTEEN

Willow grips the roll bar as Jenna maneuvers the Jeep down a desolate road, the Camaro following close behind.

How did they find us?

She got rid of the wig, the jacket, the burner phone. They'd have no way of knowing she'd take Billy's car. Her phone remains at SoulCycle and Willow left hers in her school locker.

Or did she?

Jenna cuts left onto a dirt road. The Jeep has no onboard navigation, so she prays it isn't a dead end.

Willow looks petrified, the seat belt tight against her chest. The narrow lane is dark save for the headlights, allowing visibility only a few feet ahead of them. A fork in the road appears. Jenna checks the rearview: the headlights of the Camaro are gone. Either the driver has cut the lights or it hasn't rounded the corner yet. Jenna takes a right at the fork, then slams the brakes, purposefully creating a dust trail. She then slots the Jeep in reverse and twists around, maneuvering back to the fork, then takes the left, driving slowly, so as not to kick up more dust.

She veers off the dirt road into a stretch of overgrown scrub and weeds. Here they have an advantage. The Jeep has large tires, high clearance, and off-road capabilities. A 1980s Camaro is not so well equipped. It's an odd choice for a vehicle to tail someone, since it's hardly inconspicuous. Another one of those things that doesn't feel quite right . . .

The Jeep bumps over the embankment and Jenna pulls to a stop, kills the engine and headlights.

Her heart is beating in her ears. *Thud-thud, thud-thud.*

She turns and makes hard eye contact with Willow. "Did you bring your phone?"

Willow's eyes are wide.

"I'm not mad, but if you did . . ."

Willow thrusts the device into Jenna's hands. Jenna's mind races. She can smash the phone, but it may be too late. At the same time, tracking is not as precise on country roads.

She opens the door, startled by the glow of the interior light popping on. She slaps the light off with her hand.

"Wait here," she whispers.

Willow's mouth is open, but words don't come out, like her voice box is paralyzed.

"I'll be right back."

Jenna climbs out, listens. The sound of an engine fills the air; headlights approach.

Jenna stalks through the bramble and up the embankment.

The car's headlamps brighten.

Jenna darts closer to the fork in the road. The car is getting closer. Dust floats in its headlights as it speeds toward her.

With everything she has, she hurls the iPhone across the dirt road and into the weeds, then dives into the brush, the headlights directly ahead now, barreling toward her.

CHAPTER NINETEEN

The Camaro comes to a fast halt at the fork in the dirt road, red brake lights illuminating the night. Jenna crouches low as the rumble of the V8 engine fills the air. In her head, the beat of her heart is rattling louder than the engine and she worries she's visible through the brush. She's even more concerned about Willow. Alone in the Jeep, terrified in the dark. Jenna will never forgive herself for this.

The tinted window comes down, and the woman—deceptively pretty with those cheekbones and almond-shaped eyes—appears. She looks at the left side of the fork, then the right. Then her gaze moves to the scrub where Jenna lies flat on her stomach, peering sniper-style at the Camaro through the spaces between the tall weeds.

Jenna doesn't release a breath, stays motionless.

If the woman gets out of the car, Jenna knows what she needs to do. She'd spent much of her twenties riddled with guilt and self-loathing knowing that she's an assassin, which is just a nicer way of saying cold-blooded killer, murderer, executioner. By her early thirties, she'd justified it all—the targets were bad people, the world was a safer and better place without them. But on her last assignment, her nineteenth, hiding in the closet of a Russian arms dealer, she had an epiphany: She liked her job. The revelation didn't save the Russian, but it was the moment she decided she needed to get out. The first step toward a vow to make amends, to never take another life. But tonight, for her family, she knows it's a vow she might have to break.

Jenna feels a tremor vibrate through her at the sound of the engine revving. The car juts into gear and tears down the right side of the fork.

When the taillights are at a safe distance, Jenna climbs out of the brush and runs to the Jeep.

Willow is in the passenger seat, hugging her knees, her head down.

She startles when Jenna opens the door.

Willow says, "I'm sorry, I didn't think—I didn't know my phone could . . ."

Jenna looks at her stepdaughter, who averts her eyes. "Look at me," Jenna says.

Willow's eyes, red and watery, peer into Jenna's. "You have nothing to be sorry for. None of this is your fault."

Jenna opens the driver's side window, listens.

Nothing.

"You're buckled up?" she asks.

Willow checks the strap, nods.

With that, Jenna takes in a deep breath, turns the key, and starts the engine.

It sounds to Jenna like a volcano erupting on the desolate road. She drives through the tall weeds, turning the vehicle around and climbing up the embankment and back onto the dirt road. She doesn't know if the Camaro is long gone or dangerously nearby, but she has no time to worry about it. She needs to get to the cabin and protect her family.

CHAPTER TWENTY

NICO

The sound—a sequence of *pops*—startles Nico. The sky brightens in a flash, revealing the five of them surrounding the dirt pit.

But when his thoughts clear, Nico isn't on that knoll. And the sound isn't from a cheap handgun. It's louder, from up top, outside the mine. There are more bangs, like someone's setting off dynamite on the surface. Is this another fever dream?

No, he's convinced it's not.

He hears five charges in all. His mind jumps to that safety training again. The instructor telling them to look at the sticker inside their helmets. *What did the sticker say? If you hear three shots, they know you're alive; if you hear five, they know where you are and are on the way. Is that right?*

He listens. It is now as silent as it is dark. He clicks on his iPhone flashlight and sees the dead rats again, a sight that sends a rush of fear from his asshole up his spine to the base of his neck. Oxygen is dangerously low.

He knows he's supposed to stay still. But if the rats are dying, he's not far behind. He needs to find an SCSR. They're stored in receptacles running along the mine. But the roof collapse has blocked access to the tunnels.

A thought, one of those realizations that can save your life, comes to him: the handcar. Doesn't *it* have emergency SCSRs in a compartment? He tries to stand, but he's weak. His thoughts are jumbled, another sign of carbon monoxide poisoning.

He drags himself to the handcar, which is half submerged in a pile of rocks and debris. The front end is exposed. He uses his uninjured arm to haul himself into the contraption. Holding the iPhone light ahead of him, he scans inside. The open half of the cart is covered in coal dust, but he sees a side panel with an emergency symbol on it.

He's confused again. Where is he? What's happening? But it comes back to him and he opens the side panel and inside there's the most glorious thing he's ever seen: an SCSR.

Now the challenge: remembering how to use the goddamned thing. He holds the iPhone light to the device, which looks like an oversized aluminum canteen. That's when he sees the red indicator that he's got only 2 percent battery life left on his phone.

The hits keep coming.

He's feeling confused, light-headed again. He should write a goodbye note. But to whom?

He thinks of running in the sand on that beach again. The joyous shriek as he raced away from the waves, his mom watching him.

He pops the latch off the top of the SCSR and struggles with removing the protective cover. It's wedged on like a giant cap to a martini shaker. It finally comes off, and he yanks off the bottom cover. He puts the strap around his neck and the SCSR hangs at his midsection like a tourist's Nikon camera. He remembers something about a breathing bag at the bottom. He feels for the bag and his hand grips an orange tag, which it seems is meant to activate the bag. It's so complicated.

His mind flashes to Maverick going off on one of his rants about mine safety and how the protective gear is no better than when his daddy's daddy's daddy was bringing up the black rock that powered the world.

Nico thinks of the cast of the show: Headboard (the best of the nicknames) and Kermit (for his frogface) and Doc (because of all the pills) and Bloody Joe (don't ask).

He has the mouthpiece clenched between his teeth now, but his mind floats. He thinks he hears noise from above, but he's probably imaging it.

He pictures the indignity—no, the embarrassment—of them finding his body with this thing strapped on him like a giant sleep apnea machine.

Breathing into the tube, he becomes strangely at ease, like he's in a morphine fog.

He closes his eyes. At least he thinks they're closed, because his phone has died and it's so dark he honestly can't tell. He clasps his Saint Christopher pendant in his fingers.

He sees a funnel of light. It's true, what they say about when you die. There is a light, a calm, a peace, and he waits for his body to float away.

The light gets closer, brighter. Then the voice rips him back to consciousness.

"We've got our man! We've got our man!"

CHAPTER TWENTY-ONE

DONNIE

More. That's what Donnie always craves after the first taste. More.

From that first swig he took in the tree house they'd built in those creepy woods near the freeway in Chestertown to the first line he did backstage at the Whiskey a Go Go in LA . . . he needed more.

For him, booze, drugs, sex, you name it, were like potato chips. He could never stop at one. Once he started, Donnie Danger would keep going until he was passed out or arrested.

And so it is tonight as he wanders the Florida beach after midnight, a dangerous endeavor, looking for someone to sell him what he needs.

The hotel's concierge was off duty at this hour, so his usual source for party favors wasn't available. He'd looked about the hotel, but there were no men with the unmistakable look of a dealer. So, after wandering up and down the street, after asking a cabbie where he could score and being told to fuck off, he found his way to the beach.

The moon is big and full and he walks in his Chucks, sinking in the sand. He should go to the room, get some shut-eye, call it a night like the writer did.

But he wants more.

There's a bonfire up ahead. He stumbles over—partiers at an illegal bonfire will know where he can score. There's about a dozen or so people, kids in their twenties, sharing a bottle. A guy sits, strumming an acoustic guitar. Maybe they'll ask Donnie to play.

But he arrives to standoffish stares. It's like on television where there's a sound of a record scratch and everything abruptly stops. A shirtless guy stands up, dusts off his hands.

"This is a private party," he says. He has those sculpted muscles that are more for show than strength.

"Whoa, chill, partner, I'm not here to crash your shindig." Donnie holds up his hands.

"I'm not your partner," the guy says.

A girl in a bikini comes over, grabs the guy's arm, tugging him away. "He's harmless. Come on, Brett, let's get a drink."

The guy stares at Donnie. "No one wants you. Get out of here, little man."

It comes out before Donnie even realizes it: "That's what she said."

"What was that?" The guy comes over, gets in Donnie's face.

Donnie doesn't repeat it.

"I didn't think so, you little bitch."

Donnie shuffles off. He's coming down hard now. Feeling old, feeling like the nobody he is.

As the firelight gets smaller behind him, he sees a figure approach, a feminine form.

"Hey," she says. She's wearing a bikini, has a nice figure—he's never one to miss that. She wears an unzipped sweatshirt with the hood over her head, shadowing her face.

"Howdy," he says.

"Leaving the party so soon?" she asks, looking out toward the bonfire.

"No room for an old rocker like me," he says, trying not to sound pathetic.

She pauses, like she's studying him, making a realization. "Hey, you're that guy."

"And what guy is that?"

"The, um, rock star who got drunk and fell off the cruise ship."

Donnie chuckles. He's had three albums go platinum, yet this will be his legacy. A trivia question for "Stump the Trunk," a story in *Metal Edge*.

"Have a good night," he says, giving her a mock tip of the hat. He's had enough humiliation for one day.

"Wait," she says, reaching for his arm. "Don't go," she says. "It's a nice night for a swim." Before Donnie replies, she's pulled off the sweatshirt and untied the suit top and is running toward the water.

She dives in and comes up, pulling her hair back, her bare breasts shimmering in the moonlight.

"Come on in," she calls out to him.

He ponders this. He's no fan of swimming. But he's also not one to run from a beautiful naked woman.

He kicks off his shoes and tugs down his jeans. He decides to leave on the underwear. It's a little cold out, so who knows what's going on down there.

He approaches the water, incoming waves lapping at his feet.

That's when he gets the first good look at her face in the silver light. And before he can form a conscious thought, a streak of terror races through his body.

And he turns and runs like hell.

CHAPTER TWENTY-TWO

JENNA

They arrive at the cabin at eleven thirty. There are no neighbors for five miles on either side. The structure, a classic log cabin with a rustic façade that masks a luxurious interior, is dark, no car out front, but Simon would've pulled it into the barn.

Jenna looks at Willow, who's managed to fall asleep, either from exhaustion or as a coping mechanism.

She puts a gentle hand on Willow's shoulder and her step-daughter jerks awake.

Willow seems to be out of it for a minute. As if asking herself whether the last eleven hours were an awful dream. A weird nightmare where the stepmom she can't stand turns out to be some type of criminal or Jason Bourne.

Willow's expression turns crestfallen with the realization it was not a *Wizard of Oz* fever dream. She won't wake up with her family, Toto, and her life back to normal.

Jenna opens the Jeep's door, but before she gets out Willow grabs her by the arm.

"You're not gonna, like, tell Dad about me skipping and, uh, drinking at the 7-Eleven?"

Teenagers. After everything that's happened tonight, she's worried she'll get grounded.

"I think it can wait, don't you?" Jenna will tell Simon when the time is right. She won't lie to him. He deserves to know. Not tonight, though.

Out of nowhere, a silhouette appears from the side of the house. Simon, carrying a shotgun. He leans the gun carefully against the cabin and scoops his older daughter in his arms as she races into his embrace.

He whispers something to her; she nods, hugs him again, and goes inside. Jenna feels her heart shatter a fragment when Willow doesn't say goodbye.

Jenna approaches. The sky out here is so clear, the stars brighter. In the half-light, Simon looks tired, like he's aged ten years in a single day. She swears there's more gray hair.

"I'm so sorry," Jenna says.

Simon doesn't say anything for a long moment. Finally: "I thought you said you were done? That they said you were out. Free."

She doesn't like the accusation in his tone. "I told you everything."

He thinks about this. It was never real before, she understands now. Sure, Simon believed what Jenna had told him about her past. He understood that she'd worked for a shadow outfit that did contract work for the government. But it was an abstraction. A construct that seemed more out of a spy movie or thriller novel, too farfetched to ever happen.

But that was before he saw the fear in his daughter's eyes. Before he'd had to slink away and hide like a fugitive. Before he truly understood that Jenna has done awful things that could come back to haunt her.

"What now?" Simon asks.

Jenna almost smiles. The taxman always wants a plan.

"I go figure out who's behind this."

"And when you do?"

Then I kill them. Each and every one of them.

"Then I try to get our lives back."

He looks at her skeptically but doesn't say that he knows that will never happen.

"If anyone comes, you go to the safe room." They built a hidden panic room on the main floor. The entrance is a secret panel in the back of the kitchen pantry that leads to a room armored with Kevlar panels.

Simon nods.

"I'll call when it's safe." The cabin has no internet, but the burner phone is untraceable. As long as no one used it to call any line connected in any way to Jenna.

Simon nods again.

"And if I don't hear from you?"

"You will."

"But if I don't?"

Jenna tilts her head to the side. "Then go to the FBI and give them this." She puts the manila envelope in his hand. The insurance policy she created when she got out of The Corporation, long buried in that lockbox. "And make clear that you had no idea until today when I told you."

She goes inside, finds Lulu sleeping in her room, decides not to wake her. She leans over and kisses her on the head. She stops by Willow's room to say goodbye, but the door is shut. She puts her hand on the door but turns and leaves.

Downstairs, Simon hands her a travel cup of coffee for the road. He gestures to the Glock on the kitchen table.

"You keep it," Jenna says. She has the gun from the lockbox. It's all she needs.

At the doorway, she looks at him and says, "I love you."

For the first time in their marriage, Simon breaks Jenna in two when he says nothing in response.

CHAPTER TWENTY-THREE

THE TWINS

"He's pissed," Casey says into the phone. She's ditched the Camaro and is driving a stolen Nissan on I-95.

"Expected," Haley says. "And, I mean, he's got a point."

Casey laughs. Mocking their client's voice, she says, "He was like, *Dumping a guy in the ocean? Blowing up a coal mine? I know I said make it look like accidents, but haven't you ever heard of a car accident or drug overdose?*"

Haley laughs too. "Wait till he finds out about you using that cattle killer on those douchebags at the 7-Eleven."

They have always been on the same page, Casey and Haley. They met in college. On Casey's first day on campus, people kept waving at her, saying *hey*, like they knew her. *This is the fucking friendliest place on earth*, she concluded.

Then, a girl in a sorority shirt came up and *hugged* her, referring to her as Haley, not Casey.

Casey had shoved the girl away. "My name isn't Haley."

After a few minutes of convincing, the sorority girl pulled out her phone, took a picture of Casey, sent a text. Pings came back and she shook her head. "Are you adopted?" she asked. Casey didn't answer but didn't need to. "You need to come with me."

That's how she met Haley, who'd come to campus and rushed a sorority before the other freshmen. Looking at Haley was like looking into a mirror. Except that Haley hadn't been adopted by a poor couple on a farm in Adair, Nebraska, but instead by a hedge-fund manager in Greenwich, Connecticut. They were identical twins except Haley's lowlights were expensive, her clothes designer, her teeth straighter.

Turns out they both love horror movies, both eat too much candy (both favoring Mike and Ikes), both scored 1545 on the SAT, and both applied to a small liberal-arts college in Vermont, mostly for the skiing. And they learned that the similarities didn't stop there. After a night of drinking—both being partial to gin—Haley confessed that she had an empty hole inside her that made her care about no one but herself, that she'd been disciplined in school for hurting other kids, that she liked doing it.

That's when Casey admitted that she'd worked at a slaughterhouse. That killing cattle—using a device called a penetrating captive bolt—was one of the few things that comforted her. The *whoosh* of the device driving a retracting steel bolt into their brains was pure white-noise comfort.

After Casey got expelled for breaking a frat boy's nose when he got handsy, they decided to take Haley's father's advice: *The secret to life is to find something you love and get them to pay you to do it.*

"How's Miami?" Casey asks, the white lines on the highway a blur ahead on the dark night.

"Peachy."

The sound of wind blows into the receiver. It's late, but Haley's still outdoors.

"Where are you?" Casey asks.

"The beach."

"No fair. You get a Caribbean cruise, then a beach in Miami, and I get Chestertown, Pennsylvania, and a coal mine in West Virginia. . . ."

"I'll make it up to you," Haley says. "So, what's he want us to do? Clean up the mess?"

"He said there's too much heat right now. The media is all over it. He said he needs to think about next steps."

"Is that his way of firing us?"

"Probably."

"It's funny."

"What's that?"

"He thinks it's his choice."

She smiles. They always think alike.

"I'll see you in Philly. This isn't over yet."

"City of Brotherly Love, watch out!"

PART 2

THE REUNION

CHAPTER TWENTY-FOUR

JENNA

On the drive back to D.C., Jenna's mind blazes. More questions:

She's been out for five years, so why now? Is The Corporation cleaning house? Closing shop and tying up loose ends? Is it about a past job? One of her targets' kids? Like in those shows where a son comes back decades later to avenge the murder of his father? Best served on a cold plate and all that.

But her jobs had been clean. Well, mostly clean.

Her mind flashes to the target at the Capital Grille: Artemis Templeton, a fellow resident of Savior House. Was that a coincidence? Or are they both targets? And if so, why? It doesn't make sense. She hasn't seen Arty since they were kids. He's a famous businessman now—a tech visionary who's constantly trying to outdo whatever Bezos, Branson, Musk, and the rest of the bored billionaires are wasting their money on—the only reason she recognized the adult version of him.

If she hadn't identified him, would she have taken him out? Could she so easily go back to the person—the killer—she was?

Her thoughts flutter to another killer, the attractive woman from the bus stop, from SoulCycle, from behind the 7-Eleven. She has a ghastly tool she used to murder those poor hipsters. It's Jenna's fault they're dead. That feeling of bugs crawling under her skin she'd shed so long ago is returning. She needs to fight it, cover her flesh with the repellant of compartmentalization, denial, the stuff that got her through, made it capable to start a new life. First as a single Washingtonian, then as a yoga mom in the burbs of Chevy Chase.

The sucking sound of the weapon rattles in her head. She remembers what it reminds her of: a job that did indeed go sideways.

Jenna arrives at the party, a private affair, in a short skirt and looking leggy as required. Sabine said the target was an investigator from the Securities and Exchange Commission, of all things, attending a bachelor party with his college buddies. They'd rented a space in the West Village, which had a bar on the main floor, a party room upstairs, and a basement.

The party is tame enough at first, when the girlfriends and wives are there. The men are all Master of the Universe types, members of an Ivy League secret society that isn't so secret. It's really just a fraternity filled with secret handshakes and blood oaths and so much testosterone that it makes the SigEps seem like feminist advocates. Jenna is part of the troupe hired to look pretty, give the men some eye candy, flirt, but nothing more. This after the significant others leave so the "boys can be boys."

She's made eye contact with the SEC guy throughout the night. He's twice peeled away his gaze, as if confused. He's not the same as the others. His suit isn't from Savile Row, he doesn't wear an expensive watch, lacks the swagger.

At eleven, when the wives start clearing out, the best man—Chief, they all call him—taps his glass with a pen to get everyone's attention and announces the festivities for the rest of the evening.

"Brothers!" he exclaims.

The men snap to attention with a bellowing, *"Oorah!"* like they're Marines, which is ridiculous given their uncalloused hands and muscles by Equinox.

"We're here to celebrate the death, I mean *marriage*, of our brother Connor."

"Oorah!"

"It wouldn't be a night with the Robber Barons without the Dancing Turtle, the Lazy Susan, and, let's not forget, game night!"

Jenna doesn't understand any of it, all inside jokes or rituals, but she's already finding her way to the SEC man. She says hello, holds eye contact.

She's supposed to make it look like an accident. So her plan is simple: get him alone, slip the fentanyl in his drink, and sneak out as he convulses on the floor.

But something isn't sitting right. In a room full of what she imagines contains many very bad men, he doesn't seem like one. He's kind of sweet. Uncomfortable with the company and their shtick. Like he doesn't belong. Jenna's always been a sucker for outsiders.

"College friends?" she asks, raising her voice over more cheering.

He nods, almost embarrassed. They drink and she tries to make him feel comfortable, laughs at something he says, touches his arm. When it comes down to it, men are simple creatures.

Past midnight, when she's about to make her move—invite him somewhere private—the clang of a bell rings. The leader,

Chief, slicks back his Gordon Gekko hair with a hand and pro-claims: "The flowers have arrived, gentlemen."

The room erupts.

"What's going on?" Jenna asks.

Her target gives a look of disapproval. "Maybe we should get out of here," he says.

No, this is the perfect distraction. She watches as about eight or nine girls—if they're eighteen, it's by a day—are escorted into the room. They wear heavy makeup, the way you do when you think it will make you look older, but their scared eyes and rolled shoulders tell the story. They're ushered into the basement.

Chief starts up the chant. "Game night, game night, game night."

It starts as a rumble but builds to a crescendo as the men start pounding on the bar, stomping their feet.

"Game night?" Jenna asks.

Before the SEC guy answers, she overhears one of his frat brothers say, "Remember that townie at the Vineyard? She didn't walk for a week."

Jenna doesn't like the sound of this.

"Let's get out of here," the mark says.

"Let's stay awhile. I like games."

In the basement, a group of four men and four girls are play-ing cards, strip poker by the looks of their state of dress—two girls down to bras, a guy in his boxers, another with no shirt, his hairy chest glistening with sweat.

There's a round of beer pong at a table in the back.

Jenna doesn't like it, not one bit, but everything appears con-sensual. Stock college boy nonsense. None of the weird ritualist frat boy stuff she's feared. It's time to do what she's come to do. She fingers the packet of fentanyl in her handbag.

As she's leaving, Chief, full-on drunk now, announces it's time for Target Jeopardy. There's a podium set up with a TV monitor next to it. Up pops the familiar blue categories for *Jeopardy* on the screen.

The girls are lined up in front of the podium, the men in the spectator section behind them. Maybe it's a drinking game set to *Jeopardy* questions, Jenna thinks.

But it's more grotesque. Chief stands like a deranged game show host and asks the first girl to pick a category. She's glassy-eyed, more than tipsy, and she giggles. She chooses World History.

When she gets the answer wrong, Jenna is startled as the men begin shooting paintball guns. The sound—*whoosh, whoosh, whoosh*—fills the room. The girl wails as she's pelted. She's shirt-less, down to her bra, large welts are already appearing on her back, and the firing doesn't stop until she's curled on the floor.

The next girl says, "I don't want to."

But Chief says, "Pick a category, bitch!"

Jenna looks around. The men are riled up, eyes alight.

The girl shakes her head, refuses to pick a category.

Chief makes a noise like a buzzer. "Aw, looks like you're out of time."

The firing begins again.

The other girls are bawling now, which only seems to get the men more amped up.

Jenna looks at the SEC guy. "We need to stop this."

He shrugs, grimaces, like *nothing I can do*. The paintball gun they placed on the table for him sits unused.

Before the leader asks the next girl her category, Jenna grabs the paintball gun, walks up to the podium. The leader looks per-plexed, then horrified when Jenna puts the barrel of the rifle to his crotch and pulls the trigger, point-blank. *Whoosh*.

Chief wails, falls to the floor. Jenna feels figures lurching toward her. She takes the gun and *whoosh*, a paint pellet slams one guy in the face, *whoosh* another point-blank in the chest. Both are on the floor.

Seeing what's happening, the other men start pushing out of the basement, jamming the stairwell.

Jenna picks up one of the other paintball guns and starts blasting them, screaming *"What category?"*

Jenna is yanked out of the memory when she sees the police lights as she pulls up Connecticut Avenue. The front awning of the District Inn is bordered with yellow-and-black tape. Three patrol cars crouch in the lot, bathed in blue from the strobes.

She's come to the hotel because of its reputation. A dangerous place nestled bizarrely in an affluent enclave in upper northwest D.C. The neighbors have rallied against the hotel—it's had four murders in the past year—to no avail. It's not far from Jenna's own house, and coming here has spared her having to venture to the city to find a place that takes cash and doesn't require ID.

Jenna drives past the unsightly yellow building and finds a parking space on Albemarle Street. She took Billy's number from Willow so she could let him know where to find his Jeep. She'll see if she can find a pay phone. The District Inn might have one to cater to its clientele, prostitutes and drug dealers, the rare few who still favor pay phones.

Jenna walks confidently on the sidewalk, past the Flagship carwash, the Burger King, the ZIPS dry cleaner, and stops at the perimeter. She's dog-tired after the three-hour return drive and she probably looks it, but nothing a District cop on the night shift will give a second look.

The officer manning the perimeter gives her a weary once-over.

"I'm staying at the hotel. . . . Can I go in yet?"

The officer shrugs, lifts the yellow band of tape.

She strolls inside the lobby. It's covered in a sickly haze from fluorescents. The guy working the reception desk wears a cheap suit and has a lazy eye, which seems fitting. He's watching the cops outside, who seem to be wrapping things up.

"Eventful night," Jenna says.

The guy turns his good eye to her. He seems surprised, perhaps because it's 2:30 a.m. and she's not a prostitute.

"I need a room for the night."

The guy nods, asks for a credit card.

"I'd prefer to pay with cash, if that works?" She puts down three hundred-dollar bills, a tiny portion of the cash she took with her from the lockbox. The sign on the door says $200 for a single, a steal in D.C. where rooms average at least $500 a night. She probably won't think it's a bargain when she sees the room.

The clerk sighs, frowns at the bills. "Three hundred ain't gonna cover it if you steal something."

"What could there *possibly* be to steal?" Jenna asks.

The man chuckles. "Oh, I don't know. The TV. Towels."

Jenna puts another hundred on the counter.

"One more of those," the guy says, "and you gotta be out by ten in the morning when my shift ends."

"Deal," she says, slapping another bill on the counter.

She takes the only elevator to the fifth floor. The ugly carpet in the hallway smells of rug cleaner and mold, and she's thinking maybe it would've been worth the risk to go somewhere nicer in Bethesda. But it's safer if she doesn't register, doesn't use credit cards, in case her aliases have been breached.

Inside, the room is exactly as one would expect. Heavy curtains with a layer of dust, floral bedspread, stained carpet. But she's so tired it doesn't matter. She needs a shower and some sleep.

She turns on the television and finds Channel 7, the local twenty-four-hour news station. It's not live, she knows. The news is on a loop in between infomercials.

There's a story about the shooting downtown at the Capital Grille:

"Fear gripped downtown this afternoon as shots were fired near a popular D.C. restaurant where tech billionaire Artemis Templeton was dining," the newscaster says. An image of Artemis's bald head appears on the screen. "Templeton, a pioneer in the early days of social-media technology, and who in recent years has focused on everything from next-gen artificial intelligence to e-commerce, is number three on *Forbes*'s list of the richest tech titans. It's unclear whether Templeton was a target of the shooter. Both police and Templeton have declined to comment." The report goes on: An officer has a nasty leg wound after being injured by some type of weapon. Police are looking for two white females who are persons of interest.

Jenna presses mute on the remote, then strips down.

The shower is hot and feels wonderful. The water pressure is surprisingly good in the shower-tub combo and she doesn't even mind the smell of the cheap minibar of soap. She breathes in the steam, her mind jumping about to a thousand variations of the same questions: Who wants Artemis Templeton dead and why? And more important, does Jenna also have a target on her back or was she merely considered collateral damage to the hit on Arty? She breaks unexpectedly into a crying jag, thinking about her family. She needs to stop, get it together. She can't help them if she isn't focused. Sabine's voice comes to her: *Focus on nothing but the mission.*

That's what she'll do. Tomorrow will be a big day.

After the shower, she gets between the sheets, careful not to touch the bedspread, imagining the horrors a black light would reveal. Pounding music seeps through the walls, the guests next door partying. Why not? The murder victim's likely at the morgue by now.

She unmutes the television. The news has moved to footage of a mining accident in West Virginia.

A local reporter holds a microphone to a man's face.

"We have sensors that picked up a problem. The pressure in the mine changed consistent with an explosion."

"An explosion?"

"Yes, mines often capture methane gas and that can be extremely dangerous if there's any kind of ignition, or spark. It's odd here because the mine isn't operational. It's refurbished and mostly used for the television show *The Miners*, so it's surprising but still possible there was a buildup of gas."

Jenna half listens. A TV producer evidently was in the mine at the time of the explosion. A rescue team miraculously found him alive.

Remarkably, someone is having a worse day than even Jenna.

She falls asleep before she hears the rest of the report.

CHAPTER TWENTY-FIVE

DONNIE

"I'm scared, Benny."

"It'll be okay."

"What if she—what if she doesn't wanna see me?"

"She will." Benny gazes at the house with the dead lawn and bedsheets for curtains, his expression not matching his words.

"What if there's bad guys in there?"

"Don't worry." Benny lifts his shirt, revealing the gun tucked in the waistband.

"I thought you got rid of that." Donnie's mind flashes to the shallow grave, the grisly scene from last night, something that he'll never be able to scrub from his memories no matter how high he gets.

Benny doesn't answer. He walks up the cracked sidewalk, opens the front door, which isn't locked. There's a hole where the knob used to be. The door creaks open and the place is dark. Someone groans from the light coming in.

Nico had stolen their files from the cabinet in Mr. Brood's office. This is the address on Donnie's paperwork, but maybe it's the wrong place.

There's a stench in the air. Benny takes the lead, pretending not to be terrified.

Bodies litter the floor. They're not dead but might as well be.

Why would his mom live in such squalor? He knows why but wants to pretend he doesn't.

Benny crouches over and says something to a man sitting on the floor. His legs are crossed, hands in a prayer position, like some insane Buddha.

The man doesn't say anything but points upstairs.

Benny walks slowly up the creaky steps. They're soft from damp and rot. Donnie looks up and sees there's a section of the roof missing. The drywall has mostly been removed from the walls. Copper pipe bandits.

Benny looks at Donnie like he's having second thoughts. "You know what? Let's get out of here," Benny says. "She's probably not here."

Donnie doesn't believe him. "I want to say goodbye before we go."

They're leaving Chestertown for Philly to start over. Donnie leads the way upstairs, light from a hole in the roof illuminating the stairwell. When he enters the bedroom, he sees something that brings him back to when he was a young boy. The tattoo on the nape of the woman's neck. A butterfly.

But today he's not lying beside her, spooning, cuddling. He's watching the head bob up and down, the butterfly folding with the movement of her neck as the woman kneels before the man with his pants at his knees, his eyes closed, head back.

Benny turns, takes Donnie by the elbow to guide him out.

But before he's ushered away, Donnie says, "Mom. It's me, Donnie." She doesn't reply, so he says it again. "Mom."

The woman's head continues to bob, the man's hand gripping her hair.

"Mom!" Donnie says louder.

But the word is foreign to the woman.

As it should be.

Donnie tries to shake off the memory as he brushes aside another question from Reeves Rothschild about his family.

It's nine in the morning and they're sitting in a cabana near one of the eight elaborate swimming pools on the grounds of the Fontainebleau. As always, it's a beautiful morning in Miami: blue sky, sunshine, eighty degrees. "I told you, I don't wanna talk about my childhood. Next question."

The young writer frowns. He's hunched over his laptop, looking peaked, a man who's experiencing his first hangover from a Car Bomb. "I get it, I do. But I think it adds some color if we can say how a kid from Fort Payne, Alabama, ends up in Chestertown, Pennsylvania. And how that led you to Philly and then Los Angeles with Tracer's Bullet."

Donnie is spared having to answer when one of the hotel workers—he thinks they call them cabana boys—appears. He's holding a small box.

"Mr. Danger, you have a delivery."

The man hands him the package.

"Hot damn. For once, Mickey came through for me. A new phone." It's the first time the band's manager has ever given Donnie concierge treatment, saving most of it for Tom. Donnie opens the box. He turns on the device, a flip phone that's already activated.

"He must've had a time machine to find you that," Reeves says.

Donnie gives him a narrow-eyed smile.

"Maybe you should call the FBI about that lady from last night."

Donnie made the mistake of telling Reeves about the woman from the beach. "What's the point? I'm not sure it's the same lady the agent showed me. I wasn't in the best frame of mind. . . ."

Reeves looks clammy himself, so that part he clearly gets. "Still, it could help with your friend's case."

He's right. And Donnie knows he's avoiding thinking about Benny. He fights the grief and pain by wiping his mind of the matter. He's always been good at denial or compartmentalization or whatever they called it at that treatment center. And the truth: Whenever he thinks about Benny, he feels a weight in his chest, an insatiable need to get high. It makes him ashamed, since that's the opposite of what Benny would want.

"They already arrested somebody, so I'm not sure it matters." Reeves frowns.

"All right, all right. Damn, Hemingway, you're a pushy SOB."

"I'm sorry, it's not my place to—"

"Lighten up, amigo. You're right." So much so that Donnie decides that he can't avoid it any longer. He needs to reach out to Mia, Ben's widow.

Widow. The word hits him like a gut punch. He opens his new flip phone and dials the number from memory. It goes to voicemail.

"Mia, it's me, Donnie. Please call me, dear." He leaves his number and hangs up. "Where were we?" he asks Reeves. "I've got some good stories from when we toured Japan. This one time we all got back to the hotel at like four in the mornin' and our rhythm guitarist Walker goes to his room and for some damn reason decides to take a bath. He falls asleep with the water running. One of our roadies was in the room on the floor below and woke up

because it was like a torrential rain comin' down in his room."
Donnie barks a laugh.

Reeves is taking notes, but he's not smiling. He's not too interested in the on-the-road partying stories.

They're interrupted by the purr of the flip phone. A Philadelphia area code is on the caller ID.

"Mia, darlin', thanks for calling me back so quickly," Donnie answers.

There's a long silence. Ben's wife has never liked Donnie, but he's Ben's best friend, Bell's godfather, so she tolerates him.

Finally, she speaks. "Don't call here again, Donnie."

"Wait, what? What's going on, Mia? I don't—"

"He told me what you did. This is your fault."

"Mia, please, I don't—" She disconnects the line.

Donnie stares at nothing, dumbfounded.

"Everything okay?" Reeves asks, a concerned look on his face.

Donnie sits quietly, processing. *What in the hell . . . ?* He can't ignore the ache in his chest over Ben's death anymore, can't pretend that he can pick up the phone and the Honorable Robert Benjamin Wood will drop everything if Donnie needs something. Can't pretend that he didn't hear what Mia said: *He told me what you did. This is your fault.*

Donnie says, "You're a writer, so you're good at research, right?"

"I'm okay, I guess," Reeves says.

"I need you to find out the details for Ben Wood's funeral. Can you do that?"

"Sure. He was a public figure, so it shouldn't be hard."

"Good. Do it. Then go pack your stuff."

Reeves cocks his head to the side.

"We're going to Philly."

CHAPTER TWENTY-SIX

JENNA

Jenna is out of the District Inn by ten as promised. Behind the hotel there's an off-brand rental car place, so she decides to risk using one of the credit cards. If any of her other identities are compromised and someone is tracking her cards, at least she'll be mobile in the rental car and not a sitting duck in a hotel room. She rents a Toyota Corolla, you can't get more ubiquitous than that, and heads to D.C.'s Kalorama neighborhood.

She's driven by the address only once in the three years since she saw the familiar face in *Washingtonian* magazine. The story was about the wedding of the ambassador to Brazil to his exotic-looking French-born bride. It was just like Sabine to hide out in the open, taking a Valerie Plame–like gig. The magazine did a spread of the couple's tony home, so, on a lark one day after picking up Lulu from ballet class in Cleveland Park, Jenna cruised through Kalorama and there it was, the house from the photo shoot on Tracy Place.

And today, what seems like a lifetime later, she sits in a Toyota staring at the 1920s Colonial. She considers going up to the door and knocking, but there's probably security. And in any event, it's not like Sabine would come to the door. She'd have staff. Jenna thinks of that first day on the private jet, Sabine quietly assessing fifteen-year-old Jenna. A flight attendant wearing a skimpy uniform, placing food trays in front of both of them. Jenna had been stubborn, terrified about what was going on. But she'd also been hungry. And the food looked delicious. Not like the airplane food that time her parents had taken her to Disneyland. It was some type of fancy fish, displayed beautifully. She reached her fingers onto the plate, but Sabine slapped her hand, hard.

"We might as well start now," she said in that French-Russian accent. "A woman with manners, breeding, gets what she wants."

"I don't want anything from you," Jenna told her. She reached for the sharp steak knife on the tray.

This amused Sabine. "*Mon chéri*, if you think you're better with a knife"—she tapped her own steak knife with her index finger—"go right ahead." Her smile faded. "Otherwise, sit up straight, and do what I do."

That's what Jenna learned in the first lesson of her training, which later included not only etiquette but also communication skills, exuding old-money confidence, and murdering someone without leaving a trace.

Jenna's startled by the hard knock on the window of the Corolla.

A Goliath of a man is staring at her suspiciously. Through the glass he says, "Can I help you, ma'am?"

Jenna smiles. Rolls down the window. Slipping into her yoga-mom persona, she says, "Hi, I'm looking for Kalorama Circle. I'm visiting my sister from out of town and this rental car has no GPS and I'm so embarrassed my phone's dead."

The man doesn't smile back. But he tells her to go up to the stop sign, take a right, follow Belmont, and she won't miss it. He says it quickly, with a *beat it* tone in his voice. So she beats it. A van's pulled in front of Sabine's home, and the man walks over to it, signals to the driver to move the vehicle to the street and not use the driveway. Jenna makes a point of not turning her head as she passes the house. But she still sees it. The signage on the side of the van: CATHY'S CATERING.

Jenna smiles as she turns the corner. Of course. It's Friday night in Washington, D.C.

Sabine is having a dinner party.

CHAPTER TWENTY-SEVEN

NICO

Nico's in his trailer. Shannon stands with her iPad clutched in her hand, like always. Shannon is a capable showrunner; she's been doing reality shows for a decade and should be the one filling in as EP while Nico takes some time off. But she likes being behind the scenes. She and her wife keep a low profile generally. Rural West Virginia isn't always the most enlightened place. And Davis, the fuckstick from the network, keeps insisting that he should host *The Black* aftershow while Nico recovers. The guy is such a douche.

Shannon waits for Nico to finish tapping on his phone. His seventh sports bet since he was pulled to the surface. He looks up at her.

She says, "The kid with cancer is scheduled to be on-set today. Given everything that's happened, Davis wants me to reschedule with the organization that set it up."

"He knows this kid is dying, right?"

Shannon doesn't say anything. She's not keen on getting in the middle.

"You can tell Davis I said we're not canceling, and let the cast know that they'd better be there." The teenager's last wish—to meet the cast of *The Miners*—wouldn't be on Nico's own bucket list, but he sure as hell isn't going to cancel.

Shannon walks him through other show issues and Nico pretends to listen. He wants to make a few more bets before the day gets away from him.

When Shannon wraps up, he says, "I need to tell you something."

"What's that?"

"The mine—it wasn't an accident—someone tried to kill me."

She chuckles. "I suppose it was only a matter of time."

There with that asshole thing again. Studying him now, Shannon says, "Oh shit, you're serious."

"Someone pretending to be Roger sent me a text to meet him at Mine B. I thought it was the usual Maverick nonsense. But I called him this morning and he swears he didn't send me a text."

"And someone, what? Set off an—"

Nico nods, cutting her off. "*After* they impaled me with some weird weapon." He gestures to his shoulder, which is in a sling.

She eyes him skeptically, and he gets it. Getting stabbed or shot might make sense. But pierced by a rod of steel projected through a weird weapon that looks like a Maglite? Nearly buried alive by an explosion?

"It's all gonna leak soon," Nico says. "The sheriff says he'll give me time to duck out of town to avoid the circus, but he can't wait too long. NIOSH and the other government agencies will figure out this wasn't methane buildup, that the explosion was intentional."

"Is that why you checked out of the hospital so fast?"

He nods again.

"Who?" She pauses. "Why?"

"I have no idea."

Shannon gives him another skeptical look. She's one of the few people who know about Nico's gambling. She says, "The Feds have asked for any footage we have from security cameras, so maybe that will identify who it was."

Nico doubts it. He doesn't think there are any cameras outside the mine. And he doesn't mention that Maverick told him he'd met a woman that night, "a hot tamale from out of town." That she'd gone home with him and he doesn't remember jack shit from the moment they had a drink at his place. Nothing was stolen, so he didn't think much of it. But Nico wonders if she used Maverick's phone to lure Nico to the mine.

"Have you told the network?" Shannon asks.

"Nope. You're it."

Once the news breaks, they can expect a media onslaught. There'd been an accidental shooting on a movie set in New Mexico a couple years ago and it stayed headline news for months.

"Are you okay?" she asks.

"I'm fine," he lies. He thinks of those rats with their red eyes.

"You know everyone loves you. You may not remember, but there was a massive crowd at the rescue site. Maverick, Elmo, the lot of them were there. I swear Headboard had tears in his eyes. And there's been an outpouring on Twitter."

He shrugs. The cast was there for the cameras. The rest are keyboard junkies who don't even know Nico. He's checked his messages. Mostly reporters. His ex, Natalie, hasn't called.

"I'm gonna be off the grid for a few days. Decline interview requests. Request privacy as I recover."

"I'll draft a statement."

Nico nods.

"Where will you go?"

He flips his lucky silver dollar, which he isn't so sure is that lucky, and looks at its face. "Somewhere I hoped to never return."

CHAPTER TWENTY-EIGHT

DONNIE

Donnie and Reeves sit next to each other on the United flight. It has been a long time since Donnie has flown first class and it's nice to have some legroom. Though, somewhere along the way, the airlines have managed to screw up first class. Back in the day, they'd be in mini-cabin-like pods where the seats would recline flat and a divider would make it so you didn't even have to look at the person seated next to you. Now, at least on the flight from Miami to Philadelphia International, it's basically a bigger seat, free wine from a box, and tepid beer.

"Thanks for buyin' the tickets," Donnie says to Reeves. "You'll get reimbursed, I hope?"

"Me too," Reeves says. The trip was last-minute, so he probably didn't anticipate the expense. "But don't worry about the money. This gives us a little extra private time so we can work on the book."

Donnie nods. The flight attendant offers him a beer and he gladly obliges. Better to make sure whoever pays for their tickets gets their money's worth.

"So I thought we might step back, take things from the beginning. When you learned how to play guitar . . ."

Donnie rests his head back, a smile involuntarily spreading on his face. "I was in foster care in Chestertown the first time I ever touched a guitar."

Reeves has his laptop out now. On the home screen there's a photo of a woman. She's in a hospital bed, tubes in her nose with monitors behind her, but she's smiling, a haunting, beautiful smile.

Before Donnie asks who she is, Reeves says, "You're originally from Fort Payne, Alabama?" He's already typing.

"With an emphasis on the *payne*," Donnie says, grinning.

Reeves doesn't seem amused. "How'd you end up so far from home, in Chestertown?"

Donnie's already told him to drop questions about his childhood, but Donnie supposes he can throw the guy a bone. "You mean, how'd my mom get the idea to move from one of the poorest towns in the South to one of the poorest towns in the Northeast?"

Reeves doesn't push.

"The short version is that my mom met a dude who, like all the dudes, convinced her he loved her and we'd be a family if she followed him. She did, we weren't, and next thing I know I'm in foster care and my mom's been arrested." That should be enough red meat for the writer.

Reeves types on his laptop, eyes on the screen.

"Anyhoo, my first foster family, they were a nice elderly couple, the Jensons. Mr. J played guitar and still noodled around with the church band and he taught me to play. Gave me my first guitar. I named her Susie. I've still got her."

"Susie, like the name of your second album."

"You've done your research, Hemingway, hot damn," Donnie says, smiling.

Reeves keeps typing. Not looking up, he asks, "How long were you with the Jensons?"

Donnie swallows down a lump in his throat. Not long enough.

"A year. They were a sweet couple, but not in good health. Mr. J had a heart attack and they couldn't take care of me anymore, so I got sent to a group home."

Savior House.

"Mr. J taught me the four chords I needed, and I took it from there."

"Is the group house where you met Ben Wood?" Reeves asks, taking his chances.

Donnie doesn't answer. Instead, he launches into a tired story about the time he got a DUI driving a golf cart on the way to a show in Dublin. He then excuses himself to the restroom.

As he tries to target the stream of urine into the small bowl, he's startled by a memory: the four of them at the bank of the river, on their knees, the gun barrel put to the back of Donnie's head.

Ben's voice echoes in his head. *You don't have to be scared anymore, Donnie.*

A tear rolls down Donnie's cheek.

I'm not so sure about that, Benny. I'm not so sure.

CHAPTER TWENTY-NINE

JENNA

"Are you Tabitha?" the perky woman in a stylish outfit asks.

Jenna hesitates, then remembers that she's using her Tabitha credentials—and credit card—at Saks Fifth Avenue. She called ahead, asked for an appointment with a stylist.

"Nice to meet you," Jenna says, shaking hands. The woman wears a name tag that says: BLUE.

"Your name's 'Blue'? How pretty," Jenna says.

"Do *not* get me started. My last name is Flowers. I'm Blue Flowers. My mom was into gardening."

Jenna smiles.

Blue Flowers continues, "I'm lucky she wasn't into astronomy. Probably would've named me Uranus." She offers a bright smile and says, "Follow me."

The store has a strange configuration, like it used to be something else, a three-story old-time bank. Nestled in the Friendship Heights neighborhood that straddles the D.C.-Maryland border, it's the only high-end store in the area. The area used to be synonymous with luxury retail—the Mazza Gallerie shops, Neiman Marcus, Dior, Louis Vuitton—but somewhere along the way, there was an exodus. Except for Saks.

On the walk, Blue says, "Sounds like you've had *a day*. In town for a big party in Kalorama and the airline lost all your luggage, I mean, *girl* . . ."

"You don't know the half of it."

"Well, don't worry, you're going to be the talk of that party when I'm done with you."

And for the next two hours, Jenna is Vivian Ward in *Pretty Woman*. Trying on expensive dresses, having drinks brought to her, flattery abounding.

Blue Flowers is right. Jenna, or Tabitha, looks stunning in the Elie Saab bead-embellished silk gown, the Rene Caovilla satin heels, and the Saint Laurent leather clutch.

At the register, Jenna tries not to wince at the $8,498.32 price tag. The cards have high limits. And it's no time to be frugal. As Sabine taught her all those years ago: *Beauty is a skeleton key that opens almost any door. Don't take my word for it. Studies show beautiful people make more money than smarter people, get better jobs and promotions than more qualified people, and get lighter sentences than other criminals. Throw in some confidence and manners and there's no place you can't go—invited or not.*

Tonight, Jenna will test that theory on Sabine herself.

With the Saks garment bag hanging in the rental car, Jenna drives up Wisconsin and into Bethesda. There she stops at Lululemon, where she buys some athletic wear. Black leggings, black tank, and black hooded jacket. A cat burglar couldn't find a better outfit to disappear into the night. She then walks over to Bethesda Sports on Elm and buys some running shoes. She's been there many times (Willow runs track). The manager is a notorious crank, but today he's distracted by his phone.

She's ready now. She'll go back to the District Inn, take an afternoon nap, get her hair and makeup done at Inari, then get dressed for what promises to be an interesting night out.

CHAPTER THIRTY

NICO

By early afternoon, Nico arrives at O'Leary's Tavern on Erie Avenue in Nicetown, Philadelphia. The bartender, a beefy man in his forties with dark crescents under his eyes, and undoubtedly a baseball bat under the counter, is in deep conversation with a couple of younger guys at the bar. They appear to be discussing cancel culture.

"Your generation is so sensitive," the barman says. "Someone says anything that offends you, and you've got to go to your safe space; then all these keyboard twits, overeducated white ladies, the lot of 'em, try to get you fired from your job."

The young guys—a stylishly dressed Black man and a white guy with orange stubble that looks like a chin strap—exchange a glance. It's unclear to Nico if they work for O'Leary or are customers.

"It's a little more complicated," the stylish guy says. He obviously disagrees with the bartender, but his tone is cautious, respectful. Yeah, these are O'Leary's boys.

The bartender goes on with his monologue. "Everybody's talking about discrimination, but they never mention the Irish and how we get treated." The guy notices Nico, narrows his eyes, but finishes the thought. "If you miss a day at work 'cause you're hungover they call it the Irish Flu. If you put booze in your coffee, it's an Irish Coffee. You have kids close in age, it's Irish Twins. Can you imagine if we said stuff like that for your people?" He looks at the customers, who both appear to be suppressing eye rolls.

"Don't forget the Irish Goodbye," Nico chimes in, referring to the practice of slipping out of a party without saying goodbye, something Nico's mastered himself.

The bartender eyes Nico. "What can I get you, friend?"

"I was hoping to talk with Shane. He used to take meetings on Fridays." Nico points to the back room.

Shane O'Leary, having watched *The Godfather* too many times, scheduled Fridays to deal with neighborhood or internal organizational problems. Late with payments? Get in line. Trouble with somebody in the neighborhood? Take a number. Don Corleone he's not, but there's an efficiency about his operation.

The bartender regards Nico like he recognizes him but isn't sure.

"Who do I say is asking?"

"Nico Adakai."

"Adakai? Why do I know that name?"

Nico shrugs. Back in the day, Nico's father worked for Shane O'Leary's father running book, but Nico wasn't going to get into it with this buffoon. The Adakai name may also be familiar because Nico's father disappeared under mysterious circumstances when Nico was a kid. Rumors were he got sideways with O'Leary Sr., which didn't lend itself to an extended life span.

"Interesting name," the bartender says, not taking the hint. "What is that, Mexican or something?"

Nico's mother told him his grandfather was Native American,

but his father didn't give one shit about his ancestry, so who knows? Besides, that's what everybody seems to tell their kids. *You've got Native American blood.* Nico knows nothing of Native Americans other than that they got royally fucked.

He shrugs again.

The bartender frowns, like he doesn't like Nico's attitude, but he nods at the red-headed guy with the stupid beard, who saunters off to the back room.

The barkeep starts up about cancel culture again, and Nico escapes being drawn in to the conversation as the redheaded guy reemerges and gestures for Nico to come back.

Straight out of a B movie, O'Leary sits at a table draped in white linen eating his lunch—shepherd's pie by the looks of it, as if to complete the cliché—and there's a line ahead of Nico. The man standing at the table in front of O'Leary is thanking him profusely and O'Leary's looking bored and waving him away. One of the toughs sitting on stools nearby shows the guy out. The next guy approaches.

He's wearing a leather jacket and looks like one of the toughs himself.

"You know why you're here?" O'Leary asks him. The kid is in his twenties and has large biceps, a gold chain hanging outside his tight T-shirt.

"My dad said you want to see me about the weeklies."

"Is that what your dad, my brother, said?" O'Leary flicks a glance to an older guy perched on a stool.

The kid nods. His jaw pulses.

"Here's the thing, Brendan. Your weeklies keep coming up short. Not Vince's, not Sam's, not Toby's, only yours."

"I didn't skim, Uncle Shane, I promise I—"

O'Leary raises a hand to quiet him. "I talked to the boys, to your dad, and everyone says the same thing. 'Not Brendan, he's a stand-up guy. Gotta be a mistake.'" He says this in a mocking tone.

The kid nods.

"You're family, so I give you the benefit of the doubt. But your aunt, when your cousin was little, she read all these parenting books, and you know what she always said?"

Brendan shakes his head.

"Trust, but verify."

Brendan doesn't respond.

"So, on your last pickups, we marked the bills." O'Leary puts down his fork and knife and pulls out a small penlight from his pocket. *Click-click, click-click.* A blue light goes on and off. "I'll make you a deal, Brendan. You get out your money clip, and if none of the bills glow under this light, I'll know you had nothing to do with my missing twenty Gs, and I'll give you an apology."

Brendan's face is bloodless now. His father shifts on his stool.

"Or-r-r . . ." O'Leary draws out the word, takes a long pause, letting Brendan squirm. "Or, we agree you owe me *forty* Gs and you put your hand flat on the table here."

Brendan's father is off the stool now. "Shane, we get it, enough."

O'Leary turns to his brother. "Shut the fuck up. If he wasn't your son, we wouldn't even be having this discussion."

Brendan's Adam's apple bobs up and down. His father lowers back to the stool.

O'Leary takes a bite of his food, his eyes not leaving Brendan's.

Brendan walks to the table, lays his hand flat on it. Nico thinks he might wet himself.

Without warning, O'Leary grips the steak knife and stabs it hard through the top of Brendan's hand so it pins it to the table.

Brendan screams in agony but doesn't pull away, doesn't do anything but writhe in pain.

O'Leary rises, walks around the table, and presses his forehead aggressively to Brendan's, looks him in the eyes. "Forty Gs. And if you're ever one dollar short again, I'm gonna take off both your hands, feed 'em to my dogs, and then bury you alive at the farm."

O'Leary wraps his hand around the handle of the steak knife. Instead of pulling it straight out, he yanks it to the side so it cuts through Brendan's hand. The young man collapses to the floor, Brendan's father and the other toughs coming over, lifting him by the arms, carrying him out, leaving behind a blood trail and tablecloth soaked in red.

Sitting back at the table, O'Leary dabs at his mouth with a napkin. "Ni-i-ic-c-co," he says with terrifying enthusiasm. "To what do I owe the pleasure?"

CHAPTER THIRTY-ONE

"Boys, there's a hero in our midst," O'Leary tells the room.

The others look at one another, like they're not sure what O'Leary is talking about.

"Don't any of you mutts watch the news? This guy"—he walks over, grips Nico by the shoulder that's not in the sling—"just escaped a frickin' coal mine collapse."

The crew nods, impressed.

Before Nico can explain why he's there—making sure it wasn't O'Leary who put him at the bottom of that mine—O'Leary directs Nico to follow him. They head out of the back room and to the bar. The bartender is still going on about woke politics but shushes when he sees the boss.

"Give us two Jamesons. But pack 'em for the road, will ya?"

For the road. Again, before Nico can ask, O'Leary says, "I've got an afternoon appointment. If you got the time to join me, we can catch up."

Nico feels a cold finger run down his spine. It's not an offer he can refuse.

The bartender hands them paper coffee cups with lids, and O'Leary leads Nico outside. There's a black sedan parked illegally right out front.

O'Leary presses a key fob and the Mercedes EQS's lights flash. They both climb inside. Nico's nerves are flaring now. He's relieved when none of O'Leary's boys slip into the backseat—a sure recipe for two in the back of the head. Then again, probably not in O'Leary's $100,000 sedan.

O'Leary revs the engine and they're off.

"Where're we going?" Nico finally asks.

"It's a beautiful day, thought we'd get some fresh air," he says. It's not a beautiful day. The sky is the color of granite, with intermittent showers.

"And the bar has ears," O'Leary adds. "You never know who's listening."

Nico doubts that. O'Leary nearly severed a man's hand fifteen minutes ago and surely sweeps the place for bugs daily.

O'Leary grips the wheel, zigging and zagging around traffic. The area is filled with tire stores, overgrown lots, and decaying row houses. Old trolley-car rails rivet the road, but there haven't been trolleys in years.

"So, there's something I wanted to talk with you about," Nico says.

O'Leary turns, puts a finger to his lips. "Let's wait till we get there. Cars have ears too."

Nico doesn't ask where *there* is, and his gut is roiling. This was a mistake. A miscalculation. If it is O'Leary who sent someone to kill him, he's put himself alone with the guy. They have a history, Nico and Shane, through their dads, and their paths crossed when they were kids, but O'Leary wouldn't hesitate to take Nico out if it was good for business.

O'Leary turns up the stereo. It's a pop station and O'Leary seems to be getting into the Olivia Rodrigo song. He's an odd duck—not that Nico would ever say that out loud.

Nico watches out the window as roadside ministries and murals give way to elegant brownstones bordered by iron gates. A sign says: PENN TREATY PARK, and O'Leary veers around and pulls into a lot.

Nico looks out at the large open space. Dozens of kites fill the sky, a kite festival, by the looks of it.

O'Leary parks and they climb out of the vehicle. Standing in the lot, O'Leary says, "Don't take this the wrong way, Nico, but I need you to take off your shirt."

Nico gets it. O'Leary wants to confirm that Nico isn't wearing a wire.

Awkwardly, Nico removes his sling and pulls off his shirt.

"Damn, that looks nasty," O'Leary says, examining the blood-soaked bandage.

Nico makes no reply.

"But I gotta say, no wonder the girls like you so much," O'Leary adds. "Don't worry, I'm not a *ho-mo-sex-ual*," he accentuates each syllable. "But a guy can admire another man's abs, am I right?" He nods that Nico can put his shirt back on.

O'Leary moves to the rear of the car. Fishes out the key fob. This could be it. Where Nico finds himself in another dark hole, the trunk of a Mercedes.

O'Leary opens the hatch and Nico breathes a sigh of relief. The face of a large red dragon stares up at them. O'Leary removes the kite, unfolds it carefully, and they head out to an open space on the field.

Soon the dragon's wings are outstretched and it's darting through the air.

"I didn't know you were an enthusiast," Nico says, making small talk now. This day keeps getting stranger.

"When I was a kid, it was the only good day I remember with my old man," O'Leary says. "I come to the kite festival every year. If it wasn't for my numbnuts nephew skimming from me, I would've been here all morning."

Nico nods. No matter how bad the person, we all cling to the days of innocence we remember from our youth.

"You and your dad ever . . . ?"

"Not quite," Nico says.

O'Leary nods. It's odd talking about their fathers, since Shane's might be the reason Nico's father disappeared. It remains a mystery Nico has no interest in solving, although there is one aspect to it he never understood: Once Dad was gone, no longer a threat, why didn't his mother come back for Nico?

Shane carefully hands the reins of the kite to Nico. It's then Nico realizes that his hands, his only means of defense, are occupied.

But there're too many witnesses for that. No question, Nico could still end up in that trunk with a kite string wrapped around his neck . . . but not here.

Nico navigates the dragon as it tugs the line. He's still in the sling, so it's awkward, but he does *not* want to crash O'Leary's toy.

"So, about my, ah, accident." Nico keeps his eyes on the kite, the bright red dragon like a drop of blood staining the clouds, the Benjamin Franklin Bridge in the distance.

"Yeah, you gonna sue that show? Seems like you could make a pile of cash. I mean, how long were you down there? I suspect you have some back pain and PTSD and other stuff that's tricky to diagnose."

Nico smiles. *Always an angle.* "What they haven't reported on the news yet is that it wasn't an accident." He pauses, watches for O'Leary's reaction.

"No shit. Like someone . . ."

"Set off a small explosive device."

O'Leary chuckles. "Who'd *you* piss off?"

Nico's mouth is dry. "I wanted to make sure it wasn't *you*."

O'Leary barks a laugh. "Is that why?—Is that why you came to the bar?" He laughs again, smacks Nico on the back. It sends a thunderbolt through Nico's wounded shoulder.

"Sorry, I can't think of anyone else who—"

"You owe anybody else?"

Nico shakes his head.

"Broads? Any husbands pissed off? Or crazy gals you jilted?"

Nico shakes his head again.

O'Leary shakes his head as well. "Usually it's money or broads that will get you killed." He laughs again.

"I'm glad you find it amusing."

O'Leary stares up at the other kites bobbing against the gray sky. "We do got a problem, though," he says.

"What's that?"

"If someone's trying to off you, I need to increase the amount of your payments. If something happens to you, I'll be out a lot of dough. You understand."

Nico is so relieved O'Leary isn't after him that he doesn't protest. He's not completely sure O'Leary is being serious. But then again, if he knows O'Leary, he is.

O'Leary says, "I'm sorry about your friend."

Nico doesn't understand. "What friend?"

"Oh shit, I forgot you've been in a hole. Your friend, the one who helped us with that thing, someone offed him."

Nico feels a ripple of something vibrate through him. "You

mean Ben Wood?" The kite takes a plunge and O'Leary grabs the strings from him.

"They caught the guy, one of the mopes he locked up. I think the news said the funeral's tomorrow. Gonna be a big production. That's why I thought you were in town."

Nico doesn't say anything, quickly flicks away a tear on his cheek, still watching the tail of the kite dance in the sky.

CHAPTER THIRTY-TWO

DONNIE

"Can we meet for dinner tonight?" Reeves asks. "I hear Jean-Georges is amazing." They're standing in the check-in line at the Four Seasons in Center City, Philadelphia, at the front desk on the sixtieth floor.

"For sure, Hemingway. I gotta go see Ben's wife and my goddaughter. Then I'm all yours."

Reeves nods. "I just read a story about Ben." He holds up his phone. "He was quite a lawyer before becoming a district court judge. He was on the short list for the federal appellate court."

"That was Benny. When we were kids, he was always the smart one. And in Chestertown it wasn't exactly cool to be the smart kid at school. But Benny also was six foot tall by the time he was fourteen, so nobody messed with him."

"The news says he was top of his class at Harvard Law, unanimously confirmed to the federal bench, which is pretty rare."

"When we were kids, he watched the O. J. Simpson trial and that was it. It was like when Mr. J gave me my first guitar. We both knew." Donnie smiles. "Benny would go around rhyming everything like Johnny Cochran—*if the glove doesn't fit, you must acquit. . . . If you want some food, don't shade Mr. Brood.*" Donnie shakes his head and smiles.

"One of the stories I read said he was adopted by a cop who arrested him?"

Donnie nods. "When we ran off to Philly, we didn't have any money and Benny went into the ShopRite and stole a loaf of bread and some peanut butter. The cop who arrested him was an amazing lady. Her kids were grown, so she let us crash at her house. After I joined the band, we hit the road, but Benny stayed behind. She ended up adopting him."

"That's incredible."

Donnie gives a sentimental smile. "That was Benny. To meet him was to fall in love with him."

"Why'd you guys leave the foster home?"

The hotel clerk calls Donnie up to the counter, sparing him from holding back the true answer: After Mr. Brood went missing, they knew Savior House would be closed down and the foster kids placed in new homes, separated. Exactly what happened.

Donnie secures his room key and heads toward the elevator bank. He sees a father lifting his young son to sit on the railing that separates the lobby from a coffee shop inside the atrium. The boy balances on the metal railing and Donnie feels a wave of terror rip through him.

A memory surfaces: his feet dangling over the black water slapping the side of the cruise ship below.

"Everything okay?" Reeves asks, snapping Donnie out of it.

"Sure thing, partner," Donnie says, trying to steady his breathing. "Sure thing."

An hour later, he stands at the doorstep of the beautiful mansion in Chestnut Hill. The woman at the door looks similar to when they first met in Benny's dorm room in Cambridge—smooth dark skin with large eyes framed by full eyebrows and a mouth that curls upward even when she isn't happy. But she's even more beautiful, more elegant, now. Mia had not been equally impressed with Donnie back in the day. In her defense, he'd been erratic, cocaine speed-talking. Benny, then president of the *Harvard Law Review*, didn't seem to mind. And from that first day forward, to when she'd wagged her finger in his face about the bachelor party, to her headshake at his best man's speech at the wedding, to her grudging agreement that Donnie be godfather to Bell, Mia tolerated, rather than liked, Donnie. Today, she stands at the door, lips pinched tight, eyes red and puffy.

"Can I, ah, come in?" Donnie asks.

Their home is as he remembered. Classic. Expensive. They were the *it* couple on the Northwest Philly cocktail party scene—the prominent lawyer and daughter of a wealthy business leader, the dashing federal judge. There'd been stories about Mia and Ben in the papers, Ben told him. Philadelphia's elite ate up the aristocrat marrying the poor kid from Chestertown. Ben didn't care about such things. He shrugged off the casual racism he encountered at the county club or in the courthouse when he wasn't wearing the robe and wasn't recognized as His Honor.

Mia reluctantly lets Donnie inside. In the living room, the television is on a news channel.

Mia says, "I'd offer you a drink, but you're not staying. I want you out of here before Bell is back with the nanny from the park."

"Mia, I don't understand. Why are you—"

"Save it, Donnie."

"You're clearly upset, but talk to me. What did I do, why are you—"

"This is your fault."

"Whoa, whoa." He holds up his hands. "What in tarnation are you talking about? I loved Benny. I love Bell. I don't know what you're talking about."

She falls onto the sofa, tears spilling from her eyes. There's a cocktail glass nearby and he realizes she's had a few.

He lowers slowly to the chair opposite.

She takes a pull of her drink, sniffles.

"Mia, darlin', I don't understand."

Finally: "He told me."

"Told you what? What are you talking about?" Donnie hates this, pretending, but he's not ready to come clean.

"That you did something horrible when you were kids."

Donnie shakes his head, continues to plays dumb, but an icy chill crawls up his back.

He needs to shake it off. Fall back into Rock Star Donnie. "I'm afraid I'm lost here. I honestly don't understand."

"Someone was blackmailing him—did you know that?"

Now Donnie's genuinely confused. "Blackmail? What on earth would anyone have to blackmail Ben about? He was the straightest arrow I've ever—"

"Don't." She cuts him off, the word laced with poison.

Donnie tilts his chin up, scratches the whiskers on his neck. "Uh . . . I need you to back up. Who was blackmailing Benny? Why would—"

"I don't know *who*," she says. "He told me some bad people knew something about him. About when you were kids. Something you all did."

Donnie's mind jumps to a dark rainy night, the patch of misery surrounded by woodland. "What did they want? Money?"

"If it was just about money, it wouldn't have eaten him up so much," she says.

Donnie flashes back to their last phone call. Ben didn't seem like himself. Said work was stressful. But he didn't say anything else. Or did Donnie simply miss it? Perhaps Ben hadn't trusted his on-again, off-again sober friend with a secret. His heart sinks at the thought of Ben needing to talk but not wanting to risk telling something important to a fuckup like Donnie.

Mia continues, "We gave them money, but what they really wanted was for him to fix a case."

Donnie understands now. Some criminal got dirt on a prominent judge. A get-out-of-jail-free card.

"Do you think that's why he was in Chestertown, why he was—"

"You tell me." She stares at him with something worse than hate in her eyes.

"Did you tell the police?" Donnie asks.

She scoffs. "And let that be how he's remembered?"

The nanny appears at the door and Mia snaps to attention. "You need to go. Out the back. I don't want Bell seeing you."

"Mia, please, I just want to see her and—"

"Go now, and I never want to see you again."

"Please, I—"

"Go!"

Instead of pleading any more, he slips out the back, heartbroken and bewildered.

CHAPTER THIRTY-THREE

NICO

Nico stands outside the elementary school as kids stream out of the building, a sea of shrieks and backpacks. A group of parents look on from the outskirts. Nico doesn't appear to be drawing any attention. A few looks from the moms, but no one here watches *The Miners*. Unless they're wondering about the sling, it's probably his handsome face. He's found that his square jaw and boy-next-door clean-cut attractiveness tend to elicit the benefit of the doubt. It's a strange thing how the sheer luck of genetics draws such advantages. A handsome stranger gets more curiosity than suspicion. Ask Ted Bundy.

As parents and kids reunite, Nico keeps his eyes on the brick schoolhouse. And he finally sees her. She's in a cotton dress, the sun breaking through a crack in the clouds for the first time the entire day, bathing her in a yellow glow. She's directing a group of students to the bus lines in the lot. He smiles, remembering how she used to lament bus duty. She's a special person, Natalie. You have to be, to teach. Between the overbearing parents who all think their spawn are gifted, the administrators who've never spent a day in the classroom yet constantly change the curriculum, the politicians obsessed with what you *can't* teach, and having a master's degree but being micromanaged like teenage hourlies at McDonald's.

Natalie takes a little boy by the hand and guides him to the bus.

Step 9: *Make direct amends to persons we harmed wherever possible, except when to do so would injure them or others.*

But what can he possibly do? He stole from her, opened credit cards in her name, lied repeatedly. When she broke off the engagement, the first thing he did was pawn the ring and bet it all on an Eagles game. But his real offense, as she'd put it, was always having one foot out the door.

He contemplates leaving, but he remembers the fear he felt in the mine, thinking he might never see her again, thinking he'd never get to apologize. What if he never made it out? Now another crippling thought: *What if that woman with the bizarre weapon is set on finishing the job?*

He's had several texts with Roger about the mysterious woman. The one who possibly drugged Roger and sent Nico a text from his phone to meet at the mine. His description of her is classic Maverick: lots about her breasts and legs, little about her face. She and Roger met at the crew's favorite hangout, a bar called The Hole, so maybe someone caught the woman on social media. Nico makes a mental note to search his feeds later.

Natalie is walking across the blacktop back to the building, her hair dancing in a breeze that has come out of nowhere to make her even more beautiful in this moment.

If he's going to approach, he needs to do it now.

The area clears as fast as it became crowded.

Nico walks toward her. When she's almost to the door he calls out.

"Natalie."

His voice sounds weak in the wind. He tries again, louder now. *"Nat."*

She turns, squints like she's looking for who called her name. He remembers she's not keen on parents calling her by her first name, lest their kids pick up the habit.

Then her eyes lock on him. She stands there. Not smiling but not turning away either.

He reaches her. She's even more beautiful. The freckles across her cheeks. The dimple on her left cheek.

She looks around, as if concerned that others might be watching.

"Nico. What are you—"

"I'm in town for business."

"Business," she echoes the word, skeptically.

He nods.

"They sent you on a business trip less than a day after rescuing you from a coal mine?" She eyes the sling.

So she has seen the news. And his heart sinks again—she never checked in on him. But what did he expect?

Get over yourself.

"I thought we might talk," he says.

She studies him. "I'm not sure there's anything to say."

"Look, I know this is weird, but I nearly died and—"

"And what?" she cuts in. "Now you want to talk? Make it up to me? Let's save each other the time. I'm over it. I forgive you or whatever it is you need to hear."

Her features are hard now. Tears threaten to fill her eyes.

"Nat, please. Just give me a—"

"What? Give you a chance? That ought to be the tag line for your stupid TV show. For your life."

"Did you get the money I sent?"

"I got it. Not before my credit score hit four hundred. Not before all the stress and sleepless nights worrying I'd be evicted from the apartment."

He wants to say *sorry* but says nothing.

"I'm in a good place now, Nico. I'm glad you're okay and survived, but I can't do this again."

"If we could just talk, let me—"

She cuts him off with a shake of the head.

"I've changed," he says.

She guffaws at that, collects herself. "You've changed, have you?" She glowers at him. "The FBI was just here asking about you. But you've changed?" She turns, opens the door to the school. Before she disappears inside, she turns back to him. "Goodbye, Nico. Don't ever come here again."

CHAPTER THIRTY-FOUR

JENNA

An evening breeze at her back, Jenna slinks through the majestic doors of Sabine's elegant home in Kalorama, the security detail not giving her a second look in the outrageously expensive silk gown. The party is filled with portly men in black tie looking decidedly unlike James Bond and their more attractive spouses.

A server carrying a silver tray offers Jenna a filet mignon bite. That's when she realizes she hasn't eaten in more than twenty-four hours. She takes the toothpick and tiny napkin and forces herself not to devour it like Cookie Monster. Her mind trips to Lulu, a stab of despair cutting into her, but she fights it. She needs to focus.

The sound of a cello fills the room. In the back corner, a woman moves the bow skillfully, eyes closed, lost in the music.

Jenna looks around the room. It's definitely an ambassador's party. Even in the tuxes, the men wear those obnoxious flag pins on their lapels, like all the politicos in D.C. No fashion-forward pretty boys here. Jenna plucks a champagne flute from another server and takes a sip. A small one. Her stomach is nearly empty and she needs to be sharp.

She maneuvers through the crowd, her dress flowing as she walks. Then she hears it. The familiar laugh. The French accent with its hints of Russian.

Sabine is leaning into a tall man, likely saying something cheeky. He bellows a laugh.

Jenna watches for a long moment. More partygoers approach Sabine and exchange air kisses. It will be like this all night, Jenna knows. Sabine is a magnet. And she has aged like an expensive whiskey.

Jenna takes a deep breath and sets the glass on a tray as she joins the half circle of people surrounding Sabine. She hits Sabine with a piercing stare, and Sabine doesn't miss a beat.

"Genevieve," she says warmly, "I'm so glad you made it, *mon chéri.*" More cheek air kisses.

Jenna gives a thousand-watt smile, then says to the group, "Would you all mind if I borrow Sabine?"

The others assent and Sabine gives a tight smile of her own, the first break in the façade. But she recovers quickly. "Yes, darling," she says, "I *must* show you the piece I told you about. It's in the master suite." She excuses herself and leads Jenna through the crowd and past a burly man guarding the foot of a grand staircase.

Sabine glides up the stairs. Not a care in the world.

They pass through two imposing doors and into a master suite that seems to have come out of an interior-design magazine. Sabine shuts the doors, and when she turns around her eyes flash at the sight of Jenna's handgun.

Sabine lets out a sound of amusement from her throat.

"Why?" Jenna asks.

"You're going to have to give me more than that, love." She's giving Jenna a lazy glance—a look Jenna remembers too well from her teen years.

"You said I was out. Clean. But someone tried to—"

Sabine makes a *tsk, tsk, tsk* noise and shakes her head. "I'm disappointed in you."

Jenna shakes her head, annoyed.

"Do you think you'd be standing here if *I* sent someone for you?"

It's a fair point. One that's been gnawing at Jenna since the hitter made the first mistake with the glare of the rifle scope. Then the woman with the weird weapon. The mode of execution is too flashy for Sabine's taste. Too unreliable for The Corporation.

"Let me guess," Sabine says. "You were part of that mess downtown yesterday with Artemis Templeton."

If she's lying, she's damned good. But the problem is, she is.

"I'm no fan of that bald savant, but I had no reason to kill him," Sabine says. "Put the gun down, darling."

Jenna doesn't acquiesce.

"And, honestly, I taught you better than this. The safety is on."

Jenna doesn't fall for it. Her eyes remain set on Sabine. One look away could be the last thing she ever does.

"Nice try."

Sabine smiles.

"I've been doing this since you took me when I was fifteen," Jenna says, showing she was offended at the cheap effort to distract her.

"I'm aware. And I also noticed you're in that lovely gown instead of working at the Walmart in Chestertown."

"If not you, then who?" This time Jenna does lower the gun. The truth is that if Sabine wanted her dead, she'd be dead. And, now, one yelp from Sabine will cause men with big guns to charge through those doors. "They knew about my background, about

The Corporation, tricked me into thinking you all ordered me to take him down."

"I have no idea. I've been out of the game myself. But there's no way our friends would go after Templeton. I may be out, but I'd know about that." Sabine walks toward a mirror on the wall. She wipes a finger at her eye makeup.

"It was a young woman," Jenna says. "Pretty. She uses a strange weapon. She threatened my family. Then came after me. I need to find her."

Sabine spins around. "No idea, dear. You know the contractors are always changing. I don't keep up anymore."

"She's not a girl you stole from some godforsaken group home like Savior House?"

Sabine lets out an exasperated sigh. "She's not one of ours. Really, darling, you're not a teenager anymore, so stop acting like it."

Jenna presses her lips together. Sabine still knows how to push her buttons.

"She's not one of ours," Sabine repeats. "And, for the record, you're the only one we ever trained from Savior House. I only recruited the extraordinary, the special."

Flattery, typical Sabine mind games. And probably a lie. Annie, Marta, and the others didn't disappear into thin air. "I need you to find out who the hitter is," Jenna says. "She threatened my family."

"I told you, I'm out, and I don't keep up with the competition." She offers a rueful smile like she has a secret. "*I* don't keep up, but my successor surely knows the current market."

"And who's that?"

The smile returns. "Oh, darling, you haven't kept up at all, have you?"

Jenna shakes her head. Why would she? All she has wanted is to forget.

"You know him well." Her eyes flash.

"No. . . ."

The smile widens on Sabine's lips. "Tell you what. For old times' sake, you can find him at Eighteen Highland Farm in Potomac. But don't you dare tell him you heard it from me."

Jenna believes her. Sabine's taking too much pleasure in all this to not be telling the truth.

"Lovely seeing you."

Jenna turns to leave.

"And, *mon chéri*," Sabine says.

Jenna looks back.

"Do be careful. He still has the dogs."

CHAPTER THIRTY-FIVE

DONNIE

Donnie leans over his whiskey at the Four Seasons' bar, his mind reeling from his visit with Mia. Someone had been blackmailing Benny? And Benny hadn't trusted Donnie enough to tell him about it? Mia's angry face comes to him: *Something you all did.*

He's torn from his thoughts by someone calling his name.

He turns and sees Reeves. Donnie's not in the mood for story time. On the other hand, he doesn't want to think about Mia or Benny or any of it.

"How'd it go?" Reeves asks.

Reeves is a perceptive guy, an occupational hazard, Donnie supposes, and must've sensed the visit to Mia might not go well. Donnie shrugs, takes a drink from the highball glass.

"I'm sorry," the writer says. "I know it must be hard."

"It's all right. Mia never liked me. And she's pretty devastated."

Reeves takes the stool next to him. The bartender hovers over and asks him if he wants a drink, but Reeves declines. "We can take the night off on the book if you'd like," he says.

Donnie should agree. He should go up to his room, have a big cry, and get some sleep. But instead, he decides he needs Rock Star Donnie tonight.

"It's okay, Hemingway, we've got work to do." He stands, signals to the bartender to charge the drinks to his room, and presses out of the place.

"Where are we going?" Reeves asks, trailing behind.

As the bellhop holds open a cab door, Donnie says, "To where it all began for Tracer's Bullet."

Inside the cab, Reeves looks like he still hasn't recovered from the night before. They make their way through downtown Philadelphia traffic to Chinatown. The cabbie pulls in front of a worn opera-house-looking building. Above the arched entrance is a red neon sign that reads: THE NEW TROCADERO. There are posters plastered on the doors with the name of a band Donnie has never heard of.

The club used to be called The Trocadero but has since changed hands. It seems like the only thing updated since the '90s is adding the word "New" to the name. At the ticket counter, a woman with racoon makeup pushes his cash back through the slot. "No cash, cards only."

"No cash? Times have changed," Donnie says. "When I used to play here Phil *only* took cash, helped with the taxman." He winks at the woman.

She doesn't take the bait and ask when he played there or seem to have any idea who he is.

They take a seat at the bar. Donnie revels in the familiar pound reverberating in his chest from the bass drum, the distortion pedal on the guitar tingling his fingers and toes.

Reeves asks him a question, but it's impossible to have a conversation amid one hundred decibels. "Let's talk at a break in their set," Donnie says, cupping his hand near Reeves's ear.

They have a couple beers, look around. It's a small crowd for a Friday night. A smattering of people at tables. The band is doing originals, which never goes over well when you're starting out.

Donnie drinks some more, then heads to the bathroom. He smiles when he sees that the urinals still have giant photos hanging over them of women laughing hysterically as they point down.

Back at the bar, they watch the band some more. Donnie should've brought his earplugs, since the doctor has warned him he can't afford much more damage to his hearing. But no way he was showing up to The Troc like some old man.

"Finally," Reeves says when the band takes five.

Donnie smiles. "This used to be my life at the beginning. Going club to club, often with only a few people in the crowd. This was where we played our first show."

Reeves nods. He's not taking notes, but he's always on the clock, Donnie realizes. This is only backstory, a feel for his subject's life.

The bartender comes over, asks if they want another round. Donnie nods, says, "Hey, you see that picture?"

The bartender turns, looks at a black-and-white on the back wall.

"That's me back when Phil owned the place."

With zero enthusiasm, the bartender says, "Cool."

It's gonna be one of those nights when Donnie's reminded of a truism in life: No one cares.

"How old were you when you played here?" Reeves asks.

Donnie doesn't need to think on it. It was a few months after leaving Savior House. "Fourteen."

"No one cared you were underage?"

"Back then? Shoot, they didn't care about anything."

"You were on your own? I mean, you'd left Savior House by then."

How the hell does Reeves know the name of the group home? The guy definitely does his research.

"Yep. We crashed in the van or with girls we met on the road or sometimes the house bands would put us up."

"Why'd you take the leap and leave the group home?"

Donnie shrugs. "It was time," he replies, vaguely. "Funny story: When you open for other bands, the drummers often share their kits to avoid having to set up and sound check and all that, since drums are tricky." He takes a drink, grins. "So the second time we played here, our drummer left his kit in the van and when we came out after the show, the windows were smashed and it was gone. But there was this guy sitting on the curb and we asked if he saw who took 'em. He said he thought so, and might be able to get them back for us."

Reeves seems uninterested, but Donnie keeps going.

"So the guy leaves and when he comes back about ten minutes later he says for two hundred bucks he can get the drums back. We'd only made ninety bucks for the show for all of us, but we had no choice and gave him all our cash."

"Did you get the drums back?"

"Oh yeah, he gave us an address and we found them in a boarded-up row house down the block. But that's the funny thing: When we told the house band what happened, the dudes all laughed and said the guy who'd got our drums back was in on the whole thing. He and his crew did this like twice a week to out-of-town bands." Donnie bellows a laugh. "The guy made his living selling drummers back their own equipment."

Next, he tells Reeves about Tom climbing the speakers to the balcony and leaping off into the outstretched arms of the audience.

About drinking with the boys from Cinderella at this very bar. About the bouncers of the club wearing shirts that said TROC CREW/ FUCK YOU and the regulars responding with FUCK YOU, TROC CREW shirts of their own.

The hum of an amp through the PA signals that the band's about to go back on. Reeves seems to be bracing himself.

That's when Donnie sees him. Sitting at one of the tables. He catches Donnie's eye and gives him a nod.

The FBI agent from the hospital. The one asking about Donnie's fall from the ship. The one investigating Ben's murder. Agent Rodrigo. Or was it Rodriguez?

What in the hell is he doing here? Is he following Donnie? And why would he be doing that?

A woman appears; she's holding a pen and a napkin. "Can I you sign this for me?"

Rock Star Donnie instinctively says, "I'll do anything you want, darlin'." The sound of those words, the familiarity of it all, makes Donnie's hand shake, his heart palpitate.

"Donnie, are you okay?" Reeves says, a concerned look on his face.

"I need to go," Donnie says. He thinks he's going to be sick. Not from the booze. But from the terror.

CHAPTER THIRTY-SIX

JENNA

Jenna pulls into a McDonald's parking lot. She gets some looks at her gown heading into the place. But soon she's out of the bathroom and into the black athletic gear. She carries the Elie Saab gown in the garment bag and her stomach growls again; it's the smell of the grease. She decides a cheeseburger and hot fudge sundae are in order. She smiles, thinking about Simon. On many a family road trip, Jenna lamented about how McDonald's ice-cream machines are always broken. Ever the analytical mind, Simon researched it. It turns out it wasn't Jenna's imagination. Simon explained that the machines require a complicated four-hour cleaning regimen daily and often employees don't have the time. Also, the machines require specialized training to repair them, so getting someone in to fix them takes time. A heavy sadness overcomes her, but she beats it back.

She orders her food. Of course the machine isn't working tonight.

She takes the white bag and sits in the car and inhales the

burger. She can already feel the grease saturating her pores. But damn, it's good.

She starts the car and heads down Wisconsin Avenue. She stops when she sees a Salvation Army store. It has a metal receptacle for donations out front. She pulls over and shoves the gown and shoes inside. Maybe someone shopping will find a gem. Or at least something they can sell online.

A half hour later, she makes it to Cabin John Parkway, then to River Road, and finally to Highland Farm Road and its horse fences and old-growth trees.

She passes the estate and sees that it's lit up. Someone in the security hut peers at the car.

No one travels this road unless they're visiting the estate. There's a gate and a stretch of lawn. Then another tall iron fence. The first lawn serves as a security moat for extra protection. Most intruders wouldn't make it to the second fence alive.

She takes a left and travels about a mile and pulls the car onto a side road surrounded by woodland. She kills the lights. In the dark, her mind flashes to an image of Willow's terrified face on the dirt road. Could that have been only last night?

Jenna gets out. Stretches. She tucks the gun in the waist of her leggings. It's uncomfortable, but there's nothing to be done about it.

Then she starts her jog.

The night is moonlit and air crisp. Like Chevy Chase where Jenna lives, Potomac, Maryland, isn't far from downtown D.C., but it feels like it is. Fresh air, large compounds, a sheltered life for the kids.

She's exhausted and the running doesn't revive her like usual. No amount of endorphins can regenerate her after all that's happened.

She reaches the road leading to the estate. At the edge of the iron fencing, she finds the darkest spot and scales the barrier. Years of gymnastics before her parents died, supplemented by field training from Sabine, still come in handy. But this is the decorative security. She needs to survive the moat, then get over the second fence.

Stalking low to avoid the obvious spots for motion lights or alarms, she makes it across the well-manicured lawn and to the next barrier fence. She looks up at the razor wire—this one won't be so easy to scale. She spots the guard station and the outline of two figures on the roof of the estate. That's when she hears the growl behind her.

She turns slowly. Two Dobermans stand erect, baring teeth.

Jenna smiles. "Axl." The first dog tilts its head to the side. "Slash," she says to the other. "It's me, my babies."

The two dogs charge her. Now she's on the ground, the beasts licking her, their nubs for tails moving a thousand miles an hour. She helped raise them as puppies. There's another stab of anguish, thinking about her family's dog, Peanut Butter.

She snuggles the Dobermans, tries to quiet them when she hears the creak of the security fence coming to life, an SUV pulling into the compound.

If she can make it before the gate closes, she can slip in. But there's no chance she'd go unseen. The vehicle pulls to a stop on the half-circle driveway. Two beefy men get out of the SUV and open the back door. Out steps Michael. He's put on some weight but still looks svelte.

The front door to the estate opens. A woman stands in the doorway. Even from this distance, Jenna can see she's beautiful. But that's not a surprise. What takes Jenna aback is the two kids, three or four years old, standing in front of the woman in their pj's.

The kids barrel out the door. Michael crouches low on the front walk and scoops them up as they hit him running full speed. He twirls them around and around and they giggle and a fragment of Jenna's heart breaks. He'd always told Jenna that kids were off the table.

It's then she feels the violent tug of a black bag being forced over her head.

CHAPTER THIRTY-SEVEN

NICO

Nico lies on the hotel room bed, doom-scrolling through his social-media feed. Davis has already hosted a special edition of *The Black* about the "incident." His accompanying posts remind everyone that mining is one of the world's most dangerous jobs.

No shit.

Nico searches hashtags for Maverick to see if there are any photos of him with the mysterious woman who may have drugged him and used his phone to lure Nico to Mine B. Nico never got a good look at the woman. But Maverick said she was young, hot. *Who is she? And what in the hell was that weapon?* His shoulder still throbs. He hasn't taken the pain meds since this morning. He doesn't like how they make him feel. He gets his high from putting it all down on black or 100-to-1 odds.

His thoughts go to Natalie—the FBI asking her questions at her school. He's feeling a flight instinct. Should he go to Ben's funeral tomorrow? It's risky. But he owes it to Ben.

He leans back, puts his hands under his pillow. His thoughts drift to Ben and one of the nights that changed all their lives. . . .

* * *

"Have you seen Annie?" Nico asks Jenna. She's washing dishes finishing her chores, which are on the schedule Mr. Brood tacks up on a bulletin board every Friday to ruin their weekends.

Jenna shakes her head, suds crawling up her arms from dinner duty for the younger kids.

Nico thought he'd blown it with Annie after the park incident. Watching a guy get a beatdown isn't exactly catnip for the ladies. But afterward she told Nico that he'd been brave, kissed him on the cheek. And she's wearing the necklace he'd bought for her from the street vendor. He hopes it won't turn her neck green.

Today, at lunch, he won twenty bucks playing dice behind the portable classrooms in the back of the school, so in science class he passed Annie a note and asked if she wanted to go to the movies—his treat. He waited eagerly as she read the note, tucked a strand of hair behind an ear, and glanced back at him. The note made its way down the assembly line of kids and when he opened it his heart tripped: "Only if it's a date."

So he picked wildflowers in the abandoned lot, washed his best jeans and T-shirt, showered, even though it wasn't his assigned day, and waited for her to come downstairs. When she never did, he checked her room, the bathroom, the kitchen. He's feeling anxious. Marta never came back. But he just saw Annie at school. And Ned Flanders told Arty that the foster care people said they'd found Marta, placed her in a new home. But maybe the foster care people are lying, covering for Mr. Brood because his brother runs this town. Nico needs to shake it off, he's being paranoid. He needs to get it together.

He pushes open the door to Donnie's room and finds him jamming like a madman on his guitar, his eyes closed, headphones over his ears since Mr. Brood has forbidden him playing through the amp, a rule Donnie breaches whenever possible. Donnie's eyes pop open. He stops strumming and yanks off the headset with a smile.

"Look at you, Handsome." Donnie loves nicknames. Eyeing the flowers, he says, "Holy crap, you clean up nice. You finally got the nerve to ask, huh?"

Nico nods. "Have you seen her? The movie starts in twenty minutes." It takes fifteen to walk there.

"She got a call and hurried out. I thought she was goin' to see you," Donnie says. "Hey, I got something for you." He stands, the guitar dangling by its strap as he trudges over to his footlocker. He opens it and starts digging around. "Benny got this for me when I went out with Amber that time." It's a small bottle of cologne, likely swiped from Rite Aid. Donnie approaches, opens his eyes wide, like he's asking for permission.

Nico half smiles, nods, and feels a spritz of CK One settle around him.

"She's probably out front." Donnie smiles, waggling his brows. "Don't do anything I would do. . . ."

On the porch, Nico finds Ben and Arty huddled, talking in whispers. Ben wears a devastated expression when he gets a look at Nico holding the flowers.

"Hey, have you seen Annie?" asks Nico.

Ben and Arty lock eyes, then turn their gazes to Nico.

"What?" Nico asks.

"I'm sorry, man," Arty says, putting a hand on his shoulder.

"Sorry about what?"

Then Ben says it: "It's happened again."

Nico remembers the tears rolling down his cheeks.

"She's gone."

CHAPTER THIRTY-EIGHT

JENNA

Jenna is tied to a chair, a black bag over her head.

As expected.

She listens closely. The men speak in whispers, but she can tell that someone new is in the room. Based on the short distance they dragged her, the chirp of crickets, the smell of oil, she thinks it's a shed or garage. The voice says, "Okay, let's get a look at her."

The hood is yanked off.

Yep, she's in a garage. A huge space that houses a fleet of vintage cars and several motorcycles. The chair she's strapped to is on top of a large sheet of plastic, never a good sign. An aluminum table—it looks like something you'd see in an operating room—stands nearby with what appear to be instruments of torture neatly aligned upon it.

It's then that she sees the man's cocksure smile. The same smile as when they first met nearly a decade ago. They'd been assigned to play an American couple on vacation in Berlin—to bring about the demise of a banker with a long history of working with individuals on terrorist blacklists. All their kissing and canoodling went from acting to authentic somewhere along the way. They spent five years pretending it could work between them. She'd wanted to take it to the next level—wanted a normal life, to get out of The Corporation. Get married, have kids. That wasn't who he is, he'd told her. Yet here he is with a wife and two kids.

He walks up to her, crouches to eye level, his lips near hers. "You coming to kill me?"

She stares at him a long moment. "Are you dead?"

He smiles. Steps back. "I miss that confidence. And I know you're not here for me."

"Why's that?"

"Because I've been expecting you."

"Sabine called you?"

He releases a small laugh. Shakes his head. "No. How is the old bird?"

Jenna doesn't answer.

He lets out a sigh. "It's pretty obvious why you're here. You'll remember, I'm one of the few people who's read your file. I know where you're from. Know about your foster family . . ."

She shakes her head like she hasn't the foggiest. She doesn't.

Michael scrutinizes her for a minute. "You really don't know, do you?"

"Know what?"

Michael looks at the two men standing at attention near the doors.

"Give us the room."

The men disappear.

Jenna jostles her arms, gives an annoyed look at the zip ties securing her wrists. Michael's men restrained her either as a matter of protocol or because they didn't know who she is. Michael picks up a scalpel from the aluminum table and approaches. He slips the razor-sharp blade under the zip tie, popping it off. He turns the scal-pel, holding the blade now, offering her the haft. She takes it, cuts off the tie on her other wrist, then the ones on her ankles.

He knows what she can do with a blade. If he wanted her dead, he would've never given it to her, confirming again that it's not The Corporation out to kill her.

"I take it you haven't caught the news lately?" he says.

"I've been a little preoccupied—running for my life. Protect-ing my family."

He nods. "Yes, and what a lovely little family you've adopted."

"Can you quit with the games. What's going on?"

Michael smiles again, as if admiring her cutting through the shit. Like she used to. "Cable news has been on a tear about a certain federal judge who was murdered; a rock star who fell off a cruise ship; a TV producer in a blown-up mine; and the pièce de résistance, an assassination attempt on Artemis Templeton."

She processes this. Ben became a federal judge, Donnie a rock star. She'd even seen Nico on an advertisement for some cable TV show. It can all mean only one thing: Someone is targeting the kids from Savior House. The same someone who extorted her into taking a shot at Artemis.

"Who?"

Michael shrugs.

Jenna stands, rubs her wrists, which are still indented from the zip ties. "Come on, Michael. You know all the contractors. All the jobs."

"As Sabine would say," Michael says in a mocking French ac-cent, "I'm sorry, *mon chéri*, no clue."

Her mind is spinning. Running through the whos and whys.

"The contractor is a woman," Jenna says. "In her twenties, pretty. Cheekbones. She uses a strange weapon." Jenna describes what happened. Being coerced to target Artemis, not taking the kill shot. The woman coming after her at Willow's school. Killing the hipsters. Tracking her and Willow on the way to the cabin.

"I can ask around. I don't know any professionals who'd be foolhardy enough to target Artemis Templeton, one of the richest men in the world. Much less be dumb enough to go after you."

She walks up to him now. Looks him in the eyes. She's going to say something about his family but decides against it. She realizes she doesn't care. She has her own family.

"The Corporation isn't after me." It's a statement, not a question.

"Nope."

She believes him. He could be lying. But he wouldn't have freed her. Sabine wouldn't have let her leave that party alive. Most important, The Corporation doesn't screw up. And this hitter not only let Jenna and Artemis escape but also botched two other jobs.

"You can stay in the guesthouse tonight if you'd like." He looks at her like he thinks she needs a good night's sleep. "You'll be safe here."

She nods. "I need new papers in case mine are compromised."

"And a better gun," he says, dismissing her compact Remington on the aluminum table.

"That too."

He nods.

"Thank you, Michael."

"The pleasure is all mine."

"I'm glad it's not you," Jenna says. This time it's she who offers the sideways grin. "I would've hated having to kill you."

CHAPTER THIRTY-NINE

THE TWINS

Casey sits at the bar at the Philadelphia Airport Embassy Suites. The man wears a wedding ring, but the fact that he's lingering at the bar speaks volumes. The bartender is a heavyset woman with seen-it-all eyes.

The guy wears a suit with no tie, like he ripped it off after a long day. Probably has an early flight tomorrow. Why else stay at this dump?

The bar is full. There's a group of four at the far side, people of varying ages, but they don't look like a family. The lone woman in the group stares at her phone. The guys are talking about sports. A business trip, forced friendships on the road.

The man keeps stealing looks at her. She decides to take the first step. She smiles back. It's that simple.

She wants a gin on the rocks but orders another tonic water. She reaches into her handbag for the captive bolt and feels a sense of calm at the cool metal cylinder in her grip.

Soon enough, the guy is walking over. Asks if he can take the seat next to hers. He hasn't bothered to remove the wedding ring. Just as well.

Twenty minutes later, she laughs at something stupid he says again. She says she's from the Midwest, traffic here is terrible. Did he drive? He confirms that he has what she needs. A rental car. Complains about the return desk being closed when he arrived tonight.

She downs her tonic water like it's vodka, feigns the sloppy demeanor of one too many, and puts her mouth to his ear: "Your room?"

He pays the tab quickly. She tells him to meet her outside the restroom that's off the lobby.

They walk out together and she goes into the restroom. Haley comes out of a stall. She's wearing an outfit identical to Casey's. "About time."

"Meet me in the parking lot in fifteen," Casey says. "Make sure everyone sees you at the bar."

Casey takes the long jacket from her sister, puts it on. She then puts on the baseball cap. The guy has enough drinks in him that he won't even notice. Casey leaves the restroom, puts her head down in case there are cameras, but she thinks they're only in the main areas, and links her arm around the man's as they head to his room.

Haley will go make an appearance at the bar so the cameras there—she saw two—capture her returning without the guy. Any police reviewing the footage will think she returned to the bar and the guy left on his own. In a few days, they'll find the stolen Camaro in the lot but won't connect it to this dipshit.

She doesn't need to kill him; she can slip something in his drink—like she did to that coal mine dude in West Virginia. Then she'll take his rental car.

But maybe she'll have a little fun first. Tie him up, scare him a little.

If he calls the police, the only thing he'll likely remember will be the thing she often asks to elicit fear: "Did you know that studies show there are six distinct types of screams?"

CHAPTER FORTY

JENNA

It's a gloomy morning. Jenna weaves the motorcycle through Beltway traffic, racing along the shoulder when vehicles come to a standstill.

Michael lent her the BMW M 1000 RR, and it takes all her restraint not to twist its throttle to the limit. But it's been years since she jetted on two wheels, and she's rusty. The last time was to evade the police on the lawless highways of Quezon City in the Philippines. Also, she's a mom now, and she's more mindful of safety.

All night, her thoughts were on her friends from Savior House. Ben, Donnie, Nico.

Marta. Annie.

In that moment, she's balancing on the handlebars as Nico pedals the BMX bike on the bumpy sidewalk until they skid to a stop in front of the Chestertown Police station.

Ben pulls up next to them on another bike, Donnie holding

on to Ben's shoulder as he stands precariously on the bolts that stick out from the back axle. They've decided they need to do something, make some noise about the missing girls, lest they too disappear one by one from Savior House. They're all angry, and Nico's devastated over Annie's disappearance.

The officer working the front desk seems skeptical and Nico loses his cool. Says if his missing friends worked at a donut shop the cops would find them. Ben smooths things over, and a half hour later the four are taken to an interview room.

The policewoman who takes the report is nice enough. She seems troubled, steps out to speak with someone. When she returns, she's with a man. He doesn't wear a uniform and must be a detective or something.

"Hi, kids. Thanks for coming in. I want you to know that I'm personally going to be looking into this. It was brave of you to come forward."

Jenna feels a weight lifted from her. Someone is going to do something. Maybe they're wrong and Marta and Annie and the others are safe and sound. At new foster homes or they found relatives to take them in.

"How about I give you a ride home?" the detective asks.

"We have our bikes," Ben says.

"No problem, they'll fit in the car."

Ten minutes later, the four are jammed into the back of the Crown Vic, a metal grill separating them from the front seat. The detective says, "Sorry to put you in the back like criminals. But this will remind you to keep out of trouble." He turns his head, offers a smile.

"No doubt," Donnie says, seeming to enjoy the experience.

Ben and Nico exchange a glance, appear concerned about something.

Jenna doesn't understand why until the car pulls through an underpass that borders a sludge-filled area near the Delaware River.

"Um, Detective," Ben says as the area turns darker, shaded from the underpass, "this isn't the way to Savior House. I think you might have the wrong address."

The detective doesn't say anything in response. Jenna doesn't understand what's happening, but her heart accelerates when she sees the fear in Ben's face. Donnie's brow is creased as if he's baffled. Nico is fiddling with a coin, his face drained of color.

The detective gets out of the car. He opens the trunk. The four twist around, and through the gap Jenna can see he's removing the bikes. Carrying a bike in each hand, he marches to the riverbank. He then does something that takes Jenna's breath away. He throws the bikes into the water.

Donnie says, "What in the hell is he—"

His words are choked off as the detective charges back to them. He has his blazer jacket pushed back so his holster is on display, his hand resting on the top of the pistol's butt.

He opens the back door. "Get out."

His voice isn't nice anymore. Like he's a different person.

Donnie climbs out first, Jenna sliding over after him. Ben and Nico don't emerge immediately.

"Don't make me ask again," the detective says.

Ben finally steps his long legs out of the vehicle and stands, Nico right behind him.

The detective still has his hand resting on his holster. "Walk," he says, looking toward the river.

They don't move.

"Walk, goddammit," he says.

Fear cloaks every part of Jenna. She and the boys walk slowly toward the river. She should run. They should all jet off in different directions—he can't get all of them. But it's an isolated area, grim and barren, and there's nowhere to run.

They reach the river's edge, near where the detective threw the bikes in the water.

"On your knees, all of you."

"Sir," Ben says, fear in his voice. "We don't know anything. We don't have a problem. . . . You don't have to . . ."

"Shut up."

They lower to their knees. Jenna's heart is in her throat. She has never experienced so much fear in her life.

"You wanna end up like your missing friends?" the detective says.

"No, sir," Ben says.

Jenna shakes her head, unable to speak.

A whimper comes from Donnie.

Nico's eyes are closed.

"You think anyone's gonna miss a junkie whore's kid? A kid whose father's in prison for killing his mom? A kid whose only relatives died in a car wreck? The kid of one of O'Leary's rejects?"

They don't respond, fear commandeering every part of them.

"Then you drop this. You understand?"

Jenna manages a nod. She thinks she hears Ben say something, another *Yes, sir*, maybe.

"Or the next time, it won't be only the bikes going in the water. Do you understand me?"

When there's silence, he yells, *"Do you understand me?"*

All four manage some form of affirmation.

Jenna hears the sound of steps on soft ground, then the sound of a car engine. Soon she feels Ben's arms around all of them.

* * *

Jenna is torn from the memory by the chime of the smartphone Michael gave her through the speakers in her motorcycle helmet. She reaches a gloved hand into the leather jacket—another gift from her ex—and manages to answer in time. He also gave her a messenger bag, which he called a "bag of goodies." She can only imagine what's inside.

"You in Philly yet?" Michael's voice says, sounding crystal clear in the helmet's expensive Bluetooth system. Michael always loved his toys.

"Still about an hour out."

"Huh. The way you drive, I thought you'd be there already."

She doesn't reply. She doesn't need any more nostalgic trips back to her days in The Corporation. Her days with him.

"My guys got some intel on your hitter," he says.

"Who is she?"

"No one knows much. She came out of nowhere. Basically put out a shingle on the dark web. Billed herself as a low-cost, lower-ethics provider."

"An amateur. That explains the screwups," Jenna says. Wet work is much more than pulling a trigger. It requires skill, professionalism, and experience. "Your contacts know how to find her?"

"No such luck. So your plan seems to be the best one: Let her find you."

Jenna thinks her foster brothers will attend Ben Wood's funeral in Philly. That's probably the best bait she can hope for if the hitter is still after them. She careens around a semi too fast. Glancing at the speedometer, she realizes she's going ninety. The thought of the woman who threatened her family causes her blood to run hot. She slows the bike.

"Thank you," she says.

"You can thank me by taking care of your problem without it taking care of you."

"Oh, don't you worry about me."

"Well, I will. Because here's the thing: My people all heard the same thing about this chick."

It's not like Michael to refer to women in such a way. Jenna listens.

"That she isn't doing jobs for the money or ideology or the usual reasons." He pauses. "She's doing it for the sport."

CHAPTER FORTY-ONE

DONNIE

A commotion at the front of Philadelphia's Old Pine Street Church that morning causes mourners to spin around in their pews and the reporters stationed by news vans in the makeshift media village outside to perk up.

Donnie feels the eyes of them all as he's being forcibly removed by two men in plainclothes identifying themselves as U.S. Marshals.

"Chill," one of them keeps saying to Donnie, who's jerking around, shouting, making a spectacle of himself.

"This is *not* how to respect your friend's memory," the other marshal says. They're holding his arms tight, but there's no menace in their faces. They're trying to de-escalate. Maybe it's because they know cameras are filming them, but he senses that they're decent dudes and don't want to arrest him.

He's already made a fool of himself, so he considers doubling down and fighting more. The hotel minibar had mostly whiskey, which always makes him aggressive for some weird reason. But he releases the tension in his arms, extinguishes any fight left in him. It's the sadness that ravages him—not being able to say his piece, his tribute, to the best friend he's ever had. Not being able to say goodbye to the kid who saved him over and over and over again. From the abuse. From himself.

He'll never forget Mia's face, twisted with anger, when she called the marshals over. Worse: Bell's confused expression, unsure why Uncle Donnie was acting this way.

The two marshals escort him through the massive doors and down the steps of the porticoed entrance. They release him on the brick sidewalk on Pine Street and make clear they're watching to make sure he doesn't do anything stupid.

Donnie retreats. He needs another drink. Needs something to stop this pain in his heart.

He walks down Pine and into the cemetery. It's an old one with headstones so ancient they're covered in moss, the inscriptions worn off.

When he and Benny were kids, they'd play kick the can at the old cemetery in Chestertown. They'd hide behind the tombs and in the overgrown weeds. The graveyard was nothing like this one with its well-maintained grounds. A good number of the Chestertown tombstones were kicked over or covered with graffiti. He remembers that Annie was superstitious and wouldn't play there. She'd do this funny thing where she'd hold her breath when they'd walk past the cemetery, as if a spirit might get inside her if she breathed in.

Why does everything remind him of that time in his life? Of Benny and the kids at Savior House?

It starts to rain, which is about right.

Donnie hears someone call his name. More with the "Mr. Danger" nonsense. The rain is matting his hair on his face, and he brushes it aside with his hand.

An unfamiliar young woman with a large black umbrella approaches. She's dressed in matching black with a strand of pearls laced around her delicate neck and seems to have followed him out of the church.

She looks him directly in the eyes, projecting what seems to be empathy. "I'm sorry about what happened at the service." She glances back to the scene of Donnie's latest humiliation. "The judge wouldn't have liked that." She pauses, explains, "I'm Zola. I was Judge Wood's law clerk."

Donnie stands there in the rain, not sure what there is to say.

"He talked about you a lot." The young woman gives a tentative smile.

This surprises Donnie for some reason, the thought of Benny talking about him to his law colleagues. Donnie's always assumed that he was a secret, an embarrassment to Benny.

The woman continues, "He told us how the first thing you did after your record became a hit was pay his college tuition."

Donnie feels a tear spill from his eye. Remembering Benny protesting about the money—he was so proud and wanted to make it on his own steam. Donnie insisted, saying, *Better the money goes to your education than up my nose.* He was only half kidding, but he thinks it's the reason Benny accepted the gift.

"He had your first album framed in chambers. A photo of you both when you were boys," Zola says.

This nearly levels him.

Now Zola's eyes well up. "He called me that day."

Donnie studies her. What day? he wonders. The day Ben was killed?

"He made me promise that if anything happened to him I'd tell you something. I told the FBI about it, but I don't know if they told you, so I wanted to . . ." Her voice trails off.

The hairs rise on Donnie's arms and the back of his neck. His eyes tell her to continue.

"He said to say you're the bravest person he's ever met. His brother . . ."

". . . from another mother," Donnie says, finishing the familiar sentence.

Zola offers a sad smile.

Donnie's chest shudders. Tears mix freely with the rain on his face.

"And he said—and I didn't understand this part—but he said you would."

Donnie's eyes lock on Zola's as the wind dimples her umbrella.

"He said to tell you that you all had it wrong. The proof is with Boo Radley."

CHAPTER FORTY-TWO

JENNA

From the street, behind the shield of her motorcycle helmet, Jenna watches the man at the cemetery. He was hard to miss, given the spectacle he created outside the church. Her heart aches, remembering the boy he was. So sweet. So fragile. She wasn't at Savior House for long, but long enough to succumb to Donnie's charm.

The rain's coming down in a mist, and she wipes the helmet's shield with her hand.

A woman holding an umbrella is speaking to him. He seems devastated. Even from this distance she can see it on his face. A similar expression she remembers from a rainy night twenty-five years ago on a patch of misery in Chestertown.

She watches as the two finish their conversation and head in different directions. The woman with the umbrella returns to the service; Donnie plods through the tombstones, lost in his head. In despair.

There's no sight of the killer—the young woman who should be in college and going to parties, cheering on the football team, cramming for finals, but has chosen a life of murder for hire.

Jenna glances over her shoulder. The town car is still at her six. The same car was lingering near the church earlier. *Is the female assassin inside?*

No, she doubts that. Even an amateur wouldn't be so obvious. The car is making its presence known. As if to signal that the occupant isn't intending any harm.

We'll see about that.

Grasping the handgun in her jacket pocket, she supposes it's time.

She climbs off the motorcycle. But she doesn't remove the helmet. Her eyes follow Donnie as he disappears down the street. He won't be hard to find later.

The town car doesn't follow Donnie. Yeah, it's definitely here for her.

Jenna crosses the street. The car turns on its lights.

She grips the gun, walking toward the car head on, which is now slowly heading her way. A game of chicken. She scans the area. The escape routes. The places to take cover if bullets fly. But her instincts tell her there's no threat.

The car edges closer.

She keeps walking.

Then the town car jerks to a stop; the driver gets out. He has the unmistakable bulge of a firearm holstered at his chest under his suit jacket. He walks slowly, deliberately, to the back door and opens it.

He gestures for her to get inside.

Jenna takes off her helmet. Shakes out her hair. The gun is still clutched tight in her right hand. She peers inside the vehicle.

"It's been a long time," is all the man says.

And with that she gets inside.

CHAPTER FORTY-THREE

NICO

Nico stuffs his clothes in his travel bag and proceeds to the hotel's counter to check out. He hates Philadelphia. Hates Pennsylvania. When he was a kid, he swore he'd leave and never come back. West Virginia isn't exactly paradise, but it's not here. He needs to get back to his life and the show before Davis steals his job. Before the FBI calls him in for questioning and his life really falls apart. He would've left last night if there'd been any flights out. He feels bad about missing Ben Wood's funeral, but it is what it is.

Out front to catch a cab, he's taken aback by the mob and the blinding light of camera flashes. The paparazzi shout questions at him.

"Nico, is it true the explosion was intentional?"
"Nico, how are you feeling?"
"Nico, are you afraid for your life?"
"Nico, are you worried a deranged fan is after you?"

He shields his eyes with his hand and his mind jumps back to Mine B. The bright light on his attacker's miner's helmet.

He says, "No comment," and pushes his way to the cab.

"Come on, Nico," a paparazzo says. "Give us something, don't be an asshole for once in your life."

Nico looks at him. "My dad didn't teach me much, but he said there's one great thing about everyone thinking you're an asshole."

The paparazzo waits for him to explain.

"You get to act like one. Now fuck off." He gets inside the car.

The cabbie blares his horn, moving slowly through the photographers crowding the street in front of the Ritz.

Nico puts in his earbuds, calls Shannon at the show.

"Hey, it's me," he says when the showrunner answers.

"Hey! I'm so glad you called. It's been *crazy* here." She sounds like she's walking. Shannon is always on the move, dealing with problems on the set. "The sheriff announced that the explosion was intentional and the press went bananas."

"Yeah, that's what I assumed, based on the mob outside my hotel. How in the hell did they find me in Philly?"

"No idea. It wasn't me."

Nico lets out a breath. "It'll calm down. The news cycle will turn to something else."

"I don't know about that," she says.

Nico shakes his head. No point in debating it. "I'm headed back. You should start thinking about some shows or special episodes about the mine collapse that we can milk for—"

"I don't know that the network is going to *let* you come back," she cuts in.

"What do you mean?" *That motherfucker Davis. Or maybe it's the show's insurer.*

If they think someone's trying to kill Nico, it's a liability issue for the network.

"I don't know. But they said you're on paid leave."

"Well, that's the first I've heard of it."

"I'll try to find out more, but that's all I know. And that the FBI served a warrant for the records on your company cell phone."

"For my phone?" Nico's heart rate accelerates.

"Yeah, and an agent interviewed me. Asked all kinds of weird questions. Something about some judge in Philly you knew when you were a kid. Also, they asked about Donnie Danger—you remember him, from Tracer's Bullet?"

Donnie. That's a name he hasn't heard in years. His mind ventures to the bank of the Delaware River, Ben hugging them all after the crooked detective terrorized them. "What about him?"

"You haven't seen the news? He fell off a cruise ship—was lost at sea—and somehow survived. The FBI agent asked if I knew about your friends from when you were a kid. You knew Donnie Danger?" She says this with humor in her voice.

She continues, "They asked about your vacation last month—where you went and what I knew about your childhood."

Nico's heart is in free fall. You don't have to watch many TV cop shows to know that if they have your phone records they know more about you than your parents, your spouse, or your closest friends. They know your search history, your photos, your social-media posts, your dating life, your diet, your music preferences. And they know with GPS precision the coordinates of every place you've traveled. That causes an electrical current of fear to prickle every one of Nico's nerves.

He ends the call and gets the cabbie's attention. "Change of plans. Can you take me to Chestertown?"

"Where?"

"It's in Delaware County. About an hour away."

The guy is tapping the GPS on the phone mounted to his windshield as he drives. Then he says, "It'll cost two hundred. It's a long way and I won't get any fares on the way home."

"That's fine." Nico needs to get there before the Feds. If they track his movements, then it's all over for him, regardless of whether the crazy woman with the tube weapon ever finishes the job.

CHAPTER FORTY-FOUR

JENNA

"It seems someone is upset with us," Artemis Templeton says to Jenna.

They sit in the dim light of the town car. He looks older than in the photoshopped magazine and newspaper images—or the crosshairs of a sniper rifle. But not bad, all things considered. Particularly since he probably hasn't been sleeping well since someone tried to make that bald head explode like a watermelon dropped from a rooftop. She thinks about the odd boy she briefly knew—the kid with the unusual cadence in his voice, the wooden posture. He still has that distant look in his eyes, like he's operating on another level than everyone else, but the bald head suits him. His business suit is well tailored and it's hard to imagine he's the same kid who wore short-sleeved shirts buttoned all the way to the collar and seemed to model his look on that of his childhood mentor, a neighborhood man the kids called Ned Flanders.

Jenna doesn't answer. She doesn't know how much he knows. And whether he's aware that *she* was one of the shadowy assassins who caused those dark circles under his eyes. Though she suspects he at least knows she was with The Corporation. It would explain this meeting.

"I suppose we can't chalk all this up to coincidence," she says. "Someone after all four of us . . ."

He raises his brows in agreement. "Hard to believe it's been so long."

Another life, she wants to say, but doesn't.

He waves a manila folder in his hand. "I imagine you've been asking yourself the same question I have: *Who?*"

"Why would I be doing that?"

He frowns as though he doesn't have time for games. "You didn't fall off a ship or get trapped in a mine. But no one's seen your family since the events of late."

Fair enough.

He hands her the folder. "This is my security team's report on our best guess about who hired the hitter. And I recognize it's merely that. An educated guess."

Inside the folder are photos of a man. He's in a suit and looks respectable enough. There's something familiar about him.

"Who is he?" she asks.

"One of Chestertown's finest," Artemis says. "The gentleman from the fifth congressional district."

Jenna shrugs.

"You might remember him better as one of the kids we hid from at night."

Jenna examines the photo again.

"Derek Brood," she says. The name still gives her the creepy-crawlies.

Artemis nods. "After his father disappeared, he was raised by his uncle, the mayor of Chestertown. The Broods have run that armpit of a town for decades. That didn't change after we left."

Jenna nods.

Arty continues, "That's why no one followed up on the girls who disappeared. . . . Everything was covered up by the Broods."

He gives Jenna a pointed look. She'd been one of those girls. What happened to the others? Sabine claimed that she had no hand in their disappearance, that Jenna was the only Corporation recruit from Savior House. But who could be sure with Sabine?

"Why now? After all these years?"

Artemis shrugs. "Politicians tend to be psychopaths."

"I can't believe Derek Brood's in Congress. What a disgrace. . . ."

Artemis chuckles. "Have you seen Congress lately? There's more sociopaths and carnival barkers than legislators."

Despite living in D.C., Jenna has buried her head in the sand when it comes to politics.

"As I see it, we have two choices here," Artemis tells her.

Jenna nods for him to continue.

"We see if there's an amount he'd take in compensatory and punitive damages to back down. . . ."

"Or?" Jenna knows where this is going.

"Or I give that same money to someone like you who knows how to deal with these types of problems."

This confirms he knows about her time with The Corporation. It's unsettling. But he's a billionaire and likely has unparalleled access to intel—an entire squad of former spooks and other shadowy special operators on his payroll. It's unclear why he doesn't use his own people for such work. But maybe he can't—can't tell them the reason for the hit. Or he wants to ensure it's not traceable to him.

He leans back in the leather seat of the sedan, waits for her response.

"If this is about Derek taking revenge, money won't matter to him."

"Maybe," Artemis says, like a man who knows that money often can shift the paradigm, overcome morals, emotion, sentimentality, even family ties. Particularly with the politicians who probably regularly approach Artemis with their hands out.

He glances at the folder. "It should have what you need."

Jenna doesn't look at the dossier. She'll study it later. She reaches for the door handle.

"There's something else," Artemis says.

Jenna sits back, waits for him to continue.

"We need to be concerned about the FBI. My contacts tell me that Brood—the father, not Derek—has come to the Bureau's attention."

Jenna swallows down a dry throat. "That doesn't make any sense. If Derek Brood wants us dead, why would he go to the Feds about what happened to his father? He'd be the obvious suspect if we're all killed."

"That's the question, isn't it?" Artemis releases a breath. "But maybe it's not Derek Brood talking to the Feds."

"Then who?"

"Only five people were there that night."

"Yeah, and one's dead, and the rest of us are targets. And we all have something to lose."

Artemis holds her gaze without blinking. He still brings to mind a robot—that's what Derek and his crew called him, wasn't it?

"I'm not suggesting it's any of us. But maybe someone has been talking. . . ."

"Not me."

"Of course, not you."

He could be right about the others. She hasn't kept up with

them, but it's possible one of them told someone—a girlfriend, a priest, an AA sponsor, someone.

"We need to talk to Donnie and Nico," he says. "Find out if they slipped."

"*We*," Jenna says.

Artemis's face remains expressionless. "I don't think we want me running around playing detective. It will only draw attention."

He's right, of course.

"What about your security team?"

"I'd have to tell them things we wouldn't want me to. Besides, Donnie and Nico adored you. They'll trust you."

"I saw Donnie at the funeral."

"He was hard to miss," Artemis says. "He's staying at the Four Seasons. He has a friend with him. My guys put a tracker on his rental car this morning." He hands her a smartphone. She glances at the screen and it shows a map with a blue dot.

"You have one of those for Nico too?"

"No. But he's here too, staying at the Ritz."

Jenna nods. Just as she thought, both of her foster home siblings came. For Ben.

"Look," Artemis says. "I think Derek Brood is behind this. If we can *convince* him to back off, we can make this problem go away."

Jenna thinks about this. "If he won't take the money and I have to take care of things, you can donate that money to charity."

Artemis cocks his head to the side, not computing.

"He threatened my family. This one's on the house."

CHAPTER FORTY-FIVE

DONNIE

Reeves handles the driving on I-95 South. Donnie hasn't told him why they're going to Chestertown. He's not sure himself. But Ben's law clerk's words continue to echo through his head: *He said to tell you that you all had it wrong. The proof is with Boo Radley.* The problem: Donnie doesn't have a damn clue what that means. He has huge gaps in his memory—most caused by whiskey, vodka, tequila, and white powder, not necessarily in that order. For the life of him, nothing's ringing a bell. Maybe seeing the old haunts will jog it loose. He's not keen on traveling down memory lane, but this is for Ben. And to get the money for the book he agreed to spend one full week with Reeves. The literary agent wants a draft by month's end, no doubt concerned that the clock is ticking on Donnie's fifteen minutes of fame.

A white work van speeds past.

Donnie points at it. "When we first started touring, there'd be eight of us living in a van like that, playing dive bars across the country. We'd each get seven dollars a day for food. By the end,

Tom had his own tour bus, there were two for the crew, and one for the rest of the band."

Reeves looks ahead at the road. "How was that, living on the road?"

"Nothing else like it, Hemingway. I loved it."

"Did you all have, like, homes, or . . . ?"

"Yeah, after we went platinum the first time everybody had a home base. I had a crib in LA, the rest were spread out." Donnie doesn't mention that he had to sell the LA property and currently rents a studio apartment in North Hollywood. "Three of the guys were married, had kids. But we were on the road about two hundred days a year."

"What's it like, living on a bus most of the year?"

"It's kinda like you never grow up. Other than getting from one show to the next we didn't have any real responsibilities. Our manager would take care of paying the bills for everybody's home base. We had only three rules."

Reeves turns his head, like this might be something he can use for the book.

Donnie ticks them off. "One, if you bring a girl on the bus there's an ID check and an NDA gets signed. That was the result of an unfortunate incident when our bass player met a seventeen-year-old who lied about her age after a show in Phoenix. That was a mess."

Reeves's eyes widen.

"Maybe don't put that part in the book." Donnie smiles. "Rule Two: no number twos on the bus. The smell gets in the vents and it's a big hassle to clean out the septic tanks."

Reeves scrunches his face. "I think I'll leave that out too."

"Understandable. And Rule Three: no drugs on the bus." Donnie doesn't mention that he was the genesis of that rule, but he probably doesn't need to. "Other than all that, you live for the show, then the afterparty, then you're on to the next town. You watch a crapload of movies."

Reeves follows the GPS's voice and veers off the exit for Chestertown.

Donnie feels acid crawl up his throat. It's been twenty-five years.

"Where to?" Reeves asks.

"I suppose to where it started."

Fifteen minutes later, the rental car pulls to the curb on the south side of Chestertown. Reeves seems to be in awe at the urban decay. A neighborhood of boarded-up homes. Unbelievably, things have gotten worse. Twenty-five years ago, the neighborhood was on the decline, but there were still people left from before the steel, automotive, and paper factories closed. Old couples who mowed their lawns, planted flowers, maintained the exterior of their homes—fought the losing battle of their neighborhood being taken over by drugs and crime.

They get out of the rental car and Donnie gestures to a boarded-up mansion that has a lopsided porch. Once upon a time long before the town used it for a group home—it had been a grand manor. But once the factories all closed, the place, like the town, went to shit. For some reason, a memory from the tour bus comes to mind. Watching the movie *Forrest Gump*, the scene where Jenny throws stones at the home where she'd been abused as a kid. No rock is big enough for this place.

"So, this is it, where you grew up?" Reeves asks.

"Only from when I was twelve to fourteen. Before that I was with the Jensons, and before then we were in Alabama in a trailer park that made this place look like a palace."

Reeves has a pad and pen and takes notes as they walk. He spins around, taking it all in.

"It's amazing you made it out."

Donnie examines the house. Next to the front door there's a rectangle where the paint is a different color. A plaque that read: SAVIOR HOUSE used to hang there.

"Benny said we owed it to each other to make it out."

Reeves nods, scribbles something.

"About Ben," Donnie says, "his law clerk told me something that I can't figure out." He clues Reeves in on the cryptic message she relayed to him. Nothing's coming to Donnie. Maybe the writer will have some ideas. He leaves out the part about Ben being blackmailed. That could lead Reeves down a path Donnie doesn't want him to venture.

Reeves thinks on it. "Did Ben think he was in danger, is that why he asked her to give you a message?"

"No idea. The law clerk said she told the FBI what he said, so I'm sure they're on it."

"He said to tell you that you all had it wrong, what could you have gotten wrong?"

Donnie isn't sure about this either.

"And Boo Radley?" Reeves says. "Did you all read *To Kill a Mockingbird* or something?"

Donnie shakes his head. "Benny loved to read, but I've never read it. Why?"

"Boo Radley's a character from the book. He was a mysterious neighbor of the kids in the story. They treated him like the boogeyman, but that's because they didn't understand him."

Donnie thinks about this. He's racking his brains. Benny loved books, used to spend hours at the public library. Next to the tree fort they'd built that summer, it was his sanctuary. But Donnie doesn't remember Benny reading *To Kill a Mockingbird* or talking about it.

"Was there anyone who terrorized you when you were kids?" Reeves asks.

For a split second Donnie can't breathe. He's being held underwater at the neighborhood pool. Then he's at the edge of a shallow grave. He doesn't say it, but one name comes to mind: Brood.

CHAPTER FORTY-SIX

NICO

If they track his movements, they'll find the duffel bag. And if they find the bag . . . he doesn't want to think about that. The proof is in the bag.

The cabbie drives slowly down Patterson Street in Chestertown. It looks like a scene out of a zombie movie: Cars stripped to their frames, houses sprayed with graffiti over plywood-covered windows, litter blowing on the streets. Figures ducking into the shadows.

The cabbie seems nervous. He should be.

"Look, I was fine taking you this far from Philly, but I don't have a death wish. Friend of mine was killed on the job, and no fare's worth that."

Nico says, "It's just a little more up the road."

"Looks like the cops are tailing us. I don't want no trouble." The cabbie's eyes jump to the rearview, then back to the road.

Nico twists around. There's a dark sedan that sure looks like the kind law enforcement drive.

He already paid the driver—the guy insisted on collecting the fare up front—so he just needs to lose whoever's tailing them. Nico's mind goes to Natalie. *The FBI was just here asking about you.* To his showrunner, Shannon: *The FBI served a warrant for the records on your company cell phone.* That reminds him. He pulls out his phone, powers it down. Is that enough to stop the tracking? He decides to pop out the SIM card.

"Okay, here's what I'd like you to do," he says to the cabbie. "There's an alley right up there, pull in and I'll get out."

"Not a chance, pal. No way."

Nico sighs. He looks around. He's back in the old neighborhood. He still knows the terrain. "All right. Let me out at the corner."

He looks back again at the sedan crawling behind them. The cabbie stops at the intersection. "Thanks for the ride." Nico jumps out and sprints toward the alley.

He hears the sedan's engine rev, then its brakes screeching to a stop. He twists around. There's a tall guy in a suit running toward him. Nico turns and weaves through the alley. The old chain-link fence up ahead still has the gap cut into it. He ducks through the hole, then into what used to be Meth Head Ted's yard. The dog's gone, at least. They used to make a game of running the gauntlet without Bruno biting them in the balls.

Now he's on the gravel trail behind the houses. It's a rat's maze and the guy will never catch up with him.

He hears someone shouting.

But he keeps running.

He's on Harden Street now. His heart trips when he sees the old group home. And the skinny guy with long hair standing out front. But there's no time for that. He races through the lot and to the overpass. The woods are ahead. Cutting through the trees, the smell of damp earth and fallen leaves brings him back in time. He thinks he's lost the guy. He better have.

He has to get there before they do. To dispose of the evidence.

CHAPTER FORTY-SEVEN

JENNA

Two graveyards in one day. How morbid. This one, in Linwood, Pennsylvania, isn't as stately as the one in Philadelphia. But it's a far cry from the overgrown mess of a cemetery in Chestertown where the Savior House kids would play. Even a graveyard was better than spending time in the group home with its dusty rooms filled with pressed-wood furniture and footlockers to protect the residents' minimal belongings.

She finds the gravestone, a large one for both of them. She thinks back to that night. Bowling night. The one evening her parents went out on the town. Dad had worked for Comcast. Mom stayed home and "kept house," as she liked to say. It also allowed her to shuttle Jenna to her gymnastics competitions all around the Commonwealth. Dad's job didn't pay much, but they somehow scraped together the money for the classes, the leotards, the tournament entry fees. And as much as she's shoved it all down, tried not to think about it, she allows herself a moment to cherish her idyllic early childhood. She was lucky to have had it, even if it was for only fifteen years. Better to have loved and lost, or whatever that stupid expression is. It was all stolen in the blink of an eye, when some asshole had one too many and got behind the wheel.

She pulls some weeds sprouting around the stone, brushes the marble with her hand. She feels guilty that this is the first time she's returned in twenty-five years. She holds back tears and the forever questions of whether they'd be ashamed of the life she's lived or whether they'd understand she did it all to survive. She shakes it off, literally shakes her body like she's shedding the questions, and the guilt and the pain. She has her own idyllic family she needs to protect now.

She pulls out the burner phone Michael gave her. It's probably more secure than the one the president uses, so she decides she needs to make this call. In case things go sideways.

Simon picks up on the first ring. He sounds breathless. "Oh thank god," he says.

"I'm fine. How are things at the cabin?"

"I have a teenager with no internet, TV, or cell phone, how do you think?"

Jenna loves that he's being light, trying to sound normal, which she knows is for her benefit.

"We're fine. Where are you?"

Jenna doesn't answer. "This will be over soon, and we can go home."

There's a long silence on the other end. Then a series of sentence fragments: "Whatever you're going to do, you don't have to. I have friends at DOJ, they can help us get—"

"I know what I'm doing. And this is probably the only way."

"Probably."

"If we're right about who's behind it all, yes."

"You're not sure?"

That is an excellent question from her analytical husband. Is she sure? The pieces of the puzzle fit. Who else would want all of them dead? No one from Jenna's past jobs would have any reason to take out her foster mates. It's been twenty-five years since Jenna had spoken to any of them, so it has to be someone from Savior House.

Yet something doesn't feel right. She can't pinpoint what it is, but something's causing that tingle at the nape of her neck.

"I'm as sure as I can be."

More silence on the other line.

"I'm going to take care of the problem and will be home soon." She can't help but think of Michael's words: *You can thank me by taking care of your problem without it taking care of you.*

"I love you," Simon says, words that send a surge of warmth through her. "I should've said it before you left the cabin, but I was in shock, scared for the girls, and I—"

"I love you too, Simon Raines, and I'm coming home to you."

Back on the motorcycle, Jenna rides to an area near the Delaware riverfront in Chestertown. She gets a Xanax-inducing wave of anxiety at the smell of that river, but she shakes it off. Her phone told her the congressional office is on Seaport Drive. She finds a place to park and locates a bench with a view of the office. She'll wait to see if he comes out for lunch. The file Artemis compiled said Derek Brood is a first-term congressman—one with ambition. He inherited his family's sanitation business and has done well for himself. Artemis's file says he goes to the same place for lunch every day, a steakhouse five minutes from the office.

It's a good hour before Derek emerges from the glass doors of the '70s-style government building. The sight of him takes her breath away. In the photo she noticed the resemblance to his father, but in person it's more startling. He has the girth, the gait, of the head of Savior House. Derek was always clean-cut, like his father, which was helpful in hiding their menace. He has an entourage walking with him: an Asian woman, a younger white guy in a suit, and two body men walking behind him. Why would a Pennsylvania congressman from a poor district need muscle? It's uncanny how much he looks like his father.

He was a mean-spirited kid, a bully. Could he have changed after being raised by someone else? She thinks back to a day at the park when she'd intervened when Derek was beating up Nico.

Nico. She smiles, thinking of how lovestruck he was with Annie. Following her around like a puppy. Annie didn't act like she was into him, but she was. She proudly wore that cheap necklace Nico bought for her, talked about how sweet he was. Annie had been in the system so long that she simply didn't know how to show love.

And then Annie was gone. Vanished. Jenna remembers the feeling of helplessness. Only one of them didn't lose hope after that day on the riverbank. Their knees still dirty from kneeling in the muck, thinking they were going to be executed, Ben had marched them to the public library. The incident had only hardened his resolve. *The law is how you dealt with bullies like the detective,* he told them. . . .

Jenna watches Ben as he scribbles notes on the scratch paper, his eyes glued to a lawbook he's yanked from one of the library's shelves.

Donnie has slipped out to the convenience store to swipe a bottle. He's not made for more trauma. None of them is, but it's the sweet-hearted who it hits the hardest. But even Nico holds a vacant stare now, going to the bathroom every few minutes, probably to empty his guts.

The detective warned them in no uncertain terms to back off. Jenna's instincts tell her that's what they should be doing. Not stopping at the library trying to find out how to go after the very man who threatened to kill them. But Ben is on a mission.

"Can I help?" Jenna asks Ben.

"Yeah, go get me this book." He hands her a scrap of paper that's been folded like a star. She's noticed that he has the unusual habit of folding paper. There are three stars and two scraps folded to look like flowers near where he's been reading. She looks at the star he handed her, sees he's written a library call number on it, and heads off to find the book.

On the way, she sees Donnie stumble into the library. His lips are blue from that Mad Dog 20/20 wine he drinks.

"We gotta let this go," Donnie says. "We gotta go to the house, pack our shit, and go." His words are slurred and tinged with fear and hurt.

"Come sit." She leads him to a lounge chair that has frayed arms and cushions.

"I know Benny," Donnie says. "He's gonna need to go after them. Get *justice*." He exaggerates the word. "He said his dad went to prison for something he didn't do. He never forgave himself for not being able to stop it."

Jenna understands Donnie's fear. But she thinks of Marta's eyes the night she woke up Jenna to get her safe . . . Annie telling off Derek at the lunchroom. They wouldn't walk away if Jenna disappeared.

She watches across the library as Nico comes out of the bathroom. He says something to Ben, grabs a handful of the papers, the folded stars, then throws them on the floor, and charges outside.

Ben comes over to them.

Jenna says, "Sorry I didn't get the book, I needed to—"

"It's all right. I found what we need. We gotta get the Feds interested. It's the only way to deal with corrupt local cops and officials."

Jenna nods. "Is Nico okay?"

Ben looks at the floor. "He's . . ." Ben searches for the word. "Devastated."

"He should be," Donnie says. "We need to drop this." His eyes are red and watering.

Ben crouches low. "Look at me, you redneck."

Donnie raises his glance to Ben's.

"You want them to get any more of our friends?"

Donnie shakes his head.

"You trust me?"

Donnie nods this time. "Brothers from another mother."

Ben nods. "That's right. And you know what else?"

Jenna watches as Donnie stares in admiration at his best friend.

"They're not going to get away with this."

CHAPTER FORTY-EIGHT

NICO

Nico traipses through the forest, branches smacking his face, the hum of insects in his ears. The old path through the weeds, the one they'd worn down trudging back and forth, isn't visible. But he knows he's headed in the right direction. He remembers the summer they built the tree fort—the sticky heat and fatigue of carrying lumber stolen from a construction site—Ben hauling more wood than all of them on his strong shoulders. And he remembers laying on the planks up high, watching the stars.

Today, the woods are dreary, the tree canopy making the day an even darker shade of gray. He hears a snap of twigs up ahead. Probably a deer, one of the Chestertown woods variety, thin and malnourished.

There's a brief quiet from the insects, but they start up again. Whoever was chasing Nico didn't track him here, that's for sure. These woodlands are difficult to navigate, tangled and unkempt.

He's on a fool's errand right now, he fears. If the FBI is running a cell tower report tracking his movements from the last time he was in Chestertown, it probably wouldn't ping out here. But he doesn't know that, so he needs to assume they know he was trudging through this same area a month ago. He sees his marker up ahead, the tree he carved with a pocketknife so many years ago:

N + A

It's two trees behind this one. He stalks over, looks up. It's still nearly impossible to see the fort if you don't know it's there. He finds the rusty nail that served as a foothold to start the climb and hoists himself up. It's not as easy as it was when he was a kid. Even worse with one arm. He's ditched the sling, but he can't put much weight on his arm or shoulder. But this needs to be done.

He clasps a branch, struggles to pull himself up one-handed, swings his leg over, then stands, balancing on the huge limb. He continues to climb until he finally reaches the platform.

It's four by eight. Wide enough for them to lie flat or sit cross-legged in a circle. It has plywood walls but no roof. He remembers how Annie brought them snacks. Donnie always managed to have a bottle, hiding his stash of convenience-store rotgut somewhere in the woods nearby. The summer they built the tree fort was exactly two summers after Mom took Nico to the beach that last time, and the only time since that he'd felt something close to happiness. Nico, Ben, Donnie, and Annie would spend hours talking and joking. Jenna hadn't been there long enough to face the initiation ritual of the G.R.O.S.S. club, so named by Donnie based on some comic strip he loved. Artemis was too engrossed in his coding projects to screw around in the woods.

It had been their haven. Their place to talk about their dreams. Their place *not* to talk about their lives before Savior House. The place Nico fell in love for the first time.

He looks up at the sky and inhales deeply through his nose. It smells the same. But the sky is murkier. Maybe it wasn't all as incandescent as he remembers. Maybe he's rosied up the memories. But that summer was the last time he felt something other than a void in his core. And it was that summer that also broke each of them. When Annie disappeared. When that cop took something from each of them at the riverbank.

He remembers afterward, leaving the library, pounding on Ned Flanders's door. Arty and Flanders are at the dining room table that's lined with computer monitors, the room strewn with cords. Flanders brings in a tray that has glasses of lemonade, listens as Nico rants and rages and tries not to cry.

Flanders disappears to make a call. When he returns, he says, "I spoke to a different person this time, a supervisor. She told me that her records show that Marta is in a new home," Flanders pauses. "But she has no record about Annie missing or that she or the other girls are even staying at Savior House."

"It's because Mr. Brood's brother got it fixed, he *runs* this town. Ben says we need to call the FBI."

"I'll call," Flanders says, and Nico believes him. "But we need proof that the missing girls were residents of Savior House."

Nico says, "You need proof? I'll get you proof."

Back at Savior House, Nico ventures into forbidden territory: Mr. Brood's office. He was going to kick down the door if he needed to, but he's in luck. The door is open an inch, the lights on like Brood had just been there. He needs to be fast.

He rushes to the metal file cabinet and riffles through the files. He finds a file for each of them, Nico, Ben, Donnie, but none for the girls. He goes through each drawer. But he's sure of it. There're none.

His heart jumps to his throat when he hears voices. Mr. Brood talking to someone. Nico dives under the desk and balls up as Brood and another man come into the room. The door is shut loudly and the other man sounds angry.

"I don't need this headache," the man says to Mr. Brood.

"You think I do?"

"Kids from your goddamn home go to the cops? Are you fucking kidding me? I went to a lot of trouble to get you this job. You're lucky that detective owes me. And you're lucky it sounded crazy. Some lady buying girls."

"Is it crazy? You're the one who made the deal with these people and I've got a bunch of kids missing."

"I didn't have a choice. The Corporation dealt with that problem we had during the primary."

"Your opponent's sudden heart attack . . ."

"Are you fucking stupid? Shut your mouth. And I called the French lady. They say they haven't taken any of the girls. They want the new girl, but they didn't take the others."

"And you believe them?"

"Yeah, I do. Most of those girls went missing—under your watch, by the way—long before I got mixed up with The Corporation. But it doesn't matter. It's not like we could do anything about it either way."

"Whatever you say."

"I'm just telling you what they told me. They got no reason to lie. And you best watch your tone. Mom made me promise I'd look out for you, but—"

"But what? You'll plant me and my son somewhere worse than being some babysitter at a shithole group home?"

"Quit fucking whining. You get paid plenty. As long as you keep washing the cash—and don't bring any more attention to this place."

Nico listens. The two men are quiet for a long time. Then: "What now?" Mr. Brood asks.

"Russo'll bury the report with the Chestertown squad. Maybe you and your friends keep your hands off the girls and it'll die down."

"It's your friends from Men's Club who—"

"Shut up."

Mr. Brood is quiet again. Then asks: "What about the girl the French lady wants? It's too hot right now for another one to go missing."

"She said, *'That's a* you *problem.'* I'm not telling these people no . . ."

"If The Corporation didn't take the others, then who did?"

"You think I'm fucking stupid? You promised me no more fiddling with underage girls. I worked hard to get rid of the problem last time. To get you this job around kids, for Christ's sake."

"I didn't—"

"Shut the fuck up. They're coming for the girl, Jenna, tomorrow. You pack her stuff after they get here and keep the other kids in line. And keep your hands off the girls or I swear . . ."

The door opens, the voices trail away. And Nico knows they have no choice now.

A bird squawks, bringing Nico's thoughts back to the tree fort. This mess he's in. He looks down at the planks, which are green from moss. The duffel bag—the evidence—is still here lodged in the corner. He's safe. No one knows. He sits, legs dangling over the edge, catching his breath from the climb. Looking through a break in branches and leaves below, he pictures shirtless Donnie's skinny pale torso, Ben giving him a boost to climb the tree.

Nico will wait here until dark, then climb down (somehow), and get rid of the bag.

As the sun lowers, he sits thinking about the surreal last two days: getting trapped in the mine, the rescue team showing up looking like spacemen in their oxygen masks, ruthless O'Leary flying a kite with the wonderment of a young child, Natalie telling him she never wants to see him again. And now, chased through the sprawl of Chestertown by someone—who, the FBI?—and sitting in a lopsided tree fort he helped build a quarter century ago.

Something catches his eye. A shiny object against the wall of the fort. He slides over on his rear, picks it up with his index finger and thumb, and examines it. And his heart drops. This isn't some trinket from back in the day. Isn't something Nico dropped on his last visit to the fort. It's a gold cuff link.

But it's not the cuff link that causes Nico's stomach to roil, his heart to hammer. It's the initials engraved on the gold face: R.B.W.

Robert Benjamin Wood.

CHAPTER FORTY-NINE

DONNIE

Donnie and Reeves sit at a bar eating Reuben sandwiches and drinking cold beer on Bleak Street in Chestertown. Bleak is right.

Reeves has only taken a couple bites and seems lost in thought. Maybe he's outlining the book. Taking all the material Donnie has given him so far and organizing it into some semblance of a story. Or maybe he's still processing the conditions Donnie grew up in. The bartender asks if they want another round and Reeves and Donnie respond simultaneously: Reeves shaking his head, Donnie nodding. Donnie laughs and says, "Okay, I'll take his drink too, darlin'."

The bartender—she looks like a weather-beaten New Englander—cackles.

Reeves says, "Anything reminding you of what Boo Radley means? Or what Ben was trying to tell you?"

"*Nada.*"

Reeves seems to be caught up in the mystery.

Donnie says, "I'm sure Benny read that mockingbird book, but I don't remember him mentioning it. He read a lot of books.

He'd get a pile from the library or Goodwill. I'd sometimes pinch him a new one from the drugstore."

Reeves gives a nod like he's someone who understands the love of reading. "Did he have a favorite book? I sometimes think that says a lot about a person."

Donnie thinks on this. "He liked Hemingway."

This elicits a crooked grin from Reeves, perhaps tired of the nickname.

"Benny read a book about Hemingway, and told me that the guy had said some racist and fucked-up shit, but Benny still loved his books." Donnie thinks more. "He also loved lawbooks. In Philly, we used to sneak into the law library at Temple and he'd ask the law students what they were reading and track down copies on the shelves. When Ruth arrested us for stealing food, she asked us a bunch of questions. Benny gave her a hard time about not reading him the Miranda warning, and how we could tell her that we murdered someone and they'd have to throw the whole case out. He said the 'fruit of the poisonous tree, shall set us free.' He loved to rhyme. It made him sound like a famous lawyer he worshiped."

"Ruth was the cop who ended up adopting him?"

Donnie nods. "She passed a few years ago."

"How about you, Donnie?"

"How about me *what*?"

"You have a favorite book?"

"Damn, Hemingway, you're still trying to get inside this head? Let me spare you the trouble, boss. I ain't that deep."

Reeves offers a reproachful smile.

"I went to Chestertown High, and didn't finish ninth grade," Donnie adds. "The last math class I had was called 'consumer math,' where they teach you how to add up groceries and things like that. I failed Algebra One three damn times."

"But I've read the lyrics to your songs, Donnie. Some of them"—Reeves smiles—"and I mean *some* of them, are like poetry."

"Why, thank you," Donnie says, with a hint of sarcasm combined with genuine appreciation at the remark.

"I'm being serious."

"Okay, you wanna know my favorite book? I'll tell you the *only* books I ever read for fun—and I'm gonna regret telling you because if you put this in the book I'm gonna look like an idiot."

Reeves raises his eyebrows and waits for him to continue.

"Benny used to get me these books that were collections of *Calvin and Hobbes*."

"The comic strip?"

"Yeah, the one with the kid whose best friend was a tiger, but everybody else sees Hobbes as a stuffed animal. I loved those."

"I get it."

"How's that?" Donnie asks, thinking Reeves may be patronizing him.

"There's something about seeing the absurdity of the world through the eyes of a mischievous six-year-old that's appealing."

Donnie is impressed that Reeves didn't turn up his nose.

Reeves continues, "I read a piece once about how *Calvin and Hobbes* is great literature. The comics parodied the artistic world, pondered the meaning of life, the existence of God, and the perils of mankind's self-destructive ways."

Donnie chuckles. "I don't know about all that. But Calvin had this tree fort that gave me the idea for ours." He raises a hand preemptively. "I'm not taking you there, because those woods are even scarier than the streets after dark."

Reeves doesn't debate him on that.

Donnie looks out the window of the bar into the gloom.

"Actually, the last thing Benny ever gave me was about Calvin and Hobbes."

Reeves looks at him, interest piqued.

"On my last visit to Philly, he gave me a magazine to read on the plane home. One of those ones fancy people read. Hell, I bet your bathroom at home is full of 'em. The *New Yorker* or one of those. They ran a short story some fella wrote, fan fiction I think they call it, about Calvin on his deathbed. In the story, Calvin's an old man and he's dying and his wife, the girl he always battled with in the comics, brings him his stuffed tiger to the hospital to say goodbye. It's been years since Calvin has seen the real tiger anytime he looks at the stuffed animal. But in his final moments, his best friend comes back to life when he needs him." Donnie's voice catches. It's hard to swallow. He notices Reeves staring at him. Donnie shakes it off. "I tell you what, I was bawling my eyes out on that Spirit Airlines flight. Dude next to me thought I was *crazy*."

Donnie pushes down the emotions. He thinks of Benny when they left Chestertown to head off on their own after that awful visit to the drug house to say goodbye to his mom. On the bus, Benny had packed one of the *Calvin and Hobbes* books. On its last page was the final comic strip that ever ran in the series. It showed Hobbes carrying a sled on fresh snow and saying, "The world looks brand-new!" and Calvin ending the script with, "Let's go exploring!"

CHAPTER FIFTY

JENNA

After Derek Brood's lunch meeting, Jenna stakes out the congressional office until dusk. She's moved around—strolling the waterfront, sitting on a bench pretending to read a Jack Reacher paperback, wandering around with a Starbucks cup—trying to go unnoticed.

She spied a CCTV set up for the congressional office, but the rest of the waterfront area doesn't seem to have any security cameras. She's careful to avoid ATMs—the tiny cameras on the machines are always recording anything that passes.

By dark, she thinks Derek Brood must be the hardest-working man in show business, which is basically what Congress has become.

At last, he emerges from the building. No entourage this time. He doesn't carry a briefcase, but he seems to be walking somewhere purposefully. She trails after him at a safe distance. He's heading back toward the same steakhouse where he ate lunch. She suspects this is the only area of this town that has a halfway decent restaurant, but twice in one day? Maybe this problem will take care of itself; he'll die from heart disease.

He's talking on his cell phone as he walks. Brood has an aggressive gait that hasn't changed much since he was a kid. Jenna wonders what else hasn't changed about the brute who terrorized the denizens of Savior House.

Brood waves away a homeless man who approaches him and, sure enough, he's back at the same place where he took lunch. Artemis's dossier on Brood said he's married, but no kids. Maybe he's meeting his wife for dinner. Or maybe it's where he holds work meetings, lets lobbyists slide him bundles of cash under the table.

Brood disappears inside the restaurant. Jenna needs to decide what to do. She's had all day to ponder it but can't land on how to approach this one. Wait in the back of his car? Break into his house? She needs some time with him alone. The bag of goodies from Michael contains everything she needs: Ski mask. Hood. Zip ties. Duct tape. Waterboarding cloth. Bottle of water. Pliers.

Then something grabs her attention. A young woman approaching the restaurant. *The* young woman . . . Jenna's grip on the gun in her front jacket pocket tightens. She thinks maybe she should don the mask, walk into the steakhouse, and shoot them both. Often, simple is better. One of Sabine's guiding principles.

She watches as the woman enters the restaurant.

Without thinking, she starts fast-walking toward the entrance. She's going to do it. For her family.

She keeps her head down, crosses the plaza. Her old self, along with the resignation that this is what needs to be done, has returned. She pulls out the mask as she walks.

But she slows—then halts at the sight of the man in the suit who's obviously trailing the hit woman. He has the buttoned-up look of a G-man. She remembers Arty's words:

We need to be concerned about the FBI.

With that, she aborts. She shoves the mask back in the bag, turns, and walks casually away.

It's Derek Brood's lucky day.

But not for long.

CHAPTER FIFTY-ONE

DONNIE

"I'll tell you what, Hemingway, I'll make a deal with ya."

They're back in the rental car, driving nowhere in particular. It's dark outside now, and Reeves still seems shell-shocked by the state of the neighborhood. Donnie imagines Reeves as a kid, playing tennis at a country club, going on fancy vacations. Attending an Ivy League college, then hanging with the elites at book parties on the Upper West Side.

"Sure, Donnie. What is it?"

"I'll take you somewhere important from my childhood tonight, but then I head out in the morning. I know I promised a full week—and I'll give you the full time—but it's been a rough week, so I'd like to take a little break. Think the publishing people will be cool with that?"

"I think that will be just fine." Reeves looks at him with something that resembles pity. Maybe the town's getting to Reeves. Lord knows it got to the rest of them.

"Groovy. I'll take you to the spot where Benny saved my life."

Reeves tilts his head to the side, like he's not sure if Donnie's kidding.

A half hour later, they've parked the car and are crawling through the gap in the temporary chain-link fence that surrounds the grounds.

"I'm not so sure about this. This is trespassing and I—"

"It'll be fine," Donnie says. "Cops around here have better things to do than guard a shuttered public swimming pool."

Reeves seems reluctant, but he follows Donnie to the lip of a swimming pool that is empty except for a puddle of brown sludge at the bottom. Graffiti covers the building that used to sell ice cream and Popsicles that Donnie and the other Savior House kids couldn't afford.

"We used to come here every Saturday in the summer." Donnie's mind returns to the blazing sun, the waft of chlorine. The cutoff jeans he bought at Goodwill that he used as trunks.

"I almost drowned in the deep end." He leaves out the part about Derek Brood holding him under.

Reeves pulls out a pen and his small notepad and flips it open. "I love the idea of starting the book with this. There's symbolism in starting and ending the book with you nearly drowning but surviving." He stops. Looks at Donnie. "Are you okay?"

Donnie doesn't realize that his cheeks are wet. He wipes his face with his hand. "I'm fine, Hemingway," he says in Rock Star Donnie's voice.

Reeves is studying him. Not buying it.

Donnie has the sudden urge for another drink. He lowers himself and sits on the ledge of the empty swimming pool.

Reeves sits beside him. The sky is black, the area lit by only a bulb on a lamppost that must be set on timer.

"I gotta tell you something, Reeves."

Reeves turns to him. He puts a hand on Donnie's shoulder. "What is it?"

"Can we go . . . what do you call it? Off the record?"

Reeves ponders this. "Sure. I won't write about anything you tell me unless you agree."

"On the ship. I remember what happened now."

Reeves gives him a quizzical look.

"There was a woman. I think the same woman from the photo the FBI showed me about Benny. The same one from the beach."

Reeves doesn't say anything, lets Donnie talk.

"She forced me to jump."

Reeve's eyes flash. "Wait, what?"

Donnie nods. "She had a gun and . . ." He trails off.

"You need to tell the authorities. You need to—"

"I know." He says it without conviction. If the woman who forced him off the ship is somehow the same woman who was following Benny, maybe she's the blackmailer. And if so, that means she knows what they did to Mr. Brood. If the FBI catches up with her . . . He lets the thought die.

Reeves's phone lights up and he checks the text, swipes it away. Donnie catches the wallpaper photo on the device. Like Reeves's laptop, it's a picture of a woman in a hospital bed.

"We keep talking about me, but I still don't know much about you," Donnie says, trying to change the subject.

"No one's writing a book about me."

"Hell, maybe they should be, Hemingway."

Reeves shakes his head.

"Do you mind if I ask who that is on your phone?" Donnie eyes Reeves's iPhone.

Reeves looks at his phone, clicks it so the screen goes black. "My best friend. She has Huntington's, an awful neurodegenerative disease. There's no cure yet, but there are some clinical trials that are showing promise."

"I'm sorry, man. I hope she'll be okay."

"If we can get her in one of the trials, they have this new technology where they inject viruses that attack and kill the bad DNA that causes the disease. If she was rich, she could go to another country where they're way ahead with DNA splicing."

"That ain't right. I'll never understand it."

"What's that?"

"These rich dudes who have more money than they'll ever need, but waste it on flying into space or buying more companies or mansions. They could be Batman, like a real-life superhero, going around finding people in need and changing people's lives. I don't get it." Donnie thinks about Benny, Black Superman.

Reeves looks at him.

"If I had the cash, man, I'd give it to your friend."

"You know what, Donnie? I think you really would."

CHAPTER FIFTY-TWO

JENNA

Jenna's going to have to approach this differently. If the guy following the hitter is with the FBI it means one of three things. One, the FBI agent knows the hitter killed Ben Wood—or tried to kill Nico Adakai or Donnie Danger or Artemis Templeton. Or two, he knows that Derek Brood hired the killer to take out the residents of Savior House. Or three, Derek Brood and the hitter are the FBI's informants about what happened to Derek's father all those years ago and the FBI has no idea that its confidential informants have also set out to kill everyone. Three seems the least likely. There'd be no need to include the contract killer in informing to the FBI. It would be too risky. And the agent seems to be trailing the woman surreptitiously, not coming to the restaurant to meet her.

Jenna needs to think. Get her head on straight. She thinks of Arty in the back of the town car: *We need to talk to Donnie and Nico. Find out if they slipped. . . . Donnie and Nico adored you. They'll trust you.* She needs to know what, if anything, Donnie and Nico have said to the FBI.

She unzips the bag of goodies and retrieves the cell phone Artemis gave her that monitors the tracker on Donnie's rental car. Powering on the device, she waits until the blue dot appears. The car's about ten minutes from here, parked somewhere off the interstate. She pushes the ignition button on the motorcycle and roars away.

She tracks the blue dot to a highway hotel, a chain and probably the only decent accommodations for miles. Donnie must be in for the night. She considers bribing the clerk to get his room number but is spared that indignity when a thin, long-haired man appears in the parking lot. The old rocker looks around like a teenager sneaking out of the house, worried someone might see him.

Jenna follows as Donnie pulls the Hyundai rental car out of the lot and heads back toward Chestertown. The night is cool for April and the breeze feels good as Jenna jets down the interstate, which is littered with semis.

The Hyundai takes the off-ramp and soon they're on the south side, the Hyundai and bike the only vehicles on the pothole-filled streets. Donnie slows near the corner of Fourth and Union and pulls to a stop. Jenna kills the lights and veers to the side of the road.

From a gap in the row houses appears a man. He walks to the car, leans inside, they shake hands—the exchange—then the car juts forward.

Oh, Donnie.

The Hyundai putters away. Jenna continues to follow until they hit Woodrow, where most of the businesses—the ones that aren't covered in plywood with FOR RENT signs on them, anyway—are closed for the night. But there's one that has its lights on, Chestertown Liquor. The store's windows are covered with signs for bottom-shelf liquor and lottery tickets. Donnie goes inside and comes out gripping the neck of a bottle in a brown paper sack.

Donnie drives some more and pulls in front of Savior House and sits in the car for a long time. The abandoned group home looms in the darkness. She eradicates memories creeping in. The interior light of the Hyundai goes on when the door opens and Donnie steps out. He's stumbling now and makes his way down the street.

Jenna thinks she knows where he's going.

CHAPTER FIFTY-THREE

NICO

Nico's thoughts are whirling. Ben came to the fort—he knew about the duffel bag. Probably about it all. And then he ended up dead.

Nico races through the woodland, the bag draped over his good shoulder, the contents making a dreadful clacking sound. He tears around trees and bramble until he sees lights winking through the trees. He finds his way to the path and darts toward the clearing on the knoll that's connected to Ned Flanders's house.

Beyond the weeds and past a fallen tree, there's a rusty fence. It goes up to only his chest, but his shoulder is throbbing, making the climb difficult. The grass is slick from dew and his sneakers slide as he climbs to the top of the hill. He's going to bury the bag and get the fuck out of this town and never look back.

A sliver of moon appears, giving just enough light for him to make his way to the spot. He should've brought a flashlight. He can't turn on his phone to use his smartphone light without risking a tower pinging his location.

He reaches the top and his breath is stripped from him. The

knoll—a small break in the trees between Ned Flanders's house and the woods—is pitted with holes. Six or seven of them. Each a few feet deep. Like someone was looking for buried treasure.

He doesn't have time to process or understand. He needs to move. He looks at the hole in front of him—on the same spot he'd help dig twenty-five years ago—and throws the bag into the void.

He falls to his knees and starts pushing dirt in to fill it.

Later, he's filthy and sweaty and exhausted, but it's done. He needs a shower. But that will have to wait. For now, he's getting out of Chestertown. The street is pitch-black. He's walked far enough away from the knoll, so he puts the SIM card back in his phone, powers it on, thumbs the Uber app. Unsurprisingly, no cars are available. A side hustle for Uber isn't worth venturing into this neighborhood after dark.

He'll have to walk to Industrial Highway and stick out his thumb. Or maybe the bus station. The area is familiar, and in his head he's on the way home from school with his friends. Annie's chewing bubble gum, skipping ahead of them.

He sees the park up ahead. It was a disaster and dangerous even back then. He can only imagine what it's like now. The site of his famous beatdown from Derek in front of Annie.

All the streetlights surrounding the park are smashed out. He probably should steer clear. There could be danger in the shadows. But he keeps walking, the memories pulling him ahead like a casino calling his name.

The blacktop is strewn with litter. The basketball stands and hoops—forever netless when they were kids—lie on the ground like fallen trees ripped from their roots.

He stops. He can make out the monkey bars. The octagon cage where they would sit until sundown. He swears there's the outline of a figure on top, but it's just his mind playing tricks on him.

He should go.

But he keeps walking into the park.

"You don't wanna come over here, boss," a voice says in a southern drawl. "I've got a gun."

The warning is a bluff, he knows. He also knows that voice.

"Donnie?" Nico asks.

Nico turns on his iPhone's flashlight. Shines it on his own face.

"Handsome? Is that you?"

"It is, Donnie, it is."

CHAPTER FIFTY-FOUR

Nico's sitting on top of the monkey bars next to Donnie, the two passing a bottle back and forth. They skip the small talk, and mercifully it's too dark for Donnie to notice the dirt all over Nico's hands and probably smearing his face. Or Donnie's too plastered, but it's always been hard to tell with Donnie.

"I'm sorry about Ben," Nico says.

Donnie nods. Takes a swig.

"You two keep in touch over the years?"

Donnie nods again. He doesn't seem to want to talk about it. Nico doesn't mention finding the cuff link. Doesn't mention being at the tree fort.

"What you doing back here?" Donnie asks at last.

"I've been asking myself the same question."

"I hear you, brother."

Nico says, "I don't know if you've been keeping up with the news. But what happened to me, it wasn't—"

"—wasn't an accident," Donnie says, passing him the bottle.

"Same," he says, referring to his fall from the cruise ship without elaboration. "Do you have any idea who—"

"Who's trying to kill you?" a female voice cuts in. "I know," she says.

They twist around.

"Who's there?" Donnie calls out.

The woman emerges from the shadows.

"What the hell are you doing back there?" asks Nico.

Jenna replies, "That's what she said."

CHAPTER FIFTY-FIVE

JENNA

She's been watching them in the shadows, listening. Arty's fears appear to be unwarranted.

Donnie and Nico haven't told anyone—much less the FBI—about Savior House, about anything. From what she's made out, they haven't spoken to each other in years, perhaps since the last time they were all together, twenty-five years ago.

She emerges from the darkness. Makes that stupid joke they used to love so much.

Donnie appears ambivalent. She remembers him from that night—he seemed broken. He had gone along with Arty's plan only because of Ben. And it doesn't escape Jenna that if it weren't for her—the boys trying to prevent her from being taken—all of their lives would have been different. She'd been at Savior House only a brief time, but they put everything on the line for her.

Donnie hops down, gives her a tentative look. Like he's not sure he recognizes her.

For his part, Nico looks perplexed. He says, "You're alive. . . . We thought they took you and . . ."

"I'm most certainly alive." She shrugs, smiles.

Nico seems to be calculating something. *If you're alive, then maybe Annie . . .* , but if so, he can't bring himself to say it.

Jenna thinks of what Sabine told her yesterday. *You're the only one we ever trained from Savior House. I only recruited the extraordinary, the special.*

Nico would say Annie was extraordinary, special. But not in the way Sabine meant.

"What're you doing here?" Donnie asks, breaking the awkward silence. His words have a slur to them. Not the booze. Probably whatever he bought from the guy on the corner of K and Seventh.

"I imagine the same thing you're both doing." She looks at them both. "Trying to figure out who's trying to kill us."

CHAPTER FIFTY-SIX

NICO

Nico looks at Jenna, who has grown into a beautiful woman. She retrieves the bottle from Donnie and takes a long pull. Nico can't help but think of her on the swing, which is now a nub of chain on a rusted frame. How she went after the boy who was beating him up while he lay pathetically on the ground.

They've told one another about their lives after Savior House. After the place was shut down when its director disappeared. Donnie running off to Philly with Ben, joining a band, touring the world. Nico returning to Nicetown, getting fostered by a couple who both worked in television, one as a cameraman, the other a gaffer. Jenna taken in by a Frenchwoman, and now she's married, the stepmother of two daughters.

"You know someone tried to kill Arty too?" Jenna asks.

Nico and Donnie remain quiet.

"Arty came to Philadelphia for Ben's funeral," she explains. "I spoke to him." Her legs swing under the monkey bars. She's comfortable up high without holding on. "Arty thinks he knows who . . ."

Nico's heart skips.

"Who?" Donnie asks.

"Derek Brood."

The name causes a heavy silence.

Finally, Donnie says, "But it was a woman who went after me on the ship."

"She's a contract killer."

"She's a *what?*" Donnie asks, his tone incredulous.

"Did she go after you too?" Jenna asks Nico.

"I couldn't see who it was. Coal mines are dark as hell. But I think it was a woman."

"What happened to your shoulder?" she asks.

He's not wearing the sling, so he's not clear how she knows about his injury, though maybe he's favoring his right arm.

"Let me guess," Jenna says before he responds. "It was some type of pressurized puncture weapon that looks like a tube."

Nico considers her. "How'd you—"

"It's the same woman."

Donnie says, "We should, like, go to the police or talk to the FBI guy who's investigating Benny's murder."

Nico and Jenna exchange looks, as if they both know they can't go to the FBI.

"An agent showed me a picture and said it's the same woman who was after me on the ship," Donnie continues. "I saw her again in Florida at the beach."

"Did you call the FBI?" Jenna asks.

"No, they just showed up at the hospital."

"What did you tell them?"

"Nothing. I didn't know anything to tell. Couldn't remember what happened. It's only just come back to me."

"They speak to you?" she asks, looking at Nico.

He shakes his head. He doesn't mention the FBI subpoenaing his phone records. Possibly chasing him a few short hours ago.

In the weak light, Jenna has a perplexed look on her face. She says, "If she was on your ship, how could she have been in a West Virginia coal mine at the same time?"

Donnie says, "The FBI guy was asking the same thing, since we were out to sea when Benny was killed. It can't be the same lady."

Another long silence passes.

"What are we going to do?" Nico says.

"Can you both meet me tomorrow?" Jenna asks.

Neither answers.

Donnie's looking at the ground like he's lost in thought.

Nico hesitates. He wants out of this shithole forever.

"You have a plan?" Nico asks.

Jenna doesn't answer.

They're all thinking of the last time they executed a plan.

CHAPTER FIFTY-SEVEN

JENNA

TWENTY-FIVE YEARS AGO

Jenna puts on makeup, which she rarely wears. She's also borrowed a lower-cut shirt from one of the other girls who's more boy crazy. She looks at herself in the mirror, purses her lips, and heads downstairs to the chime of the dinner bell.

There are two long school-cafeteria-style tables in the dining room. Derek Brood and his crew of assholes catcall when they see Jenna. Mr. Brood, who always sits at the head of one of the tables, calls for quiet. They say grace and pass around bowls of whatever slop the kids on kitchen duty have come up with. Jenna sits across from Ben and asks him a question with her eyes: *Did you get the gun?* He nods. Next to him, Donnie stares absently at his plate but doesn't eat. He's been drinking during the day again, they've all noticed—his breath smelling of grapes, the cheap wine he swipes from the convenience store and stashes near the tree fort in those scary woods.

There's an empty chair where Annie usually sits.

Nico looks destroyed. His face has dirt on it and his fingernails are dark with grit. Mr. Brood tells him to go get cleaned up. Nico stands, the chair scraping on the floor.

"Where is she?" he demands of Mr. Brood.

This isn't part of the plan. Ben tells Nico to calm down, but he's staring daggers at Brood.

"Where's who?" Derek says. "That slut girlfriend of yours? She ran off. Probably at the bus station sucking—"

Nico lunges for Derek but is held back by Ben and Donnie.

"Enough!" Mr. Brood says. "Nico, I know you're upset. I've reported Annie missing to the agency and the police. I'm sure she just needed a break and will come back. It happens sometimes."

Nico's expression has hardened now. His gaze turns to Ben and he nods, then walks upstairs to clean up.

Arty appears in the doorway to the dining room. He usually doesn't eat with them. He spends most evenings a couple blocks away at Ned Flanders's house.

Derek takes notice. "I didn't know robots need to eat."

Derek's crew laughs too hard; it isn't even funny.

Arty apologizes to Mr. Brood for his tardiness. Mr. Brood gestures for him to sit.

It's true, Arty is an oddball, and, truth be told, he is a touch robotic.

"How's your project going?" Mr. Brood asks.

"Mr. Jones says we're going to get the funding."

"Good for you, Art." Mr. Brood addresses the table: "You see that, kids? You find something you're good at, work hard, and it will pay off."

Derek mumbles something under his breath. Mr. Brood swings his arm so the back of his hand smacks Derek in the mouth.

Jenna tries not to react, ignores the violence. Focuses on the plan.

It was Arty who devised the plan, after Nico told them all that the lady was coming for Jenna tomorrow:

Step 1: Nico digs a hole in the secluded clearing in the woods behind Flanders's house. Check.

Step 2: Ben and Donnie buy a handgun. Check.

Step 3: Jenna lures Mr. Brood to her room at lights-out.

Arty told them that Marta said Mr. Brood touched her. Hence Jenna's makeup and cleavage.

After dinner, Derek goes out. He's Mr. Brood's son, not one of the foster kids—or "loser orphans" as he likes to call them—and isn't subject to the same rules.

At lights-out, Jenna asks Mr. Brood if she can speak with him about something. In private.

Mr. Brood comes to her room. After he enters, Jenna closes the door, but he casually walks back over and opens it.

That's when Ben appears from the closet, Donnie behind him. Ben strikes Mr. Brood with the butt of the gun, which is supposed to knock him out, but it doesn't. Mr. Brood takes Donnie down easily with a punch to the chest. He then charges Ben, tackling him to the floor.

Jenna's heart is pounding. She's supposed to be the bait. But they need her help. She looks for something heavy that she can hit Mr. Brood with and finds nothing.

Donnie is curled up, gasping for air, while Mr. Brood straddles Ben, his fist raised. Brood is a big man, six foot, more than two hundred pounds.

Jenna is about to jump on Brood's back, to scratch at his eyes like her father taught her, when Arty appears in the room. He has what looks like a car battery with shoulder straps attached to it draped over his small frame. In each hand, battery cables. He walks to Mr. Brood, who's still on top of Ben, and jams both ends of the cables on either side of Mr. Brood's ribs. Both Brood and Ben scream.

Arty pulls back the cables, and Ben manages to push Brood off of him. And Arty shocks Brood again. But Brood doesn't go down. He's so damned big. He grabs Arty by the neck and begins squeezing. Arty doesn't dare shock Brood now because the current will run through both of them.

Jenna comes from behind and kicks Mr. Brood between the legs, which causes him to buck forward. He claws at Arty, then bites Arty on the shoulder, eliciting a wail. Brood manages to stand up, his mouth red with blood. He makes the mistake of no longer being in physical contact with Arty, who takes the opportunity to touch the ends of the battery cables to Brood's neck.

Brood vibrates and makes an unusual sound like a scream that's choked off. Arty removes the cables and that's when Ben hits Brood with the butt of the gun again, taking him down.

Minutes later, Mr. Brood is in a wheelbarrow, ranting at them through his gag as they roll him into the woods.

PART 3

THE TRUTH

CHAPTER FIFTY-EIGHT

THE TWINS

PRESENT DAY

"We need to take care of him," Casey says into the burner phone. She's at an Airbnb in what passes for the nice side of Chestertown. Her sister, Haley, is sprawled out on the bed watching a show on her laptop.

"Are you crazy?" the client snaps. "An FBI agent? The Feds'll throw every resource they have at it."

"I'm not seeing much of a choice. He followed me into the restaurant. He knows." She glances out the window, watches bugs bounce against the porch light.

"Are you sure?"

"I told you, the benefit of hiring us is two sets of eyes. And, yeah, he followed me all the way there and waited outside until we left." Casey wrinkles her nose, thinking of the low-quality beef at the steakhouse where Derek Brood took her for dinner. She adds, "That Lara Croft wannabe bitch was also following and backed off when she saw him. It's not going to take long for the agent to put everything together." Casey snaps her finger at Haley to pause the show on the laptop. She cups the receiver and says, "Don't watch the rose ceremony without me."

They both love *The Bachelor.*

An audible breath blows into Casey's ear over the phone line.

"This has all gotten out of hand."

She makes no reply. She catches Haley's glance and rolls her eyes at the client's whining. She waits as he wrings his hands.

"You know where to find him?" he asks.

"Yeppers," she says. Haley followed the agent after he left the restaurant. He's staying in a hotel off the interstate. It's only two mile markers down from the hotel where the old rock star is staying with the writer.

"Okay," he says.

Casey disconnects the line, falls onto the bed next to Haley. The laptop bounces and Haley catches it before it tumbles to the floor.

Casey looks at the screen. One of the contestants, a thirsty bitch named Dallas, is frozen, her face distorted. "If he gives her the rose, I'm going to lose it. . . ."

Before they resume the show, Casey says, "We need to be careful with this one. We'll need some space, somewhere secluded. Find out what the agent knows."

Haley thinks about it. They face each other and simultaneously say, "Semitruck."

They're two peas in a pod.

Haley says, "I wanna play the runaway teen hooker."

Casey replies, "You got to last time. And we need you to play the corporate executive." Though they are so much alike, their divergent upbringings suit them for certain roles.

Haley hits play and the show resumes. They both swear at the screen as Dallas, wearing a slinky sequined dress, totters down from the group of girls and accepts her rose.

CHAPTER FIFTY-NINE

DONNIE

Donnie wakes up in the Holiday Inn Express. The room has two single beds and a sofa sleeper. The bed next to his is empty, but it's been slept in. And there's a sound coming from the sofa, a male form under a blanket—Nico. It's coming back to him: the playground with Nico and Jenna, the decision to stay together, safety in numbers, the bed spins before he passed out. He rises, stumbles to the bathroom, and relieves his bladder. He wonders where Jenna is. She's the one who insisted they all cram into Donnie's small room at the interstate hotel.

He's still wearing his clothes from yesterday. Raising his arm, he smells his armpit. *Whoa.* He needs a shower. But first he needs to regroup.

He's feeling unusually restless today. Not the hangxiety or boozanoia you get sometimes when you drink too much, but a genuine sense of impending doom. He supposes that's understandable. Jenna said that Derek Brood hired the crazy lady who forced him off the boat and probably whoever tried to blow up Nico in the coal mine *and* whoever tried to assassinate Artemis

Templeton. Did Brood also have Benny killed? The news said they'd made an arrest of some dude Benny had put away. But that FBI agent seemed skeptical about that.

Donnie opens the curtains a crack. The room is on the ground floor and faces the parking lot. Jenna is pacing outside as she talks on her phone.

"You got any aspirin?" Nico says, sitting up, his eyes squinting from the light.

"Sure, Hollywood." Donnie digs into his travel bag. The bottle of Advil rattles as he tosses it to Nico, who misses the catch.

Nico downs the pills without water. He looks around the room.

"Where's Jenna?"

"On a call outside." Donnie gestures to the window.

Nico looks pale, clammy.

There's a knock on the door, sending a wave of panic through him. But it can't be the crazy hit lady. Jenna's outside and would warn them. Donnie peers through the peephole. It's Reeves.

Donnie opens the door, steps outside. He doesn't want Reeves to see Nico. It will invite more questions. Donnie sees Jenna eyeing them from across the lot, phone still pressed to her ear.

"I'm headed out," Reeves says. "I wanted to say goodbye before the Uber gets here." He hands Donnie the keys to the rental car.

"Cool, man. We'll connect next week?"

Reeves nods.

"I'm looking forward to seeing what you put together for the book," Donnie says.

"Me too. You've given me a lot of material to work with."

"Try not to make me look too stupid, okay, Hemingway?" Donnie grins. They shake hands.

The Uber pulls into the lot, and Reeves heads over. Before he gets in, he stops, calls out. "Hey, Donnie."

"Yeah?"

"It was an honor to hear your story."

"Shucks, man." Donnie gives him a crooked smile.

The Uber disappears, and Donnie returns to the room.

"Who was that?" Nico asks, seeming both curious and concerned.

"A writer."

"Writer?"

"Yeah. Long story, but we're working on a book about my life, if you can believe that."

Nico raises a brow.

"Don't worry. It's about the band."

"Is that why you're here? I hope he's not going to dig into—"

"Don't worry, Hollywood. It's all good."

Nico tilts his head to the side. "What if he—"

"Don't worry. The book won't get into anything before I joined Tracer." It's a lie, but not a big one.

"Then why are you in Chestertown?"

Donnie decides it's safe to tell Nico about his conversation with Benny's law clerk and the cryptic message he left for Donnie.

"He said we all had it wrong. He said, 'The proof is with Boo Radley.'"

"What the hell does that mean?" asks Nico.

"You got me, boss. Boo Radley apparently is a character in a book. I thought coming back might rattle something loose."

"And . . ."

"And no such luck."

"I hate this fucking town." Nico sighs.

"Me too, Hollywood. Me too."

CHAPTER SIXTY

JENNA

In the hotel's parking lot, Jenna looks out at the interstate, the steady hum of traffic making it hard to hear Artemis on her cell phone.

"You are sure?" he asks in that monotone voice of his.

"As sure as I can be. I don't think either of them reached out to the FBI. Donnie said the agent came to his hospital room, showed him a photo of a woman who was on the cruise ship. But there's no way she could've been on the ship and in D.C. when the hitter tried to take you out." Jenna still hasn't told him that she was the shooter. That the woman who set her up for the job knew about her past with The Corporation and threatened her family.

"You believe him?"

"I think so. Donnie hasn't changed all that much and doesn't exactly keep things close to the vest."

Artemis makes a noise of agreement, no doubt recalling the whimsical southern boy from their youth. "What about Nico?

My team says he's a TV producer but owes a sizable sum to the O'Learys."

"Who are the O'Learys?"

"A Philadelphia crime family."

"What's the debt for? Drugs?"

"No, gambling."

The other reason people borrow money from bankers who wear leather jackets and gold chains and carry brass knuckles.

"Nico said he hasn't spoken to the FBI and when Donnie mentioned reaching out to the agent Nico shot it down quickly." She notices that Donnie is outside the hotel room now. He's talking to someone, a guy who looks like a college professor—blazer with jeans, wavy hair that touches his shoulders.

"Okay, I guess we need to *approach* Derek Brood." Artemis says *approach* like it's a code for something.

"The agent's following him, so I'm not sure about the best play here," Jenna says.

"In business, sometimes you have to go directly to the top."

Jenna listens . . . waits.

"I'm going to set up a meeting," Artemis finally says.

"Just like that?"

"You'd be surprised how quickly people drop everything when I call."

"Okay, a meeting. Then what?"

"I'll have a business discussion with Brood. If that doesn't work, well, you'll have to join the meeting. And you'll need to bring Donnie and Nico. Like before." Artemis clearly wants them to be part of whatever happens so they all have something to lose.

"And how will I know if your negotiation is successful or unsuccessful?"

"Easy."

Jenna waits.

"If it's not a success, he'll bring the woman who's been trying to kill us all."

CHAPTER SIXTY-ONE

THE TWINS

Casey wanders the lot. Semis are lined up to create an oversized maze at the truck stop. They need a truck. It's the best portable interrogation site around. Isolated, windowless, easy to clean, hard to trace.

She's mussed her hair, donned a tank top and fishnet stockings she ripped. For this role, she needs to look like a teen who's trying to look like she's young and for sale—fishnets are how television depicts prostitutes, and how Casey imagines a runaway would offer her wares.

The universal signal—Casey learned it from five minutes on the internet—is flashing headlights. She also learned the going rate for a lot lizard is 30/60/90—each for a sex act more awful than the last.

When no one flashes their lights, she decides to be more aggressive. She climbs the steps to a rig, knocks on the window. The trucker rolls down the glass.

"I'm sorry, but I'm not interested." He has a lined face, beard, displays his wedding ring.

Casey considers jolting him with the stun gun, her second favorite weapon of choice after the captive bolt, but he's a big guy.
The hand he displayed with the ring is as big as a bear's, and the
current from the mini stun gun that's designed to look like a tube
of lipstick might not take him down. Casey steps off and continues roaming the lot. She hadn't anticipated it taking so long. It's
lunchtime. Maybe that's the problem. She might just have to steal
a truck. She's driven a rig—her uncle is a long-hauler—but she
doesn't know how to hot-wire one.

She goes inside the diner. Finds a spot where she's hard to
miss. She looks like she's been on the streets for a time, but with
her curves and face she's not your average lot lizard. Someone
will bite at the hook. She orders a water and gets a frown from
the waitress.

"You can't sit in here unless you order food."

Bitch.

Casey isn't hungry, so she decides she'll head back to the lot.
But a voice from one of the booths says, "You hungry? Go ahead
and order, I'll take care of it."

A man in his late twenties—a clean-cut white trucker with a
friendly smile—waves at her.

The waitress seems like she may say something to Casey,
warn her perhaps, but instead asks impatiently what Casey wants.
She orders pancakes.

"Pancakes in the afternoon?" the guy says.

Casey shrugs.

He smiles. "I like breakfast all day too."

Casey minds her own business, plays hard to get.

The food arrives, and Casey eats like she's starving. Uses her
fingers.

"Where you headed?" the man asks.

She shrugs.

"Strong silent type. I get it."

She eats, her eyes rising to catch his.

He wears a vest and jeans and it's hard to tell if he's a creep or Good Samaritan.

"I'm going to New York," she says.

He nods. "What's in New York?"

She shrugs again.

He pulls out a wad of bills. Puts the money on the table for his check, then walks over, drops a twenty for hers.

"This ought to cover it. Safe travels," he says, and heads to the door.

She almost calls out to him, but patience is the key.

The man makes it to the door, stops. "I'm headed north," he says.

And there it is. She keeps eating.

"I can drop you in Newark if that helps?"

She doesn't reply.

He lingers for a beat, then says, "Well, good luck to you."

"Wait," she says, before he's out the door.

The waitress is watching, shaking her head like she's seen this a million times before.

"What do I have to do in return for the ride?"

The guy looks baffled, then understands. "Oh my. You don't have to do anything. I'm—It's not like that."

Casey nods, pays the check, then follows him out.

On the way, he tells her his name is Chet.

Still in character, she doesn't offer her name.

His rig is parked next to about ten others side-by-side in the lot. He climbs the steps to the cabin, gestures for her to go to the other side.

Ten minutes later, they're on I-95. Breaking the quiet, she asks, "What are you hauling?"

"I just dropped off a load in Wilmington, and I'm heading to New Jersey for another."

Casey nods. That's what she needs. An empty trailer. She feels for the lipstick stun gun tucked into the pocket on her skirt.

"You have family in New York?" he asks.

"Something like that."

"I hear you. I've got a lot of *something like that* in my life too." He smiles. It's a nice smile. He's handsome in a plain, almost dopey way.

"Want me to turn on some music or something?" he asks.

"Whatever you'd like."

He says, "I like the quiet. Out here, on the road, you turn off the radio and it's like you're on a deserted island. No bosses, no parents, no TV, no social media. It's peaceful."

He looks ahead at the interstate like he's taking it in. Like it's a scenic villa in Italy or some kind of long-hauler's pilgrimage trail.

"Does it get lonely?" she asks. Casey spent the first eighteen years of her life on the farm feeling a deep sense of loneliness. Until she found Haley, reunited after the twins had been so cruelly separated at birth. She's learned that it's common, twins separated at birth. Great for social scientists who do nature-versus-nurture research, but not so much for the twins themselves.

"Lonely?" He thinks about this. "Not really. I pick up hitch-hikers sometimes. And we have the CB. But I'm fine on my own."

It sounds nice. He's nice. She contemplates getting out at the next truck stop, finding a different rig. Then she imagines Haley mocking her for going soft on this dude.

"Oh crap," she says. She digs through her backpack.

"What is it?"

"I left my wallet at the diner. It's got my ID."

"Oh no." He looks at his watch. "I can take you back."

"No. I can get back there. Pull over at the next stop and I'll figure it out."

He thinks more, then acquiesces, no idea how lucky he is.

At the exit for the next truck stop, he veers off the interstate, slows to a stop in the lot. He smiles again, looks at her. "I really don't mind taking you back."

"No, you have a job to get to. I can handle it."

"You be careful out there."

She nods, then turns to open the door.

In an instant, she experiences a wave of panic as she feels an arm clenched around her neck choke-hold-style, and a cloth clamped against her face. She feels a burning sensation on her cheeks, nose, and lips, and before she can fight him off her world goes black.

CHAPTER SIXTY-TWO

JENNA

Back in the hotel room, Jenna sits cross-legged on the bed. Nico sits on the sofa, and Donnie shuffles on his feet, emanating nervous energy. She can't help but flash back to Savior House, the kids sitting at the long dining room table as Mr. Brood held court.

"I spoke to Arty," she tells them.

They say nothing.

"He has a plan."

Both men look down, no doubt remembering the last time Artemis Templeton had a plan.

"He's going to set up a meeting with Derek, offer him money to drop this."

Nico raises his eyes. "He thinks that will work? Whoever is trying to kill us hired a contract killer. Maybe more than one. They went on a cruise ship, blew up a coal mine, you said they went after your family. I don't think this is about money."

Jenna shrugs.

Nico continues, "Derek agreed to meet?"

"Arty's reaching out to him, but he seemed confident he could set it up."

"Where? Somewhere public, I hope? If not, Arty ought to make sure his affairs are in order," Nico says.

Jenna agrees that somewhere public would be the safest course. But she also knows it *won't* be a public meeting, in case Jenna has to execute the backup plan.

Donnie remains quiet, his eyes still on the matted carpet. Finally, he asks, "What if he won't take the money?"

Jenna figures he already knows the answer. "Arty will convince him. He suggested it would take a lot of zeros."

"But what if he doesn't take it?" Donnie asks again.

Nico and Jenna share a knowing glance.

Jenna says, "In that case, Arty asked that all three of us come. That we try to convince him to stop this nonsense."

Donnie stares out at nothing, and Jenna pictures a younger version of that same vacant stare on a rainy night twenty-five years ago.

Nico clears his throat. "I'd bet on Arty getting it done."

Jenna's burner phone pings with a text. "It's set," she tells them. "Tonight at seven o'clock. Say what you want about Artemis Templeton, he makes things happen."

"Maybe that's the damn problem," Donnie says.

Ignoring that, Nico asks, "Where do we meet?"

"Seven o'clock . . . at Savior House." She waits for the questions, the concerns, about the locale—their now-shuttered group home.

Instead, Donnie goes into the restroom. There's the sound of the faucet. When he comes out, his face is wet, like he's doused himself.

He moves to the door.

"Where you going, Don?" Nico asks.

Donnie doesn't answer. He opens the door, goes outside, then closes it behind him.

Nico gives Jenna a curious look.

Jenna goes to the window, moves the curtains, and looks outside. She sees Donnie's rental car tearing out of the lot.

CHAPTER SIXTY-THREE

THE TWINS

Casey opens her eyes. Everything is blurry and she's disoriented. Before she comprehends what's going on, she feels hands around her neck. When she sees the trucker's face, it all comes back to her like a knife to the chest. The trucker pulling over to let her out, the chloroformed rag over her nose and mouth. The rig isn't moving. Maybe she's only been out for a few seconds. She has no idea.

The trucker looks her deep in the eyes, squeezes her neck hard enough to show he's serious. It's strange how his face has changed, morphed from the aw-shucks guy-next-door into a dead-eyed killer.

Still holding her neck, he says, "You're going to get in the back and do what I say."

Casey nods. She sees her skirt is hiked up, but the fishnets are still on, like she regained consciousness sooner than the trucker expected. He releases his hold on her neck, shows her a large hunting knife.

"I'll do whatever you want. Just don't hurt me."

"Get back there and take off your clothes. If you scream, I

won't hesitate to use this." He raises the knife. The long blade is smudged with dirt or maybe blood that's gone brown.

Casey's heart is beating, adrenaline flowing. Her face feels sunburned, tender.

She climbs into the cabin behind the front seats, which is separated by a curtain. In the back, there's a mattress. Then she notices the handcuffs. The jug of lubricant. The sex toys.

She takes off her tank top, baring her breasts.

The trucker appears excited, but he makes himself look out the windshield checking the lot before climbing in back with her.

He grabs her by the neck with one hand again, looks her in the eyes.

She gently puts a hand on his. "You don't have to be rough. Slow down. Let's do this right."

But his grip doesn't loosen. He doesn't *have* to be rough; he *wants* to be rough.

He removes his hand and starts unbuttoning his pants. It's then that Casey removes her skirt, taking the lipstick stun gun from the pocket and putting it on top of her pile of clothes as if it fell out.

Chet's about to pounce.

Casey pushes herself back against the wall, spreads her legs. While he's distracted by that, she palms the lipstick, untwists the cap with one hand.

He's crawling toward her, breathing heavily. She startles when he jumps on top of her. As he's about to violate her, she jams the stun into his neck. She triggers the device, struggling out from under him. She holds it against his neck as Chet sputters, spasms, and collapses, incapacitated now. Casey's eyes land on the hunting knife that he left within easy reach.

She scolds herself for being fooled. For thinking of letting him go. Lesson learned: Show no mercy.

He's motionless but she gives him another three million volts, just to be sure. He vibrates like a man on the electric chair, then goes still again.

Naked from the waist down, he moans, drool bubbling at the corner of his mouth.

Still naked herself, Casey places the stun gun directly on his cock.

"I know you didn't want me to make any noise," she says, looking him straight in his widening eyes. "But I'm fine if *you* want to scream."

CHAPTER SIXTY-FOUR

NICO

Nico shushes Jenna as he watches the local newscast on the hotel room's television. On the screen is a photo of Ben Wood in his black robe, looking dashing and distinguished.

"There've been new developments in the murder of a prominent Philadelphia federal judge. The primary suspect in the murder, Damon Angelos, was released due to insufficient evidence. Angelos, who had threatened Judge Wood during his sentencing in an unrelated case nearly a decade ago, was arrested shortly after Judge Wood's body was found in Delaware County. A spokesperson for the Philadelphia Police Department has declined to comment other than to say that Mr. Angelos is no longer a suspect."

Jenna says, "The hit woman's frame-up apparently didn't stick."

The newscaster continues, "Angelos's release comes on the heels of another development in the case. Police released video footage of Judge Wood the day before his body was found in an industrial area of Chestertown."

An image of Ben paying for gas and a bottled water at a gas

station appears on the screen. "The judge was caught on the security camera at a gas station in Chestertown, ending speculation that he had been carjacked and taken there."

The screen flips to another image of Ben, this time in a building lined with bookshelves. "That same afternoon, the judge was captured on video at the Chestertown community library. Police are asking anyone who may have seen Judge Wood that day or has any additional information to contact them at the number on your screen."

Nico considers this. Why the library? Ben used to spend a lot of time there, but why now? He pictures Ben lugging an armful of books into his room at Savior House. Then it hits him: "Boo Radley," he says, aloud.

Jenna gives him a quizzical look.

"Ben's law clerk gave Donnie a message from him." Nico stops. "Ben referenced a character from a book. She said, 'The proof is with Boo Radley.'"

"From *To Kill a Mockingbird*?" Jenna says.

Nico thinks so, nods. "He gives a message about some book after he was at a library. . . ."

"Maybe he left something hidden in the book or something?" Jenna says, as if thinking aloud.

"It can't hurt to check it out."

Jenna doesn't answer but instead grabs the motorcycle helmet and charges outside, Nico on her heels.

CHAPTER SIXTY-FIVE

Nico's holding on to Jenna's waist as she races the motorcycle through the streets of Chestertown. She chivalrously offered him the helmet and he didn't refuse. Her hair flows in the wind like she's some kind of superhero. She kind of is, he thinks. And he's glad she's here. She inspires confidence. He doesn't know what happened to her—where life took her after Savior House. Perhaps it was the military or some other field training, since she seems unflappable. She has mentioned her family, but she's otherwise been vague about her past.

Fifteen minutes later, they pull into the empty lot of the Francis L. Rizzo Library. Nico remembers going to the library on that day he doesn't want to think about, Ben insistent they needed to go.

They go inside and the place still smells the same, aged paper and printer's ink. The building is old, but well cared for. To the left is the kids' section. Beanbag chairs dot the floor and face a bulletin board covered with cutout letters that say: OUR BOOKS ARE BETTER. A poster with the Cat in the Hat says: READ. To the right are rows of bookshelves and smaller bookstands displaying hardcovers and audiobooks. Straight ahead, a librarian sits at a reference desk.

Jenna makes a beeline for the reference computer. She taps on the keyboard, finds what she's looking for, and points to the call number. She then leads Nico to one of the shelves, passing the library's current patrons: an elderly man reading a newspaper at one of the tables and a homeless guy asleep in a lounge chair.

Jenna runs her fingers along the books and stops. She pulls two books from the shelf, both copies of *To Kill a Mockingbird*. She hands one to Nico and starts flipping through the pages, examining the spine, looking for a note tucked in or message written inside. Nico does the same thing with his copy.

They do this until both come up empty.

"It was a long shot," Jenna says.

"I thought we were going to find something. I mean, he was here. And Boo Radley. What else could it mean if he wasn't referring to the character?"

They return the books to the shelf and approach the reference desk. The librarian—a thirtysomething woman with dimples and sparkling eyes—looks up from her paperwork. "Can I help you?"

Jenna takes the lead. "I hope so," she says, smiling. "We're doing a podcast about the murder of Benjamin Wood, and we understand he visited the library, and we hoped you might be willing to talk to us."

She regards Nico. "Are you on that show with the miners?"

It's not like Nico to get flustered, but the librarian is gorgeous. At first he thought she looked like one of those perky Pilates women, but he notices she has tattoos sleeved on both arms. Famous literary quotes and images, by the looks of them.

"That's me." He grins.

"My brother's a big fan of the show," she says. "I'm not much of a reality TV person, myself, but I've watched a few episodes with him and those coal miners—well, they're characters."

"You have no idea," Nico says. "Maybe we should send your brother a selfie?" He widens his mischievous smile.

Her eyes light up. "That would be hilarious." She's already tapping on her phone.

Nico takes the phone, turns around, and takes the shot of the two of them. He examines the photo and is surprised that the librarian has her tongue sticking out like the guy from Kiss and is making the sign of the horns with her hand. A pose only a big brother would appreciate.

He returns her phone and she looks at the shot. "Oh, he'll love this. Thank you."

Nico says, "So, we wondered if you remember anything from the day Judge Wood visited the library."

"Like I told the FBI agent, I didn't even see the judge that day."

"You didn't see him at all?" Jenna asks.

"I wish I had. But no. The FBI apparently tracked the judge's phone here. They asked for our security camera footage." Her eyes move to the cameras mounted on the ceiling.

"We saw the video of the judge on the news. Have you seen it?"

"Oh yeah."

"Do you know where he was in the library, what section?" Nico turns and gestures around.

The librarian hesitates. "We don't give out information on customers—what someone chooses to read is their own business. But I suppose it's okay to tell you where he was since the video's been made public. He was in the back there." She points to the far corner away from the shelves.

They thank her and walk over. The section has a sign that

reads: DELAWARE COUNTY PROPERTY RECORDS. There are stacks of large ledgers and books that look like boundary plats and other land archives.

"What do you think he was doing over here?" Nico asks.

Jenna shakes her head like she hasn't a clue. "I mean how often would anyone be looking through this stuff? Most records are probably available online." She walks over to a large bound volume that's on top of a reference table. She opens it and flips the pages absently. It seems like a complicated dead end.

Still, she flips through the volume slowly, stopping at a page that's bookmarked. The makeshift bookmark is a scrap of paper someone has folded into a five-pointed star.

"This is Carver Street. That's two blocks from Savior House."

Nico stands next to her. He picks up the bookmark.

Jenna has a flash of a memory of Ben at the library, a group of folded stars on the table where he was reading.

The memory is confirmed when Nico puts his finger on some writing on the star:

Brood-Robot LLC-Fagin Jones

"You think Ben wrote this?" Nico asks. Before Jenna answers, he adds, "What's it mean?"

"I have no idea," Jenna says. "But it lists an LLC, and I know someone who's an expert at tracking companies and identifying people."

"Who's that?" Nico asks.

"An adorable tax lawyer."

CHAPTER SIXTY-SIX

DONNIE

The rental car is vibrating. Donnie's foot is to the floor and he hasn't slowed since he peeled out of the hotel parking lot. His thoughts are swimming, his chest having a hard time capturing air, his knuckles white on the steering wheel. He needs to slow down. Breathe.

He takes controlled breaths, trying to level himself off, trying to stem the panic attack or whatever this is.

He can't do this anymore. It's all too much. Benny is gone and nothing he does is going to change that. If Derek Brood wants Donnie dead for what they did, so be it. He's survived Derek before and he'll do it again. But he's spent more than half his life trying to escape what they did that night, and he'll be damned if he's going to do it again.

He needs a drink.

He eyes the landscape. There's a billboard for a strip club off Exit 43. He's always been popular at the clubs; one of Tracer's Bullet's songs is a staple for pole dancers. It's no "Pour Some Sugar on Me," but a close second.

He decides against it. The dancers love social media, and he doesn't need attention right now. He's still in the afterglow of his fall—correction, push—off the cruise ship, so there's a risk paparazzi would notice the posts and show up.

He sees a sign for Lester. There's gotta be a hole-in-the-wall bar there. Every forgettable drive-over town has a dank bar where patrons mind their own business. He takes the exit and follows the signs into town.

Sure enough, there it is, a bar called Drink. *If you insist*, he thinks. He parks the car on the street and heads inside.

At the over-glossed bar Donnie orders a Maker's Mark from the bearded barman. The customers include a barfly who wears too much eyeliner, an old-timer with a face like an old leather shoe, a tattooed guy crouching over his drink like he's in the prison mess hall. If any of them recognize Donnie, they don't show it. Donnie takes his drink to a table in the back.

The familiar sting of the whiskey reaches his sinuses and warms his insides. He doesn't want to think about it all, but he can't turn off the questions in his head. Will Jenna and Nico and Arty kill another Brood? What about that gal trying to kill them? Will they off her too? Where does it stop?

His mind floats to Benny again. *It's okay, I'm here.*

But you're not here. I'm scared, Benny.

He finishes the drink, walks over, orders another.

On his fourth Maker's, he's feeling the familiar soupy sensation in his head. The barfly keeps glancing over, but he's not in the mood. His thoughts go to Reeves Rothschild, wondering what the writer will make of the fragments of life that he's shared with the young man. The past few days, he's opened old sores, exposed some of them to Reeves, and now it feels like they're infected again. Maybe his true fear is that when he reads the pages he'll realize that his career, his life, are a joke, the punch line him falling out of a boat. He closes his eyes, massages his temples with a hand.

When he opens them, there's a man standing in front of his table. It's the FBI agent. Rodriguez is his name.

"Can we talk?" he asks.

Donnie considers protesting, telling him to piss off. But instead he kicks the chair opposite, sliding it open a gap, an invitation to sit.

"Get you a drink?" Donnie offers.

Agent Rodriguez shakes his head. "Not while I'm on duty."

Donnie frowns, downs his Maker's. "Suit yourself. But I'm getting another." He stands.

"You know what? Sure, I'll take a beer."

"What kind?" Donnie asks.

"Surprise me."

Donnie returns with two glasses of whiskey. "Surprise!" he says, setting down the drinks.

The FBI agent lets out an exasperated sigh. But he reaches for the drink, takes a sip, winces like it's rocket fuel.

"I was hoping we could talk," Rodriguez says.

"Talkin' is a two-way street, man," Donnie says. "Last time, our conversation went one way."

The agent nods, gives a *fair enough* expression. "You have questions? Ask away."

Donnie takes a pull of his drink. "All right, who killed Benny?"

"That's what I'm trying to figure out."

"I thought y'all made an arrest. One of the criminals he put away."

"The FBI didn't make that arrest. Philly PD did. Based on an anonymous tip. They've since had to release the suspect."

Donnie narrows his eyes.

The agent continues, "It looks like a setup. Someone must've researched defendants who'd previously threatened Judge Wood. During his sentencing eight years ago, some dipshit threatened the judge, and it was reported in the newspapers. Google Ben's name and the word 'threat' and it's the first link that pops up."

"And what? You think whoever killed Benny researched it and dropped a dime on the guy?"

"Looks that way. The guy has an airtight alibi. He was in Kansas City at the time, visiting his brother."

"So, who, then? That woman in the picture you showed me?"

"Possibly."

"Who is she?"

"I don't know."

"Well, what *do* you know? You came all the way here for a reason."

The FBI agent retrieves his phone, shows a photo to Donnie. It's a skeleton, displayed on a sheet or blanket. The agent swipes his finger and there's a close-up of the skull, which has a hole in the forehead the size of a quarter with hairline cracks shooting out from its circumference. He swipes again and there are five shell casings that appear to be covered with mud or dirt.

"Damn, who's that?"

"We're not sure."

Donnie shakes his head, puts on his best poker face.

"We had our computer forensic team do a deep dive into Judge Wood's computer—his phone's still missing—and they found these photos."

Donnie tries not to react, but his thoughts trip to what Mia told him: *Someone was blackmailing him.*

"I don't understand," he tells Rodriguez. "Maybe it was from one of his cases or somethin'."

"We considered that. But there was a message with the pictures. It said there's DNA from the victim's teeth and the gun and Ben could purchase it for one hundred K and help fix a case. Two days after receiving these photos, Judge Wood withdrew one hundred thousand dollars from his account."

Donnie shrugs, tries to look befuddled. "His wife's rich, so that's not a lot of money to them."

Agent Rodriguez frowns.

"So you think whoever sent the photos killed him?"

The FBI agent cocks his head. "I don't know. But that doesn't make much sense to me. Why kill him? He withdrew the funds, so it looks like he either paid the blackmail or planned to."

"I'm sorry, boss, but I'm not following ya."

"You know what I think?" the agent says.

Donnie drains his glass, waits for him to continue.

"I think that Judge Wood did something when he was younger and, given the bones, I can only surmise it was something terrible, and someone knew and was blackmailing him. Maybe others were involved with whatever happened to that skeleton." He gives Donnie a pointed look.

"Interesting theory."

"And maybe Judge Wood tried to figure out who was blackmailing him and found something new. Does Boo Radley mean anything to you?"

"No, why?" Donnie lies.

"No reason," the agent lies back at him. Obviously, the law clerk told the agent the same thing she told Donnie about Benny's message.

"You have *any* idea who was blackmailing him?" Donnie asks.

The agent hesitates, like he's considering how much to share. "Let's just say we think we identified a case Judge Wood might have fixed—a highly unusual dismissal of a racketeering charge against a member of the O'Leary family out of the Nicetown neighborhood in Philly. You know anyone from Nicetown?"

Donnie shakes his head.

"And the photo of the bones, well, it was sent from a computer in West Virginia. The URL's from a computer owned by a TV network."

Donnie still isn't following.

Then it hits him hard, like a semitruck barreling down the highway.

Nico.

CHAPTER SIXTY-SEVEN

NICO

"Where are we going?" Nico asks Jenna as she hides the motorcycle in the tall weeds on a vacant lot a block from Savior House.

"To Mr. Get off My Lawn's place," Jenna says.

Nico smiles, remembering all the crazy names they had for the characters in their Chestertown neighborhood. There was Meth Head Ted, who was in dire need of dentistry, Ned Flanders, the guy who was helping Arty with his computer projects, Urkel, the Black guy with thick glasses who worked at the bodega. They had more nicknames for folks than coal miners. Mr. Get off My Lawn was the neighbor across the street from Savior House. A crank who sat on his porch with a perpetual scowl, complained about the group home ruining the neighborhood, threatened them if they so much as stepped a foot on his grass.

They push through a rusted chain-link gate to the backyard, which, like the rest of the neighborhood, is unkempt and half-dead.

Jenna pulls open the screen door, which hangs on only one hinge, then kicks the doorknob, causing the lock to splinter and the door to burst open.

There's the clicking sound of tiny feet, and Nico shudders as he thinks back to those rats in the mine. The past three days truly have been a surreal disaster.

Jenna sweeps the house for any unwanted tenants, both of the two- and four-legged variety. Then she pries open a board covering the front window, giving them a clear view of Savior House.

"What now?" Nico asks, glancing at his phone. The meeting with Derek Brood isn't for three hours.

Jenna looks at him like it's a dumb question: "We wait."

An hour passes and Nico glances up from his phone and notices Jenna staring at him. He's already made several bets on DraftKings.

Jenna says, "I have a teenager and she spends less time glued to her phone than you."

"Um, am I supposed to be doing something else? Forgive me, I don't know stakeout etiquette."

Jenna frowns, continues contemplating him. "Can I ask you something?"

Nico shrugs.

"I don't remember . . . why were you at Savior House? I mean, what happened to your parents?"

Nico doesn't know why she's asking. It's an odd question all things considered. What does it matter?

"My old man, he was, for lack of a better word, a fiend."

"He abused you?"

Nico isn't much for therapy hour, but there's nothing else to do. "Not so much me. Mostly my mom. She took it for years, but finally she had to escape."

He remembers the day at the beach. He thumbs the Saint Christopher necklace that matches the one she wore.

"Did you ever reconnect with them?"

Nico releases a cynical laugh. "My dad disappeared, an occupational hazard when you work for the O'Learys. And my mom, no, I never saw her again."

For years, Nico was so angry at her. He once did some internet sleuthing and found out she was alive. She was not on social media, but there was a local newspaper story about Gloria Adakai organizing a bake sale with funds going to a domestic abuse shelter in Los Angeles. She'd always dreamed of living on the West Coast. He considered reaching out, but she's an old woman now. If she wanted to locate him, Nico isn't hard to find.

"Your parents?" Nico asks.

Jenna shakes her head. "Car crash. What I wouldn't give to see them again . . ."

Nico decides to change the subject: "I've googled 'Fagin Jones' and 'Robot LLC' and come up with nothing. Assuming it was Ben who wrote the note, what's with all the cryptic messages? I mean, why not spell it out?"

Jenna shrugs. "He was a judge, didn't want anyone to know, I suppose. And the note from the library was just a note to himself, he knew what it meant. Anyway, we'll see what my husband finds."

Nico feels a wave of guilt. Maybe if he hadn't been so shameless, so greedy, Ben would still be here. Maybe if he wouldn't have gotten in so deep with Shane O'Leary.

Maybe if he'd admit that the reason he never reached out to his mom is that he knows the hard reality: that she has no interest in seeing her cowardly son—the one who didn't protect her.

Nico examines Jenna as she peers out the window. What would the oddsmakers give the chances of Derek Brood backing down, taking Arty's money? And what happens if he refuses?

What odds would they give on Nico coming out on the other side of this, particularly with that FBI agent seeming to know that he blackmailed Ben?

Nico loves the thrill of beating the odds. But this is a long shot not even he would take.

CHAPTER SIXTY-EIGHT

THE TWINS

Outside the dive bar, Haley waves to Casey, who's driving the semitruck. Casey's face is tomato red and she's wearing a trucker hat. That driver picked the wrong girl. . . .

Casey pulls the rig to the side of the road. The vehicle is too big for the area and risks grabbing a cop's attention, so they need to be fast. They're losing daylight and Casey's sideshow with the truck driver cost them time.

While Casey was with the trucker, Haley tracked the FBI agent. He's going to notice her tailing him sooner or later, so it's now or never.

The agent has been inside the bar for about an hour. Haley risked peeking inside and she saw him talking to the guy from the cruise ship. Haley smiles, remembering him plummeting into the Atlantic. *Who would've thought the geezer could survive? Good on him.*

Across the street, Casey is opening the back of the rig, lowering the ramp. They'd better hope no cops come by. She feels a stab of worry that Casey hasn't gotten rid of the trucker's body.

Finally, the agent emerges from the bar. His jaw is set, like he's having a day, and he takes no notice of the rig.

Haley walks across the street, making sure he can't miss her. He's been on their trail and she's counting on him noticing. Halfway across the street, she can virtually feel his eyes snag on her.

She walks slowly up the ramp and inside the big rig's trailer. It's empty and has railings running along each side to secure cargo. She feels the slightest shift in the floor as the agent climbs into the trailer. She keeps her back to the entry, giving him plenty of time.

"Turn around slowly," the voice demands.

Haley twists around. "Oh my god, you scared the crap out of me." She smiles.

The agent stands, jaw tight, hands gripping his service weapon. "Put your hands up."

Haley smiles again. "Are you serious right now? Is this a joke? Did my sister put you up to this?"

"This is no damn joke: Hands up, on your knees."

Haley's eyes widen. "Okay. You don't have to be rude about it."

She raises her hands, lowers to her knees. The agent keeps his gun trained on her. With his left hand he reaches around for cuffs strapped to his belt. She didn't know FBI agents carried handcuffs. You learn something new every day.

"Turn around," he commands.

"How am I supposed to do that? I'm on my knees and—"

"Do it!" A tinge of fear creeping into his voice.

Haley makes an exaggerated shuffle on her knees and puts her back to him again.

"Hands behind your back!"

Before she moves them, there's a loud buzz, and a scream. Haley turns her head and the agent is sprawled on the bed of the trailer. Casey's holding the stun gun and still pressing it against the nape of the agent's neck.

"Careful with that thing," Haley says. "You hit the metal and you could zap us all."

"Wouldn't that be something."

"Your face . . . what the hell?" Haley says, examining her sister.

"Chloroform burn."

The agent groans. They drag him to the side, use his own handcuffs to secure him to the rail.

Standing before him, Haley says, "You ever watch the Spider-Man movie where three Spideys from different multiverses meet?" she asks the agent.

He doesn't respond.

"Yeah, well . . ." Haley points to her sister, then herself. "Here's the bad news: Both versions of us are evil."

CHAPTER SIXTY-NINE

DONNIE

Donnie doesn't recall the last time he's been this angry. When his blood has been so hot that he wanted to punch something, someone. In this case Nico Adakai. The betrayal nearly demolishes him. Nico and Benny were friends. They all looked out for one another. They loved one another. How could he? And blackmail? Nico would be risking himself if he ever told what Benny—what they all—did on that rainy night.

He's going to drive back to the hotel to kick the shit out of Nico, then get the hell out of Pennsylvania. But after the half-dozen drinks, he can't get behind the wheel, something he damn well should've thought about before stopping at a bar named Drink. He needs to think more, grow up, stop acting like some stupid kid who can drink himself into a stupor and sleep it off in the car.

Agent Rodriguez rattled him. The FBI man knows there's a skeleton with a bullet hole in the skull. Knows that someone—Nico—was blackmailing Ben with those photos. You don't have to be frickin' Sherlock Holmes to figure out what happened twenty-five years ago on that knoll. The agent's so close. Why would Nico do such a thing? Donnie doesn't know or care.

He thinks about the blackmail message. Saying that Nico had DNA from the teeth. Mr. Brood *did* bite Artemis in the struggle. Is that possible? Extracting DNA from teeth buried for a quarter century? The message also said that the blackmailer had the gun. That doesn't make sense: Ben hid the gun near the tree fort in Donnie's secret spot.

Holy shit.

Donnie remembers the day. It was after they went to find his mom, before they caught the bus to Philly, that Ben hid the .22 in his spot in the woods. Benny knew about the place because it's where Donnie hid his booze and anything else he didn't want Mr. Brood to find or Derek and his goons to steal. The first time Donnie showed the secret spot to his friend, Benny said, *That's some Boo Radley shit.* Donnie had no idea what Ben was referencing, which wasn't all that unusual, and it's probably why he didn't remember it until now.

Donnie's wrenched from the thought by a woman's voice. "Are you Donnie Danger?"

The barfly is standing at his table now. "That's me, darlin'." Even now he carts out Rock Star Donnie. He's so pathetic.

"Can I buy you a drink?" She bats her bloodshot eyes.

"Sure, beautiful."

She sits, asks for a selfie with him, and he obliges.

After, he says, "Can I ask you a favor?"

"Of course."

"You have Uber?" he asks.

"Pardon?"

"You got a ride app on that thing?" He gestures to her phone.

"Yeah."

"Tell you what: You get me a car and I'll give you cash for the fare and get you backstage passes next time we play in Pennsylvania."

"Can I come with you wherever you're going?"

"I'm sorry, beautiful, but you don't want to go where I'm goin'."

CHAPTER SEVENTY

JENNA

Jenna and Nico have been inside the ramshackle property across the street from Savior House for nearly three hours and the smell is starting to get to her. The sun is coming down and the entire neighborhood has an eerie end-of-the-world feel. She studies Nico. He's predictably grown into a handsome man with broad shoulders and chiseled features, the archetype of modern beauty standards. But she can't help seeing the boy he was, the sadness in his eyes, which she finally understands.

He notices that she's gazing at him.

"Can I ask you a question?" he says, then looks back outside through a crack in the boarded window.

"Sure."

"Do you think there's any chance she's still alive?"

Jenna looks at him and knows he means Annie. His features are those of a teenager again, a lovestruck, heartbroken kid. Abandoned a third time in his life: first by his mother, then by his father, then by Annie. Jenna suspects there's been more abandonment in his life since then.

"I honestly don't know."

"If the others weren't taken by the people who took you, then where could they be?"

Jenna doesn't answer. If Mr. Brood was willing to hand Jenna over to The Corporation, then he probably was willing to let others go with even more questionable caretakers. Could The Corporation have recruited Annie or the others at Savior House who disappeared? And if so, where are those girls now? Living normal suburban lives like Jenna? The most likely answer, as much as it roils her insides, is that they were sold into the sex trade, and the life span for trafficked victims isn't long.

Her thoughts are interrupted by the buzz of her burner phone.

"Hey," she says.

"Hey," Simon says back.

She's glad to hear his voice again. To talk before she and Nico go into the house of horrors across the street.

"I got the information you needed."

"That was fast."

"I've taught the girls to play poker, read Congress's thousand-page new tax bill, watched seven episodes of *Backyardigans* with Lulu, and witnessed Willow mope around about not seeing a kid named Billy. . . . So your research project was the best thing that's happened all day."

Jenna feels a fissure in her heart.

Simon continues, "Robot LLC."

The company's name written on the folded star at the library.

"It's a shell corporation, part of a web of related entities. It may be impossible, even for me, to ever find the source. But I did find something."

"What's that?"

"It's a single-purpose company, meaning it was created for only one purpose."

"And what was that?"

"To buy a parcel of property."

Jenna hears Lulu's voice in the background asking him something.

"Can I talk to her?" she says. "Never mind. I'll see her tomorrow." Jenna's superstitions are kicking in.

Simon continues, "The buyer was the corporation itself, but it does list the seller. His name is Park Jones."

Jenna doesn't recognize the name. "Never heard of him."

"I ran a search. The guy's dead but was a major creep. He used to work in Big Tech in the early years, was a pioneer. But he also had a thing for underage girls."

The worst kind of monster.

"I'm sending you an article about his conviction. He apparently was fired, moved back to live with his parents, and inherited their house. It's an unusual transaction for a shell company. Buying a low-value home in a blighted community."

Jenna's heart trips as she opens the newspaper story on the phone and recognizes the man's face instantly. The man they called Ned Flanders.

"Let me guess, the house he sold is in Chestertown? On Carver Street."

"Yes, how'd you know?"

Jenna's interrupted by Nico.

"He's here," Nico whispers, staring through the crack in the board.

Jenna peers out and watches as the car pulls to the curb in front of Savior House. Derek Brood gets out of the sedan and looks around. He seems nervous, but that could simply be standing on this block after dark.

"I've got to go," she says to Simon. "But I need to say something."

He waits.

"You're the love of my life," she says, powering down the phone without waiting for his reply.

They watch as Brood goes to the front door, which is plastered with NO TRESPASSING signs. There's a Ring camera mounted above the door, but it appears to be covered with spray paint. Brood fumbles with some keys and unlocks a padlock and multiple dead bolts. He opens the door and stands in the entryway before going in, like he's listening. He may be concerned about squatters, meth cookers, or vagrants or the other dangerous inhabitants of abandoned homes on this side of Chestertown.

An interior light goes on as he steps inside and shuts the door behind him.

"Why the hell did Arty ask him to meet here?" Nico asks.

"Because it's secluded, I guess. He said Brood still owns the property."

"Is Arty really gonna come?"

Jenna shrugs. She's realizing how little she knows, and it's making her nervous. And Nico's question is a good one: Will Arty dare make an appearance? He was reluctant to show his face at the funeral for Ben. And he's kept material details about Savior House from his own security team. Would he come on his own without his body men and protection? If Jenna were on his detail, she'd advise against it. But even as a kid, Arty didn't follow conventional thinking.

The thought is answered when a black town car pulls to the

curb. A tall man in a black suit gets out of the driver's side and opens a back passenger door. Jenna can't see on the other side of the vehicle. She can hear voices but not what's being said. The driver comes back around the vehicle, his gait reluctant, shaking his head.

The town car pulls away, leaving Artemis Templeton, who walks inside Savior House. Unlike Derek Brood, he isn't timid about it. He opens the door like he owns the place and strides in.

"What now? Should we go in?" Nico says.

Jenna shakes her head. "Now, we wait."

"For what?"

Jenna's eyes fix on the figure appearing from nowhere in front of Savior House. Every time Jenna sees the woman, bolts of rage flow to her extremities.

"For *her*."

CHAPTER SEVENTY-ONE

The pretty hit woman strolls into Savior House almost as casually as Arty did a few minutes before. She's not carrying a gun or the bizarre weapon. And she's not dressed in tactical gear but a blouse and slacks, business-casual attire. Cool as a cucumber.

Jenna encountered some eccentrics in her time with The Corporation, but this woman is by far the most unique.

She and Nico watch as the woman disappears inside Savior House.

Jenna feels for the pistol in her pocket. "You okay with the gun?" she asks Nico.

He reluctantly took the handgun Jenna pulled out of her ex, Michael's, bag of goodies. She's still digesting what Simon told her about Ned Flanders, real name Park Jones, the man who used to live down the street, the man who owned the stretch of land where they took Mr. Brood. The scientifically minded man who'd mentored young Artemis.

"I've only fired a gun once in my life," Nico says.

They both pause, silently acknowledging the long-ago event.

"Just stay near me," Jenna says.

They walk quickly and quietly to Savior House and the front door creaks open, but not loudly. There are voices coming from what used to be the dining room. Jenna points to the hallway that leads to the kitchen, which provides another entry into the dining room.

Nico nods, he remembers too.

They sidle down the hallway, through the kitchen, and stop out of sight. Listen.

A panicked voice says, "Susan, my god, what in the hell are you doing?" That's Derek Brood's voice, and it sounds like his father's.

"Sit!" the woman's voice says.

Jenna isn't clear what's going on.

"We can talk about this," Brood says. "Put the gun down."

Jenna stealthily makes it to the entryway, peers inside.

Derek Brood, walking slowly, hands in the air, takes a chair—the only piece of furniture in the room—in the center of the dining hall.

The hit woman has her back to Jenna and hasn't seen her yet. Jenna's breath is taken away when she realizes that the woman—who's a foot taller than Arty—stands behind him and has her forearm around Arty's neck, a gun to his temple.

Jenna steps quietly behind the woman and puts the handgun to the back of her head.

The woman stiffens.

"Slowly," Jenna warns as the woman lowers the gun from Artemis's head and Jenna gestures for Nico to grab it. He scurries over and takes the gun gingerly like he's picking up a spider.

The woman releases her grip on Artemis's neck and he pushes away from her.

"What the hell's going on?" Derek Brood says, standing again. "Susan said she was your real-estate rep," he tells Arty. "That you wanted to buy Savior House and rejuvenate the entire area. What the—"

"I can explain," Artemis says. "Please, sit."

Jenna's mind is reeling. Derek Brood seems sincerely mystified by the turn of events. Jenna and Nico lock eyes. Her old friend looks equally confused.

Jenna still holds the muzzle of the pistol to the hit woman's head.

Artemis looks at them both. Like he's pondering what to do as the ones and zeros come together in that computer of a brain.

"We all need to talk this out," Arty says. He looks at Jenna. "You can let her go."

"I'm not letting anyone go until you tell me what the hell is going on."

Artemis offers a disappointed look. He moves toward her. Jenna moves the gun from the woman to Arty's center mass. "Don't fucking move."

Finally, she understands. It wasn't Brood who hired the hit woman.

It was Artemis.

That's when Jenna feels the blow to the back of her head and she hits the floor.

CHAPTER SEVENTY-TWO

DONNIE

The Uber pulls up to the area where the street ends and woods begin. The driver says, "Here?"

"Yeah, this is great," Donnie says, still feeling the booze. It's getting dark, a few minutes past seven. He wonders if Jenna and Nico went through with the meeting at Savior House.

Donnie gets out of the car and heads into the thick vines and weeds and trees. It's been so long since he's been to this patch of gloom, but there's an immediate familiarity. He stumbles on some bushes. He needs to get himself straight. He smacks himself in the face, which works sometimes, and continues navigating through the branches and scrub.

Could the gun still be here after all these years? Is that why Benny was back in Chestertown—to see if the blackmailer was bluffing? Lying that he had evidence of what they had done. And did Benny hide something *else* in the spot? It has to be what he meant by "Boo Radley."

Donnie spies the tree, the one Nico carved with the N + A.

Nico was such a sap back then. Now he's a Benedict Arnold who deserves an ass kickin'.

Two trees down, Donnie sees the familiar base of the giant maple tree. He gazes up and is taken momentarily back to hot summers with the G.R.O.S.S. club—Get Rid Of Slimy girlS—a name he'd stolen from *Calvin and Hobbes*. He didn't think girls were slimy, he quite liked them even at fourteen, but the tree fort was inspired by the comics, so it was fitting.

He travels past the tree fort and four trees to the right, and there it is, the knothole about three feet from the ground in the old tree: the Boo Radley hole.

Donnie swallows, his mouth dry. A headache is creeping at the back of his skull. He thrusts his hand inside. He feels the metal and retrieves the small handgun he and Benny secreted there more than two decades before.

For a moment, he's back on the knoll. Arty is peering into the shallow grave like he's gonna do it but only stands there, arm extended, the light rain beading his face. Jenna takes the gun from him, says, "We agreed. We all have to"; then there's the sickly bang of the gun. Jenna hands the firearm down the line; Ben takes his shot, then Nico, then Arty, who thrusts the weapon into Donnie's hands. Donnie stands frozen until Benny laces his finger over Donnie's and squeezes the trigger.

His mind snaps back to the woods around him. He feels light-headed. He tucks the old .22 in his waistband and sticks his hand back inside the knothole. He feels the glass of a bottle and tugs it out of the hole. He examines a half-empty pint of peppermint schnaps and shudders. You never forget throwing up that stuff. He thrusts his hand back in the hole and feels around. Ben was in Chestertown when he was killed, when he called the law clerk.

He wanted Donnie to come to this hiding place for a reason. Donnie's fingers land on a thin slab of metal and plastic, and he pulls out the phone. It has a gold chain tangled around it.

Donnie looks around, worried that the FBI agent or someone is gonna jump out from behind a tree, but there's no one out here but Donnie and the insects bouncing off his skin.

He untangles the chain from the device, powers it on. The FBI must not have been able to track Ben's device because it was off or because of no signal in the woods. When the screen pops on, it asks for a password. Donnie tries Bell's name, then Mia's. He thinks on this more, then tries "Calvin."

The phone flashes to a screen. The camera app. A video shows up as the most recent image.

Donnie takes a deep breath before playing the video, and that's when he notices that the gold chain has a decorative name engraved into it:

Annie

CHAPTER SEVENTY-THREE

JENNA

Jenna comes to on the dining room floor of Savior House. She must be seeing double because there's two of the hit woman now: one standing over Derek Brood, the other crouching low, looking Jenna in the eye with the hint of a smile. Nico's sitting on the floor, back to the wall, his hands behind him. He looks despondent, defeated.

Artemis walks up to Brood, whose face is covered in blood. "I'll ask you again. Where are the bones?"

Derek looks at his lap. "I told you, I have no idea what you're—" He's cut off by his own deafening scream . . . as the hit woman's weapon makes a *whoosh* and there's the sound of cracking bone as she removes it from Derek's thigh.

"You know what, Derek." Artemis crouches in front of their old nemesis, who appears to be losing consciousness. "I think I believe you."

Derek's chest is shuddering, he's blubbering now.

"You know what else?"

Derek dares to look up into Artemis's eyes.

As she watches, Jenna is trying to clear her head. To formulate an escape plan.

Arty raises his voice. "I said: Do you know what else, Derek?"

Derek shakes his head timidly.

"Your father was a buffoon, which is the only reason he got stuck babysitting a bunch of kids. Your uncle was probably relieved when he disappeared, except that he was stuck raising another buffoon."

Arty stands straight. "But at least your dad wasn't a bully."

"Please . . ." Derek moans as the hit woman raises the tube weapon.

"No compute, no compute," Arty says in a mechanical voice. "That's how robots talk, right?"

"I was just a kid. . . ."

"And so was I." Artemis says it again: "Where are the bones?"

"I . . . don't . . . know. . . ."

Artemis looks at the hit woman, nods. The other woman—she must be the hit woman's identical twin—has eyes on Jenna, watching for any sudden moves.

Again in a robot voice, Artemis says, "Terminate."

The hit woman puts the cylinder weapon to Derek's temple and *whoosh*.

Derek slouches lifeless in the chair.

As the woman pushes Derek onto the floor, Artemis's gaze goes from Jenna to Nico.

"Which one of you is next?" He touches his chin. "Bring her to the chair."

One of the ghastly twins drags Jenna off the floor and onto the chair.

Jenna's head is still pounding, she's concussed, but the adrenaline has heightened her senses, her fear, as the hit woman jams the tube weapon at the center of her chest.

CHAPTER SEVENTY-FOUR

DONNIE

Still in the woods, Donnie watches the video on Benny's phone. It has a night-vision filter that casts everything in a green tint, but it's surprisingly clear. Ben filmed a figure on the same knoll where the five of them had put Mr. Brood in the ground.

A woman's voice rises above the chirp of crickets through the tinny speaker.

"This is not what we signed up for," she says.

It's dark and the white coveralls she's wearing are covered in dirt. She holds a phone in one hand, talking to someone on speaker mode. With the other hand she scoops up a pile of what look like rags, but when the camera zooms in they appear to be decaying clothes containing human bones.

"Quit whining," the voice through the phone says.

"Um, fuck off. I've been doing all the dirty work while you get a tan," the woman says. "There's like so many remains here. The clothes look like they were teenagers."

"Not our concern," the voice on the phone says.

"Spoken like a woman sipping a margarita poolside on a cruise while I'm digging up human remains."

The video jostles as Ben moves closer. His movement stops as the camera focuses in on the wheelbarrow. As the image resolves, Donnie sees that it does not hold kindling. The wheelbarrow's filled with bones, including at least three skulls. A Black hand appears in the video; Benny seems to be taking something from among the remains. Something delicate, shiny. The hand freezes when the woman calls out.

"Who's there?" Her voice has the lilt of concern.

The video turns black but is still on as it jostles up and down, the sound of footfalls, heavy breathing.

Benny's running.

The camera goes black.

When it turns back on, Ben is looking into the screen. He appears to have his back pressed against a tree.

Into the camera, he whispers, "Donnie, if my law clerk got you my message and you found this, it means something's happened to me. Contact Agent Rodriguez with the FBI, the Philadelphia field office. Tell him to look into Park Jones. I think Jones took Annie and the others."

Ben's quiet for a moment, like he's listening for someone coming.

"Arty lied to all of us. Take care of Mia and Bell. Take care of yourself. You'll always be my brother from another mother."

A voice chimes in from the background. "I *see* you," it says in a singsong tone. "You can come out. Don't worry, I won't hurt you."

It was a ghoulish lie.

Donnie holds back a sob as the screen goes black.

CHAPTER SEVENTY-FIVE

JENNA

"Where are Mr. Brood's bones?" Artemis says.

Jenna's heart trips as one of the twins moves the weapon from Jenna's chest to her neck. If the device shoots the steel bolt into her carotid artery, she'll die within seconds. The other twin simply watches, no longer holding her gun on Nico, like he isn't a threat.

"I have no idea what you're talking about, Artemis," Jenna says. She tries to keep her voice flat, unemotional.

"I believe you."

"Like you believed him?" Jenna looks at Derek Brood's body, now a mound on the filthy dining room floor.

Artemis doesn't reply. Jenna's mind jumps to the boy pulling the wagon full of computer equipment down the sidewalk, the boy bullied in the school's lunchroom who would later become one of the world's richest men, an innovator, a man before his time. With her life seemingly over now, Jenna is struck by the fact that this house where she will die instilled something in each of them that helped them reach their full potential.

Artemis looks at Jenna, his expression blank like always. "I believe you because you don't need the money," Artemis says. "And because you didn't take the shot."

Jenna says, "I have no clue what you're—"

"Who do you think coerced you into taking the hit on the bald man at the restaurant?"

Jenna understands now: Artemis set up a fake assassination both to divert any suspicion away from him and to draw Jenna out into the open.

"I was worried that with all your training you'd see that the bullets were blanks, that you'd realize the glare from the other scope was too obvious, that you'd realize the hit was designed to draw you out. I guess you're rusty."

Jenna gives Artemis a lazy glance. "Honestly," she says, "if you wanted to take me out, you could've done better than hiring these half-wits." She takes a sideways glance at the woman holding the weapon to her neck, then at the other twin.

The woman with the weapon at Jenna's neck tenses, like she's going to pull the trigger.

Artemis looks at the twin holding the cylinder weapon, shakes his head with a firm *no*.

Jenna barely flinches. "So let me guess, the bones—someone dug them up from where we left him and didn't blackmail only Ben, but you as well?"

Artemis shrugs.

"And what, you decided it had to be one of us, and you decide to take us all out?"

"It was the most logical solution."

"For such a smart guy, it's pretty fucking stupid."

"On reflection, maybe you're right. But twenty-twenty hind-sight . . ."

Artemis nods to the woman, who places the weapon at Jenna's

temple. Jenna has the sudden sense that this is where it will end for her. She swallows a sob, realizing that she'll never see Simon or Willow or Lulu again. Realizing she'll never get to eat those pancakes, never get to help Willow through the pain of losing her mom, never get to watch Lulu wave goodbye from the school bus. She needs to fight. For them.

"Where are the bones?" Artemis asks her again.

Jenna is about to leap from the chair, risk the bolt penetrating into her skull.

But then a voice breaks the brief silence.

"Stop!" Nico bellows. "I'll take you to them. Please, just stop."

CHAPTER SEVENTY-SIX

NICO

Artemis stares at Nico. "I should've known that the simplest explanation was the correct one: The degenerate gambler needed money and blackmailed me." He looks at Jenna, who's still on the chair with the tube weapon—the hydraulic bolt gun that had pierced Nico's shoulder in the mine—pressed to Jenna's head.

Jenna's gaze, which Nico can only describe as part heartbreak, part betrayal, turns to Nico. Shame envelops him.

Artemis nods at the woman with the weapon, who presses it hard into Jenna's head.

"Where are the bones, Nico?" Artemis says. "I swear I will put a bolt through her brain if you don't tell me in the next three seconds."

The hit woman looks amped, the anticipation, the glee, vibrating from her.

When Nico doesn't answer, Artemis turns to the twin.

Jenna closes her eyes.

"All right, stop!" Nico yells. "I'll take you to the site. But you have to promise to let her go. This is on me. And, so we're clear, I was never going to tell anyone."

"How brave of you, Nico," Artemis says. "It only took twenty-five years."

Nico feels like the miserable person he is. "Promise me."

Artemis smiles again, but Jenna looks disappointed, as if suddenly understanding there's no promise Artemis will keep.

Artemis gestures at the other twin to help Nico to his feet. Without releasing the zip ties, she hoists him up.

"She comes too or I swear I won't take you there," Nico tells Artemis. "And if I don't call someone by midnight, there's an automatic email that will go out to the FBI that tells them everything."

Artemis appears skeptical of that. And rightly so: There is no email, and if Nico dies, everything will likely remain hidden forever.

"I can take you there right now, but you have to promise."

"Scout's honor," Artemis says, dryly.

With that, he gestures to the door, and the twins march Nico and Jenna out of the house.

CHAPTER SEVENTY-SEVEN

JENNA

Nico leads the way through the back alley, around the park, and down a dirt path to a meadow behind a dilapidated house.

Artemis stops, stares at the house where the man they all called Ned Flanders lived, the man who recognized Arty's brilliance and mentored him. The closest thing Arty had to a father figure, and ultimately a relationship that fostered the technology that supported the then newly emerging social-media sites, technology that made Artemis a rich man by his mid-twenties.

The pixels are now coming together for Jenna. Ben Wood was being blackmailed and it prompted him to revisit the events of that night, and he uncovered something none of them had known at the time: Ned Flanders's real name was Park Jones. He was a child molester who'd befriended a boy who had easy access to young girls. She thinks of Ben's handwritten note at the library: BROOD-ROBOT LLC-FAGIN JONES. Ben loved to read; he'd referenced Boo Radley. And Fagin is an infamous character from a Dickens novel—a despicable man who used children to commit his crimes. Flanders used Artemis to lure girls.

And Artemis must've agreed, since he needed Park Jones. So Marta,
Annie, the others . . . it's so awful, Jenna can't finish the thought.

But the theory is confirmed when she sees the holes dotting
the knoll. The final resting place of the missing girls, no doubt.
Arty created a shell company to buy the property to ensure no
one ever discovered the bodies, the crimes he had been party
to. But when Nico blackmailed him with photos of Mr. Brood's
bones, Arty needed to remove all the remains on the property
and destroy all possible evidence linking him to the murders.

Something she can only describe as blind rage is consuming
Jenna now.

Nico leads the group not to one of the holes, but instead, to a
mound of freshly tilled soil. The spot from all those years ago . . .

Nico looks down at the dirt. "Here," he says.

"Here?" Artemis lets out a wooden laugh. "You dug up
Mr. Brood, and what?—then brought him back to the original
gravesite and reburied him?"

One of the twins walks to a shed near the house and returns
with a shovel. She jabs it into the dirt so it stands upright. The
other twin removes Nico's zip ties.

Artemis gestures to the shovel. "Get to it, then."

The other twin still has the tube weapon pressed against
Jenna's spine. She watches, shaking her head, knowing that Nico
is not only retrieving the bones Artemis is after but also digging
his own grave.

The woman whispers in Jenna's ear, "I'm going to enjoy bury-
ing you alive."

Jenna feels a rivulet of sweat drip down her side. Her mind is
racing, teasing out how she can attack without that bolt driving
through her vertebrae, without Nico being torn to shreds by the
other hit woman's gun.

Artemis looks out at the other holes. A field of weeds now pockmarked by tilled soil, bordered on one side by Flanders's ramshackle house through the brush, bleak woodland on the other side. "You should've filled in those holes," he says to the hit woman with Jenna.

"We kinda got tied up with the judge and didn't think returning was a good idea," she says like a snarky teenager. "Don't worry, no one will ever find what was left of the others."

"Still," Artemis says, but drops it.

Nico continues to dig as Jenna plays out different scenarios. She could lunge forward, charge at Arty, and the twin with the gun might not shoot for fear of catching him in the cross fire. No, she thinks these chicks wouldn't care if they did. Frankly, she wonders if Arty is going to make it out alive.

Alternatively, she could do a backward head-butt, crush the other hit woman's nose, and dart away. But the woman would likely instinctively set off the weapon, which would send Jenna to the ground with a severed spinal cord. And that would surely result in her being buried alive, as promised.

If she can catch Nico's glance, he could swing the shovel, hit the one sister, and Jenna could get away, race into the woods, be done with the lot of them. But again, the weapon digging into her back presents an inescapable peril.

Then, she spies something that may give her a way out: a man with scraggly hair hiding behind one of the trees.

CHAPTER SEVENTY-EIGHT

DONNIE

The air is ripped from Donnie's lungs when he sees them. The two identical women. He now understands how Ben was killed while Donnie was attacked on the ship: It wasn't the same killer. There are two of them. And they're marching Jenna and Nico out of Savior House and down the street. He sees Arty as well, but no Derek Brood.

It was reckless to come back. But he couldn't let Jenna, or even Nico, walk into a trap with Arty, the person who betrayed them all. And though his heart feels like it will explode out of his chest, his mind filled with doubts that he can save them, he owes it to Benny to try.

He follows in the shadows as they go to a house he remembers from when they were kids, their neighbor's place. What was it that they called the owner? Some character from *The Simpsons*? His house bordered the woods and had an expansive meadow in the back that led into the bramble where their beloved tree fort hung in the canopy.

Donnie follows at a safe distance as the group moves to the

back of the house. When he catches up, he takes in a breath but just as quickly loses it when he sees the holes in the field. He'd glimpsed the hidden graveyard in Benny's video, but it's even more chilling live.

Who killed them? Mr. Brood? Donnie now doubts that. It was a fiction created by Artemis to make them think Brood was selling the girls to a mysterious woman for sex slavery or whatever. But they'd been only two blocks away the whole time, buried less than six feet under. Was Artemis the killer? It didn't make sense. He'd never shown interest in girls, in anyone sexually, for that matter. It was one of the reasons they called him The Robot. So, who?

Right now, it doesn't matter. He has the gun from the Boo Radley hole. Ben led him there. And now he's going to stop the people who killed his best friend.

He ducks low in the shadows. He sees Jenna. Her eyes are darting around. He can almost see the calculations going on in her head, figuring out how she'll break free.

He can't let the others spot him. But if he can show himself just enough to catch her eye . . .

He sees Artemis directing Nico, who's pulling a duffel bag out of a freshly dug hole.

Donnie stares at Jenna and she locks eyes with him.

All attention is on the duffel as Artemis unzips the top and peers inside.

This is their chance.

Jenna nods at Donnie, who fires the gun in the air and charges the knoll.

CHAPTER SEVENTY-NINE

JENNA

The gunshot echoes in the night. The next seconds are a whirl-wind.

Jenna simultaneously arches her back and thrusts her head into a reverse head-butt. Her skull connects hard and she hears the crunch of cartilage at the same time as the deadly *whoosh* of the cattle gun. The steel rod connects with her back, but she's managed to put enough distance from the device that it sends a shock wave of pain through her without piercing flesh or bone.

At the same time, Nico swings the shovel, connecting with the other twin, who fires off a shot that doesn't seem to hit any-one. Nico scrambles out of the hole and onto the twin who's still got the gun. She's bleeding from the head, stunned, and he claws at her hand for the pistol, prying it loose.

For his part, Donnie is pointing the gun at Artemis, whose hands are raised.

Back to the other twin, her nose gushing. She's staggering toward Jenna with the tube weapon.

Nico shouts, "Drop it!" and fires in her direction.

She stops, catches her sister's gaze, then drops the strange weapon. Nico and Donnie corral the twins and Artemis next to the hole where Mr. Brood was buried. Jenna tells them to shoot if anyone so much as moves an inch. She makes her way over to the shovel, crouches low, and saws the zip ties on her wrists off on its sharp blade. The plasticuffs pop off.

She walks over to Donnie and gently takes the gun from his hand.

"This isn't about Mr. Brood," Donnie tells her, his breaths coming in rasps. "It's about Annie. And the others."

"We know, Donnie."

CHAPTER EIGHTY

DONNIE

After Donnie tells them about Ben's video, about the skeletal remains, about Ben taking Annie's necklace from one of the bodies, Nico steps toward Artemis and puts the gun to his head.

Artemis stands there unemotional, not even bracing himself for the head shot.

Donnie watches as Nico's face reddens as he tightens his hand on the pistol, but he pulls away.

Donnie looks at Jenna, asking with his eyes, *What are we going to do?*

They can't go to the police, Donnie knows. They can't execute them. But they can't just let them go.

From the woods, a figure emerges.

"Oh shit," Donnie says.

Jenna already has her gun on the man.

"Hold up, hold up," Donnie says, both to stop any of them from any sudden moves and to prevent Reeves Rothschild from seeing what's happening.

"Hemingway, what are you—"

"I was curious why you stayed, so I followed you. What's going on?"

"It's not what it looks like. Those two." He points to the twins. "They killed Benny, tried to kill all of us."

Reeves is processing the new information. He looks to Artemis, perhaps recognizing the famous tech billionaire.

Donnie turns and glances at Jenna, at Nico, for guidance. Then he feels the cold muzzle of a gun pressed to his head.

"I'm sorry about this, Donnie. I really am," Reeves says.

CHAPTER EIGHTY-ONE

JENNA

The man holding the gun to Donnie's head is vaguely familiar, but Jenna has no idea who he is. He demands that Jenna and Nico drop their weapons, but they don't oblige. The stranger has a gun at Donnie's head. But something in his tone suggests he won't use it.

"This isn't what we agreed to," the man tells Artemis. "I was supposed to find out what he knew. Not . . ." He looks around.

Artemis shrugs. "You're in it now. And if you want your wife to get the treatment, then . . ."

The man looks desperate. His eyes dart to Jenna, Nico, Artemis, the twins. "I'm sorry, Donnie. But she's dying. He can get her the DNA treatment in Europe."

Donnie doesn't say anything, seeming strangely at peace with the fact that this man has betrayed him.

The stranger pulls himself together. "All of you, drop your guns or I'm gonna do it." He makes a show of pressing the gun to Donnie's head. "I don't want to, but I will."

Nico throws down his gun. A chill goes through Jenna. One

less gun on their side. Artemis stares at her, a look of faint amusement on his face.

Jenna sees no way out. She knows that if she drops the weapon they're all dead. The man says he'll shoot Donnie, but will he? He doesn't seem to have that in him. Though it sounds like he's doing this to save someone. His wife? It's then that Jenna believes that he might pull the trigger. We're all capable of the unthinkable when it means protecting our families. She feels a tremor in her hands, fear seizing her. But she needs to fight for her family too.

She looks over at the twins, who are glowering at her. The one with the red face and bloody nose will bury her alive. The one with the gash on her head from Nico's shovel may well do worse.

Jenna thinks back to Michael's warning: *They aren't doing jobs for the money or ideology or the usual reasons—they're doing it for the sport.*

Jenna moves her gun in Artemis's direction. He's staring at her in that unemotional way of his. She allows the muzzle to drift toward the hesitant newcomer.

The man fidgets, takes a half step back, his gun still on Donnie. "I'm telling you, I *will* shoot," he says softly, with a lingering resignation in his voice Jenna cannot deny. "I have nothing to lose, nothing left, if my wife dies."

Nodding, Jenna lowers her weapon, then she pivots, twirls around like a discus thrower, and in one swift movement hurls the handgun as far as she can. All eyes follow the arch of the gun as it sails high into the woodland that separates the knoll from Ned Flanders's backyard.

With everyone looking in the direction of the flying weapon, Jenna dashes off in the opposite direction—deep into the woods.

There's a pause, then several *pops*. One of the twins, no doubt.

But the shots miss. Jenna's already too far away and through the tree line.

Jenna continues to run, not knowing what she's going to do but knowing she must do something because the twins will be coming for her.

CHAPTER EIGHTY-TWO

DONNIE

"How could you, man?" Donnie says to Reeves. The writer has a gun pointed in the direction of both Donnie and Nico, who stand near the edge of one of the unturned graves in the knoll. "I thought we were . . ." He wants to say *friends*, but they barely know each other. The whole book thing was a setup, he realizes, funded by Artemis.

The twins have darted into the woods after Jenna, and Artemis paces near another one of the holes as if contemplating his next steps.

"Was there ever a book?" Donnie asks.

Reeves shakes his head at the question.

"Are you even a writer?" Donnie asks.

Reeves is watching Artemis pace, answers without looking at Donnie. Nico stands quietly as if lost in thought.

"What I told you about me is true. I had a novel that critics loved, but no one bought. I took a gig ghostwriting a business book for Artemis Templeton. Then my wife got sick. I asked for his help. He said he could pull some strings."

Donnie remembers the photo of the woman in the hospital room on Reeves's phone and his laptop. "I told you things about me, man," Donnie says.

Reeves looks at him, his eyes steely now. "But you didn't tell me everything, did you?"

Donnie exhales. "So, what, you're gonna let them kill us? Let them get away with killing Benny? Do you know what was in these holes?" Donnie gestures across the knoll.

Before Reeves answers, Artemis comes over. Donnie's heart sinks when Artemis takes the gun from Reeves. He thought they might have a chance with Reeves. But Artemis is another matter.

Artemis looks at Reeves. "I'm sorry it ended this way," he says. "And just so you know: Your wife never had a chance even with the treatment."

Reeves opens his mouth to speak when there's a loud bang. Reeves's face is distorted in shock and disbelief as Artemis pushes him into the hole.

Donnie's screaming now: "You ain't gettin' away with this, man! The FBI agent, he's on to you. He knows about those psycho chicks and about Benny and about all of it."

"You mean the FBI agent in that hole over there?" Artemis directs his chin to the far end of the knoll. "One of those *chicks* found out everything he knows and took his files. You're lucky she won't be extracting your secrets."

Terror vibrates through every part of Donnie.

"Mr. Danger, Mr. Adakai, I'm afraid it's the end of the line. Get in the hole." Artemis looks down at the grave. "Go without trouble and I'll make it quick. If not . . ."

Well, this is it, Donnie thinks. They say your life flashes before your eyes when you experience a near-death experience but all that Donnie can see is Benny. A montage of him reciting Johnny

Cochran closing arguments, lounging in the tree fort with his nose in a book, riding that bus to Philly.

Donnie's about to jump into the hole when he hears a roar. In a blur, Donnie sees Nico charging Artemis and both men fly into the grave. Donnie is shell-shocked, but he makes out the words. Nico's voice:

"Run, Donnie!"

CHAPTER EIGHTY-THREE

JENNA

Jenna races through the woods making sure to leave an obvious trail of trampled brush and snapped branches along the way. As part of her time with Sabine, she underwent survival training. They dropped her in a remote wilderness area, in a dangerous neighborhood, in a war zone, and forced her to fend for herself. Each time she emerged bloodied but stronger.

Unseen insects flick against her face. Her muscles are sore, wrists raw. There's a bump on the back of her head from one of those awful twins. They called each other Casey and Haley. She thinks Casey is the one with the tube weapon, which means she's the one who'd threatened Jenna's family. The other twin, Haley, is the one in business attire, the one who'd masqueraded as Artemis's real-estate manager and lured Derek Brood to the house.

She hears movement behind her, not far now, and drops to her belly behind a fallen tree. She inches into some shrubbery growing up against the dead tree.

Against the soundtrack of her heartbeat, she hears voices.

"I say we kill him too."

"Who?"

"That bald asshole. He killed young girls—the world will be a better place."

"I don't think he killed them."

"You weren't there. I dug up those bodies."

"He said it wasn't him. Said it was the neighbor. The judge said the same thing . . . at least when he wasn't screaming."

The women go silent as their footfalls grow closer.

"I'll think about it. But killing him will bring a lot of heat."

"No more heat than killing a federal judge. When did you get so timid?"

"Whatever. But he's only paid us half, and we could use the rest."

They stop in front of the fallen tree, mere feet from Jenna on the other side. Jenna holds her breath. It took them less time to find her than anticipated, but that's okay. Jenna's thoughts go to Willow's terrified face in the Jeep as they hid from one of these dreadful women. Both will pay for that.

The voices grow even closer. Jenna will have only one chance. She steadies her breathing and rises quietly to her feet, crouching low.

"When I find that bitch I'm gonna—"

The words are stolen from the woman's throat as Jenna springs up from behind the downed tree, her arms extended like a T, and hits both twins in their throats with knifehand strikes.

The twins reach for their necks and double over in unison, like some twisted TikTok video. They're barking coughs as Jenna knees the one on the right, Haley, in the face, taking her to the ground. That should hold her for the moment. Jenna knows her right-handed strike was the strongest, but in unison neither is the crippling blow a single thrust would have been.

Which means she needs to move. It's Casey that Jenna is most worried about, the one Jenna struck with her weaker hand.

As she turns to look, Casey is coming at her, brandishing the cattle gun like a fencer with a rapier, the device *whooshing*, the steel rod retracting and firing, sliding in and punching out.

As the tube gun comes back around, Jenna takes a swipe at it with her arm, pushing it aside, then leaps forward and goes for the eyes, presses her thumbs into the sockets. Casey screams, dropping the cattle gun and clawing blindly at Jenna's hands and arms.

Out of the corner of her eye, Jenna sees the other twin groping for something in the folds of her jacket.

Jenna digs her thumbs deeper into Casey's eyes, then grabs her head and slams it into the closest tree. Casey staggers sideways and falls, moaning, both hands cupping her eyes.

Haley has pulled a gun from the jacket and is getting to her feet. As the weapon and woman come up, Jenna charges, running-back-style, and they tumble into the undergrowth. Jenna grapples for the gun with one hand, repeatedly slamming her free elbow into the woman's face until she goes still, the weapon falling into the dead leaves.

Jenna hears movement behind her. *These fucking twins. It's almost as if they feed on the violence—live for it.*

Casey has abandoned her cattle weapon and drawn her own gun. One eye is swollen shut, blood trickles from the other. Squinting, she aims her weapon at Jenna, but it's wobbly.

"Shoot her, Casey!" her sister shouts. "Shoot her!"

Jenna dives right as the gun fires. She looks at her own torso. She isn't hit.

"*No!*" Casey cries.

Jenna takes a quick glance back and sees a large red stain blossoming on the blouse of Haley's once immaculate business getup. Casey accidently shot her twin. Without wasting another second, Jenna scoops up Haley's gun from the leaves and takes the shot, hitting Casey in the forearm, which spins her around. Jenna races over and pistol-whips Casey. She collapses to the ground again.

Jenna knows she should take care of both of them, finish this. But that's not the person she wants to be anymore.

As she works through the options, despite being shot, Haley is miraculously on her feet, her blouse soaked in blood. She's found her sister's cattle gun and wields it with a renewed vigor. She stabs it at Jenna, who dodges around the deadly bolt. Jenna raises her pistol, but the cattle gun swings back the other way and knocks the gun loose. Jenna dodges a third pass and is about to charge when she is grabbed from behind, and her arms pinned to her sides.

Casey grips Jenna as she bucks and kicks, trying to free herself. "Put this bitch out of *our* misery," Casey says to her sister. "Finish her."

Brandishing the cattle gun, Haley grins.

Jenna is reined in once more. The tube gun is rising, stopping at Jenna's abdomen, then rising again. To Jenna's solar plexus, her chest, her chin.

The rest seems to unfold in slow motion.

Still pinned from behind, Jenna shifts her head to the side, twists her body down and around, thrusting her hip back. At the same time, she plants her leg just beyond Casey's foot and pulls forward. The twin falls forward onto Jenna, who twists more until Casey's head comes front and center and directly into the barrel's sight as Haley pulls the trigger.

Jenna hears the distinct hydraulic *whoosh* and crack of the steel bolt striking home. The arms holding her fall away and Casey drops to the ground; a large red dot marks her forehead, blood trickling out.

She turns back to Haley, who's in shock at killing her own sister. Jenna aims a kick at her kneecap, hears the telltale crunch of bone, and watches as the woman folds, hitting the dirt hard.

Lying supine, the twin whimpers, the red on her shirt turning dark scarlet. Jenna hears Haley gasping to say something, but she never gets the full word out.

CHAPTER EIGHTY-FOUR

Jenna darts through the trees, back to the knoll. She's taken care of the twins, so that leaves Artemis.

She doesn't have time to put all the pieces together as she hurries back, but she knows this much: Nico anonymously blackmailed Artemis and the billionaire decided that the easiest way to figure out who was behind it was to kill everyone associated with that night. But he didn't count on Ben also being blackmailed and learning the truth: that Artemis had tricked them all into killing Mr. Brood. That he manipulated them to believe it was Brood abusing the girls, then selling them off to the likes of Sabine or other boogeymen. And even tonight he manipulated them: making them think that Mr. Brood's son was responsible for the failed efforts to take them out one by one.

Jenna reaches the knoll and she sees no one. But there's a sound . . . groaning, it seems. *Where's it coming from?* She listens carefully. It's definitely a groan. Then she realizes it's coming from one of the holes.

She runs to the edge of the fresh grave and finds the tangled bodies of Nico and Artemis. Both appear to be bleeding. Jenna's heart jumps when an arm—Nico's—juts up and out. She's startled again when a figure appears next to her, extends an arm, and tugs Nico out.

Donnie.

A moment later, all three kneel at the edge of the grave, pushing the dirt back in with their bare hands.

Jenna can't help but think of that night twenty-five years ago, the rain coming down. Donnie speaking for them all:

What have we done?

CHAPTER EIGHTY-FIVE

ARTEMIS

In the last moments of his life, Artemis has no regrets. His work will live on forever. Did he make mistakes? Every great inventor does. Did he betray friends? Again, show him an innovator who doesn't do whatever it takes to change the world. He stares up at the sky from the bottom of the hole. He's losing blood, losing consciousness. There's nothing that will save him. As he takes his last breath, dirt raining down on him, his mind retreats to the house where it all started:

"I think you are making a mistake," Artemis says to Mr. Jones.

They're in Park Jones's dining room, which is jammed with computer monitors and equipment.

"Let me worry about that," he says, tapping on the keyboard. He's wearing a cardigan and plucking at his mustache. The other kids are right: With his sweater, glasses, and mustache, he looks like Ned Flanders.

"They want you to call Social Services about Marta to report her missing. It's only a matter of time before they get someone to pay attention. If another one goes missing, someone's going to realize they're not all runaways."

"You're a smart kid, Artemis, but just do what you're told. Tell her to come over tonight."

"What am I supposed to say?"

"I don't know—tell her what you told the others."

"Annie's sharp, she's not going to—"

"Get it done. Tonight." Park stares at him over his glasses.

"I think you are miscalculating."

"No, I think *you're* miscalculating. I pick up that phone over there and make one call and the deal will be cratered. I'll tell my contacts your code is crap."

"But that would be a lie. The code will change everything. How people communicate."

Park Jones chuckles, shakes his head. "Created by someone who's hardly a poster boy for communicating."

"At least I don't hurt girls. You and Mr. Brood."

"Watch yourself."

"No, I think you'd better watch *your*self. I know where the bodies are buried, quite literally."

"You should choose your next words carefully, Artemis Templeton. I've spent a lot of time, money, and contacts helping you, but that can change."

"It better not. I'm the one who stopped the other kids from asking too many questions, the one who scared them into thinking Mr. Brood is to blame. But if you keep doing this, the truth's going to come out."

"You'd better hope not. If it does, you're going down with me, kid."

An hour later, there's a knock on the door. Artemis answers it.

Annie's there, wearing the cheap necklace Nico bought her. She looks distraught.

"Is Nico okay? Where is he?"

"I think he'll be okay. Derek beat him up pretty good."

"Oh my goodness, where is he? Did you call anyone else?"

"I think he'll be fine. He's in the room in the back. . . ."

EPILOGUE

NICO

"Hi, Nico," the small crowd perched on metal folding chairs says in unison.

He stands at the podium, offers a fleeting smile, and says, "It's been eight months since I last gambled."

The room fills with light clapping as he looks at the circle of faces. It's mostly men, but there are a few women attending the GA meeting. Some of the attendees are in business suits, others in work uniforms, others in shorts and flip-flops. Every color of skin is represented. The draw of the game—the thrill that your next hand will be the big one—doesn't care about race, religion, or socioeconomic status. This Los Angeles crowd doesn't look so different from those who come to GA meetings in West Virginia.

Nico's in LA to talk to the network about his future. He's guessing it isn't so bright. Three years ago, he flew over for the same meeting and they met at Nobu amid celebrities and a thousand-dollar tab for run-of-the-mill sushi. This time, the network set a late afternoon meeting at its offices in Century City, which isn't a great sign. *Oh well.*

Nico looks out at the other gamblers taking it a day at a time. He keeps his talk short. He usually tries to be upbeat. Everyone at these meetings has tales of hitting bottom. Few involve the depths of a coal mine, but many are even more bizarre, sadder. Nico can't tell them the whole story, of course. That will forever be buried on that knoll in Chestertown, Pennsylvania.

After the GA meeting, he'll head over to the Hollywood Roosevelt, which is hosting a fan conference for a few of the network's reality shows. Comic-Con it isn't—he'll likely sign posters and participate on a panel about the show—but it'll make the network happy. Then comes the dreaded meeting with the suits. *The Miners* is still doing well in the ratings, though the aftershow tanked when the audience revolted against Davis. He wonders if that douche will be in the meeting today. *Whatever.*

By two o'clock, he's wrapping up at the fan event at the Roosevelt. The organizers have shuttled him down to the poolside bar to take photos. The DJ has the music on too loud and Nico can't wait to get out of there.

He's done a few of these fan events, and ever since what happened in the mine he always secretly hopes his ex, Natalie, will show up. He hates how they left things. But he can never explain the truth. The world will never know it. Jenna's former employer sent a cleanup team. No one on earth seems to have missed the ghoulish twins. There have been a few reports about Donnie's missing writer but, again, no major stories. No big search. Most of the attention has been on the disappearance of the FBI agent and Artemis Templeton. The agent was investigating the O'Leary family, and many suspect that Special Agent Rodriguez is wearing concrete shoes at the bottom of the Delaware River. He didn't deserve what happened to him, but such is the curse of Savior House.

The only serious media attention has been devoted to the disappearance of the eccentric tech mogul Artemis Templeton, but he's rumored to be alive and kicking on a secret pilgrimage to create the Next Big Thing.

Nico says his goodbyes, then makes his way to the lobby where he'll wait for the network's driver to shuttle him to Century City. There's a fountain bordering the stairs. Nico retrieves his silver dollar and examines it before climbing up. Then, for some unexplained reason, he flips the coin into the fountain.

He finds a seat in the lobby, which has an old-time Hollywood feel, complete with photos of cinema icons in black and white outside the elevator banks. He gazes about the room, imagines Natalie walking over, sitting across from him.

An older woman approaches. She holds her head low. She's not exactly the target demographic for *The Miners*, so he wonders if she's mistaking him for an actual celebrity.

He smiles as she raises her head.

It's then he notices it. Around her neck, the chain with the medallion.

An identical match to the Saint Christopher he wears around his neck.

She walks toward him, and he thinks she's going to reach out her hand, say, "I hope you can forgive me."

But she passes without a word.

And with everything he's done—the chain of events he set in motion that hurt so many—he knows one thing: It's what he deserves. But he's determined to be better. For Annie and the others.

DONNIE

Donnie sits backstage at the 9:30 Club in Washington, D.C. He's staring at the set list he's written out. He released the songs on the internet two days ago—well, he didn't, his new manager did.

It's risky doing a set without playing even one of Tracer's Bullet's hits. The crowd might revolt.

But if they want to hear Tracer's Bullet, watch Tom shake his aging ass onstage, they should go buy a cruise ticket.

He examines the set list again.

He named the song collection—there's no such things as "albums" anymore—*Savior House*. Eight new songs from Donnie Danger:

- Drowning
- Brother from Another Mother
- That's What She Said
- Finding Mom
- High in the Trees
- Ghost Writer
- Overboard
- The Innocents

A knock comes on the dressing room door. In pops Pixie. He poached her from Tracer's Bullet. She was happy to be off the cruise-ship circuit and away from Tom. Her eyes are alight with pre-show energy. "I sneaked a peek at the crowd and—"

"Ah. I don't wanna know. If there's only ten people out there or a thousand, I'm gonna give it everything I got."

Pixie doesn't say anything for a moment, but she looks worried. "Before we go on, I wanted to thank you."

"Thank me? Hell, what for?"

"For including me. These songs. They're . . ." Pixie's eyes well up.

"Don't you go gettin' sentimental on me."

She shakes it off. "Okay. If I'm not being sentimental, maybe I should ask whether you need *that*." Her eyes move to the bottle of Jack on the dressing room table.

"There's the little tyrant I know and love," Donnie jokes.

There's a knock on the door. Their manager pops her head in. "Five minutes."

Donnie stands up. Bounces on his feet. He gives Pixie a sideways grin, then grabs the bottle, takes a swig. "I don't need it. But like Popeye said, *I yam what I yam.*"

Pixie frowns. Nods in resignation.

"I'll be out in a minute," Donnie says. Pixie throws her arms around Donnie, then, without a word, heads out to the area behind the stage entrance.

Donnie stares at the set list again, at the last song, "The Innocents." That's how he chooses to remember them. Nico sitting on the monkey bars barefoot, cracking *That's what she said* jokes; Jenna hiding her grief about her parents, protecting them from Derek Brood; Benny escaping into his books, being Donnie's brother from another mother; even Arty, brutally bullied, manipulated by a man who claimed to understand his unconventional mind.

Donnie looks at himself in the mirror, which is bordered by lightbulbs like an old-time Hollywood dressing room. He doesn't need self-affirmations to pump himself up. He has the songs. Out loud, he says, "I'm not scared anymore, Benny."

And in the reflection behind him appears a tall Black man. Donnie whirls around—no one's there, of course. But in his head, he hears Ben's voice: *The world looks brand-new. Let's go exploring.*

Donnie gets his guitar from his tech on his way to the stage. The band's in a circle with their hands stacked at the center, like a football team before kickoff.

Donnie doesn't join in. He struts onto the stage, where he's met with a roar louder than any other crowd he's ever heard. The room is electric, and for the first time Donnie can remember he feels comfortable in his own skin. He doesn't need to pretend to be Rock Star Donnie. It's who he really is.

He heads to the mic and says, "This one's for Annie. And the others."

JENNA

"*Girl*, I can't even. If I looked like you for my prom. I would've dumped my date and called Timothée Chalamet to come pick me up." Blue Flowers, the Saks Fifth Avenue stylist, stands in the lounge area of the fitting room with her mouth agape. Willow's perched on the platform in front of the trifolding mirror. It's the fourth prom dress she's tried on, and it's exquisite.

She steps down, spins around, and looks to Jenna. "What do you think?"

Jenna feels a surge of emotion. Things have been better between them. Willow's still traumatized by what happened. She's seeing someone for occasional panic attacks and anxiety. But the only good that came out of those awful twins entering Jenna's life is that it brought her closer to her stepdaughter.

Jenna and Simon told Willow as much of the truth as they dared. It was more of a Netflix glamorized version, where Jenna was in the CIA—one of the good guys—and the people after her were dedicated to destroying truth, freedom, and the American way. She wasn't sure Willow believed it all—Willow's a smart girl—but she accepted the explanation without too many questions.

"I think you look beautiful."

"It's so much money, though."

"Not with my friends-and-family discount. Right, Blue?"

The stylist picks up on the ploy quickly. "Half price for friends and family."

Willow beams. "Okay. I love it. Do you think Billy will?"

Jenna thinks of the shaggy-haired boy she first met behind the 7-Eleven. He's been a fixture at their house, since. And despite how they met—the kids skipping school and drinking behind a convenience store—he's a sweet boy. He complements Willow. He knows when to give her space, knows when to draw close.

And most important, Willow's crazy about him. A little too crazy, so Jenna and Simon are constantly on guard, listening for when it gets too quiet while the kids are watching television alone in the basement.

"He's going to love it."

"He better, or I'm calling Timothée for you," Blue Flowers chimes in.

Jenna pays the tab while Willow's in the changing room. If the stylist notices that Jenna is using a different name than before, or that she'd previously claimed to be from out of town, the salesperson says nothing.

Handing Jenna the credit card, she says, "So, was the man you were excited to see at the party last time you were here Willow's father?"

Jenna smiles. "Yes," she lies, deciding that it wouldn't be a great idea to say that the person she went to see at the party was a Frenchwoman who recruited her to work for a shadow organization when she was fifteen years old.

"You did rock that gown."

Jenna smiles.

"And your stepdaughter is *gorg*."

A text causes Jenna's heart to jump a beat. It's from an unfamiliar number. It says:

> Your dry cleaning is ready.

That's The Corporation's code to contact home base.

She considers clicking on the number that sent the text, but Willow appears from the dressing room beaming.

On the car ride home, Jenna's mind is on the text. What could they possibly want? She'll get Willow home and find out.

"Can I ask you something?" Willow says, pulling Jenna from the thought.

Jenna looks at her stepdaughter.

Willow's face reddens a shade. She hesitates but continues, "A lot of the couples are staying overnight at a hotel after prom."

Jenna says nothing, lets her talk.

"Billy said he'll, like, wait as long as I need—wait until I'm ready—before we . . ." Willow trails off.

Jenna realizes that her stepdaughter's confiding in her about sex. Her chest swells, but she knows she can't show the emotion. She needs to play it cool.

"As he should," she says, trying not to sound judgmental.

"But it's prom, you know? It's romantic and . . ." Again she doesn't finish the sentence.

Jenna smiles. "I understand. You'll all be dressed up, taking limos downtown, getting photographed at the monuments at sunset, the last time you'll all be together. . . ."

"So, how do I know if I'm ready?"

Jenna blows out a breath. She never attended prom. Never had a normal high school experience, a sweet teenage boyfriend. Her thoughts go to Sabine forcing Jenna to take dance lessons, etiquette training, so that she could look like she belonged at any ball in the world. The text gnaws at her again.

"I think you need to trust your intuition. Don't do something because you think you should. Sometimes the most romantic things are the mundane, the unexpected." She thinks about falling for Simon on their second date when he took her bowling.

"You're smart," she adds. "Smarter than I ever was at your age. And I think you'll know if it's time."

Willow nods. There's a long pause. "Can we get sushi for dinner?"

And with that, Jenna's first bit of parental advice comes to an end. She nods, determined not to cry.

At home, they find Simon in the dining room. It's odd because he never goes in the dining room. He thinks it's too formal. Lulu's in the corner, playing with her dolls, also unusual.

"What are you doing in here?" Jenna asks, smiling.

Simon gives a tight smile in return. "Oh, I just wanted a change of scenery. How was shopping?"

"I found the perfect dress," Willow says.

Simon smiles again. Something's wrong. He'd normally ask to see the dress, ask Willow to try it on, make a bigger deal out of it.

"Everything okay?" Jenna asks.

Before Simon answers, Willow says, "Dad, we were thinking of ordering from Raku. Is that okay?"

"Sure," he says.

Something is definitely wrong; Jenna can see it in his face.

"You want the usual?" Willow's already scrolling the Door-Dash app.

"Yes, but also get me this new roll I've been hearing about."

"What's it called?" Willow says, scrolling the menu.

Simon's glance fixes on the door leading to the kitchen. "I think it's called 'Alas Babylon.'"

Adrenaline courses through Jenna. She looks at Lulu, who's still playing dolls on the floor, to Willow, still distracted ordering dinner on her phone.

Simon isn't visibly restrained, so there's a reason he's not doing anything. He'd fight to the death for his family. Yet his hands are folded calmly on the table. He looks down and makes a mushroom-cloud-explosion gesture with his hands.

Now Jenna understands. There's an explosive device. If he does anything. If *she* does anything . . . *boom.*

He looks again to the kitchen. Jenna stealthily pads over and pushes the swinging doors in.

She thought both twins were dead, but one stands here. She holds a device in her hand. It's not the cattle killer. It's a detonator.

"I'll come with you," Jenna says. "Just don't hurt them."

"Oh, I'd love to kill each and every one of them in front of you. But that would be bad for business." She gestures to the back door.

Jenna wants to go back to the dining room, say her goodbyes, get one last look at them, but she needs to get this woman as far away from her family as possible. Jenna makes her way outside, the woman following behind. It's then Jenna notices the limp. She flashes back to the woods, her foot connecting with the woman's knee, collapsing the joint in the wrong direction. *Is this one Casey or Haley?* She can't remember. It doesn't matter.

"One move and I will blow this house sky-high."

Jenna raises her hands. "I told you, you can do whatever you want to me." She means it. Her heart is breaking. She'll never see her family again, she knows. But at least she had this last, perfect day.

The surviving twin leads her to Jenna's car in the garage. With one hand still gripping the detonator, she uses the other to give Jenna a pair of handcuffs. Jenna takes them and clicks them on. Her only goal now is to get this wretched woman away from here.

She gestures for Jenna to take the driver's seat.

Jenna has never felt so powerless in her life. She wonders how far the detonator can transmit.

As if reading her thoughts, the woman says, "It has a ten-mile radius. Don't worry, we're going less than five. I told your husband that if he calls anyone or leaves the house, you're dead and he and his girls will be in a million little pieces scattered across the neighborhood. He doesn't seem to get that you're already dead."

Jenna doesn't say anything. She reverses out of the garage and follows the directions the woman gives her. Soon they're only a couple miles away, in an industrial area of Rockville, Maryland. She passes a glass-repair shop, a kitchen-remodeling center, and a plumbing supply company.

With the detonator still in hand, the twin motions to an open warehouse, and Jenna drives inside.

Jenna considers bargaining with her. Explaining she was only defending her family. But the woman's eyes are dead. Her twin is dead. She's been planning this for some time. This is revenge, but also something else: a clear message intended for the wet-work market.

"Get out."

They both climb out. The woman walks to the warehouse's double doors and pulls them shut.

There's a rope draped over a support beam. At the end of the rope is a metal hook. The woman gestures for Jenna to clasp the hook to the chain of Jenna's handcuffs.

Before Jenna does so, she contemplates charging the woman, swiping the detonator out of her hand, killing her. But she knows it will never work. Her mind jumps to an image of Simon making pancakes. Lulu on the bus waving goodbye, Willow in her prom dress, asking her advice on the car ride home. She clasps the hook around the handcuff chain.

The woman comes over and yanks on a rope, which tightens, and Jenna starts to rise from the floor, the cuffs digging into her wrists. The woman is having trouble raising Jenna with only one hand. She sets the detonator down and yanks the rope and Jenna's feet now dangle eight feet from the ground. The woman ties off the rope and then walks toward the corner of the warehouse.

This is Jenna's chance. If she can get down, she can get the detonator, then take out this disgusting specimen of a human being.

She twists her wrists, but the cuffs have clicked tight from her weight. The rope is thick and there's no way to cut it. And the beam is solid.

She watches as the woman removes a tarp from something in the corner. It's a dolly with an industrial barrel on it. She gets behind the dolly and slowly—seeming to use great care—rolls the barrel over until its open mouth is under Jenna's feet. If Jenna could get lower, she could wrap her legs around the woman and snap her neck. But she's too high.

The woman moves away from the barrel and back to the rope.

"Do you know there are six types of screams?"

Jenna doesn't respond.

"For my sister's sake, I wanted to hear you make every single one of them. This was the best I could come up with."

That's when Jenna understands. Inside the barrel is liquid.

Acid.

She's going to lower her into it—slowly.

A wave of panic smashes into her. She starts to buck and kick, flails for what seems like an eternity. She finally stops in exhaustion and looks at the woman, who has a smile on her face. She's getting off on the terror.

It's then that Jenna decides she won't give her the pleasure. She gives up the fight and closes her eyes. As she feels the rope lowering, she says a prayer for Simon, for Willow, for Lulu. For her parents. She's had a better life than she deserved, given all she's done.

She will not cry and she sure as hell won't scream.

The rope lowers slowly.

It jerks to a stop. The woman is toying with her. Jenna keeps her eyes closed. She won't give her the satisfaction.

But then she hears something. Movement, a familiar voice. A French accent tinged with Russian.

Her eyes pop open and she sees Sabine. She's accompanied by a man, who swiftly puts a black bag over the twin's head. The man turns and Jenna sees Michael give her what can only be described as a casual wave. He picks up the detonator and carefully places it in a metal box.

Sabine looks up at her. Jenna isn't sure if this is real or if it's a hallucination, her mind protecting her from comprehending that she's being melted in a vat of acid.

"Just like when you were a teenager, ignoring my calls," Sabine says.

Jenna remembers the text when she was at Saks. The Corporation was trying to warn her.

One of Michael's men—Jenna recognizes him from the night she breached her ex's estate—wheels away the barrel from under her and lowers Jenna to the floor. Releases the cuffs.

Sabine says, "You're lucky Michael didn't take kindly to these amateurs pretending they worked for us or he might not have been keeping an eye out when she went back in business."

Jenna doesn't say anything; she's still processing.

"I thought I owed you this much, *mon chéri*. Now let's get you home to your family."

Jenna feels something release in her chest—gratitude? forgiveness?—but says nothing.

She needs to make it home in time for sushi with a sexy taxman, a blossoming teen, a charming five-year-old, and a dog named Peanut Butter. To appreciate this life. For herself. For her parents. For Annie. And the others.

ACKNOWLEDGMENTS

To get this novel into your hands required the work of many talented publishing industry professionals as well as the support of family and friends.

Thanks first to my literary agent, Lisa Erbach Vance, to whom I owe this wonderful career. Through her skill and tenacity, my novels have been published around the world and adapted for the screen. Other writers would be so lucky to have such an amazing representative.

Of course, thanks also to my publisher, St. Martin's Press, Minotaur. I have the privilege of working with one of the finest editors in the business, Catherine Richards, whose expert pen and vision elevate my work. And let's not forget associate editor Nettie Finn and copy editor Barbara Wild. All of my novels have also benefited from St. Martin's extraordinary marketing and PR team: Martin Quinn, Stephen Erickson, and Kayla Janas. Thank you, thank you, thank you.

Two other publishing professionals deserve special mention:

Joe Brosnan, who started me on this journey, and Ed Stacker, my private editor/secret weapon.

Many people helped me try to understand and capture the worlds of Donnie, Nico, and Jenna. For Donnie, I'm indebted to the rock band Kix, a staple from my youth, when I blasted "Cold Shower" and "Girl Money" from the cheap speakers of my rusted MG Midget. Kix inspired many iconic bands of the 1980s and 1990s, never receiving the full recognition they deserve. Members of the band graciously took time to talk to me about their early years and recent resurgence. Also, thanks to Keith Marlowe, my old law school buddy—and guitarist of the terrific band The Miners—who educated me on Philadelphia as well as the city's club scene in the 1990s. I also drew inspiration from Dave Grohl's excellent memoir. Donnie is, well, Donnie, and not based on any real person, but these gifted musicians helped me get my head into one of my favorite characters I've written to date.

As for Nico, Christo Doyle gave me a glimpse into the world of a TV producer. Like Nico, Christo has had major TV hits and even an aftershow for *Gold Rush,* but the comparison ends there. I must also express gratitude to J. Davitt McAteer and Celeste Monforton for providing information on coal-mining disasters. And many thanks to Joshua Caldwell and West Virginia University's Academy for Mine Training, who showed me the academy's state-of-the-art mine rescue center and provided insights into the life of coal miners, brave and hardworking individuals who risk their lives every time they go to work. All errors, and the many embellishments, are my own.

With respect to Jenna, I drew inspiration from some fictional favorites, including Jason Bourne, Nikita, Jack Reacher, Lisbeth Salander, the Gray Man, and Orphan X, among others. I relied again on esteemed author Barry Lancet for assistance with Jenna's fighting capabilities. And I turned to UK lawyer, friend, and fashionista Elena Jacobson for advice on Jenna's attire for the Kalorama party.

Special thanks to additional professionals who helped me along the way. For expert medical advice I once again bothered John Thieszen, M.D. For legal, I always go to the best lawyers in the world, my friends at Arnold & Porter.

And to the other friends and family who have cheered me on through every book: Paul and Trish Adair, Laney and Juan Altamar, Reeves and Brooke Anderson, Dan Barnhizer, Lisa and David Blatt, Mara Bralove, Deb Carpenter, Amy and Christo Doyle, John Elwood, Jenny and Garrett Evenson, Debbie Feinstein, Charles and Juli Franze, Steph Gangi, Todd and Candy Golden, Brian Hook, Stanton Jones and Carolina Chavez, Jeff Karlin and Sheila Scheuerman, Yong Sang Kim, Robert and Sae Knowles, Kat Lindsey, Jon Lindstrom and Cady McClain, Chris Man and Adam Marquez, John and Patty Massaro, Tony Mauro, John McCarrick, Sean Morris, Evie Norwinski, Brian Panowich, Elissa Preheim, Alexis Rodriquez and Craig Hoetger, Laura and Karl Roske, Mara Senn, Greg Smith, Craig Stewart, Lynn Swanson, Carmen Venecia, Rob Weiner, Andrea and Mark Williams, and Rob Wood.

One of the great things about this job is that you get to know other writers. Thanks to Sarah Pekkanen for our weekly "author walks" where we talk plot and business and kids. To Kimberley Howe for her friendship and support, and for running the International Thriller Writers organization, which helps so many writers. To other friends I met through ITW (Liv Constantine, Ethan Cross, Todd Gerber, and Tosca Lee, to name a few). To Jenny Hillier for being such a positive force in the universe. To Lee Child and Lisa Gardner for their endless support of me and so many writers.

To Gayle Lynds and John Sheldon for mentoring so many. And to Thomas Cooney and Lain Hart for creating the wonderful Leopardi conference in Recanati, Italy.

None of this would be possible without readers, librarians, booksellers, and the always creative and positive Bookstagram community. Thank you for your passion for stories and keeping reading alive.

I am lucky to have such a supportive family. To my kids, Jake, Emmy, and Aiden, who keep life interesting. Pub day for my books is always bittersweet because I reflect on how much each of you has grown since the book before. But I get prouder every time.

Last, to my wife, Trace. Thirty-five years, and there just aren't the words. . . .